AS THE SPARROW FLIES

SOJOURNERS' SAGA BOOK I

BY CHAD CORRIE

DARK HORSE BOOKS

Published by
Dark Horse Books
A division of Dark Horse Comics LLC
10956 SE Main Street
Milwaukie, OR 97222

DarkHorse.com

Library of Congress Cataloging-in-Publication Data

Names: Corrie, Chad, author. | Burgess, Dan, artist.
Title: As the sparrow flies / writer, Chad Corrie ; cover art, Dan Burgess.

Description: Milwaukie : Dark Horse Books, 2024. | Series: Sojourners' saga
    ; volume one
Identifiers: LCCN 2023006858 (print) | LCCN 2023006859 (ebook) | ISBN
    9781506740157 (trade paperback) | ISBN 9781506740188 (ebook)
Subjects: CYAC: Graphic novels. | Survival--Fiction. | LCGFT: Fantasy
    comics. | Graphic novels.
Classification: LCC PZ7.7.C6734 As 2024 (print) | LCC PZ7.7.C6734 (ebook)
    | DDC 741.5/973--dc23/eng/20230519
LC record available at https://lccn.loc.gov/2023006858
LC ebook record available at https://lccn.loc.gov/2023006859

First edition: May 2024
Ebook ISBN 978-1-50674-018-8
Trade Paperback ISBN 978-1-50674-015-7

1 3 5 7 9 10 8 6 4 2
Printed in the United States of America

ALSO BY CHAD CORRIE

THE WIZARD KING TRILOGY
Return of the Wizard King
Trial of the Wizard King
Triumph of the Wizard King

GRAPHIC NOVELS
Sons of Ashgard: Ill Met in Elmgard

STANDALONE NOVELS
The Shadow Regent

SOJOURNERS' SAGA
As the Sparrow Flies

CHAPTER ONE

Crows and Ash. Submit or Be Slain.

I f not for the crows, the fields would have been silent. They circled above in the reddening sky, swooping down now and then whenever a suitable opening presented itself. The freshly slain bodies gathered into heaps across the field were a tempting sight. A handful would land on a mound and start exploring a body until another would arrive and send the first group back into the air. The process ensured none would claim much of anything from the dead, leaving them whole for when they were put to the torch. Elliott had seen it many times since becoming Sir Pillum's squire three years ago.

The neat mounds were outside the town, between it and their camp. The common brown tents used by the infantry formed the outer part of the encampment, with the knights' white pavilions at its core. The camp was assembled a short distance from the town's walls but not far enough to jeopardize their hold over it. Not that they had any worries of losing control. The battle was over, and, like everyone else they'd encountered, the townsfolk couldn't stand before them.

Elliott sat on his simple folding chair, polishing his master's shield. The infantry's tents were shorter than the knights', which, along with the wide paths between key junctions, allowed him a decent view beyond the camp's confines.

If not for the mounds of dead, it would have actually been a fairly pleasing sight. But such things were a distraction from his work, and he pulled himself from them. Sir Pillum's shield had seen some heavy strikes today, but Elliott would have it looking presentable for Selection. After three years of practice he could hammer out small dings or buff out small scrapes with ease. It was the polishing that took most of his effort. Yet no matter how hard he tried, he couldn't keep his mind on his work.

Soon enough he was studying the crows. They wouldn't touch the bodies of the infantry or the Salamandrine, only the enemy. The fallen soldiers of Pyre deserved more dignity and had been tucked away under tents reserved for such purposes, where they'd be free from any further defilement. Those who had secured the bodies—fellow soldiers and those squires who saw to their fallen masters—had finished their tasks about an hour ago, giving them plenty of time to join the rest for Selection. It was a squire's honor to witness it on behalf of their fallen master.

Elliott doubted Sir Pillum would fall in battle before Elliott became a knight. His master was a mighty man of valor who seemed unstoppable on the field and was just as zealous regarding the things of Pyre. Few could find a better knight to serve, and Elliott knew he was quite fortunate in having been assigned as his squire. And he'd served well, ever hopeful of being found worthy of elevation into the Salamandrine's ranks. He'd technically be eligible by year's end, when he'd finally turn sixteen. But there was no guarantee of acceptance just because you reached a certain age. He had to be found worthy.

Looking back now, Elliott was amazed at how fast the last three years had passed. Though he couldn't see how it was possible, Sir Pillum had told him the time of his service would go faster than he first thought. And though during the years it seemed that things were actually slowing down rather than speeding up, he now stood on the cusp of some great days to come. But until then he had to keep to his tasks, do his duty to Pyre and his master—all of which would reveal and remove any impurities that might still cling to any hidden parts of him so he could be found pure and worthy enough to earn the title and place of a knight.

It was the highest honor anyone could hope to achieve outside the priesthood. And while he was devout, Elliott knew he wasn't cut out for the greater responsibilities and honors given priests. The proving of the Salamandrine was challenging enough; the priesthood was on another level. Not to mention priests had to answer to Pyre and Salbrin directly. He knew his own shortcomings and never deemed himself able to presume such a place. Becoming a knight was honor enough.

Few could stand against the Salamandrine's might. They were the greatest warriors to walk Annulis and held something no others possessed: the favor of an unstoppable deity. Pyre was the mightiest of gods and had shown this truth time and again as Salbrin and his generals had led them to victory after victory. Those who dared war against them instead of embracing Pyre's truth quickly learned their lesson. Just as those who had stood before them today had . . .

Shoving his daydreaming aside once again, Elliott focused anew on his task. He worked the cloth and special balm over the red bird emblazoned on the shield's white surface. The bird rested in the center of the shield, wings spread and head cocked to the left. It resembled something crafted of living flame, making it a fitting emblem of their god and their most sacred mission.

But this wasn't the only thing that marked a knight's shield as unique. All of them were shaped like tilted squares with the points of their corners facing up, down, left, and right. These points were capped with sharp steel and used as weapons in battle. Sir Pillum was particularly fond of this tactic, as Elliott could attest after scraping dried blood from the points more times than he could count. He'd even had to sharpen them a few times over the years after such continuous enthusiastic use.

Though this was nothing when compared to what the clothing suffered along the way. Travel alone could soil any garment, but with the fighting and everything else, a dedicated group of camp workers was necessary to continuously mend and wash garments on what Elliott could only assume was an hourly basis, given the size of their force.

No, he was content enough working on making *one* knight's gear presentable, not dealing with knights, infantrymen, priests, and everyone else alongside. And it was a truth he'd often remind himself of whenever he found himself thinking he might be getting overwhelmed in his chores. What he had been given to oversee was nothing in comparison to that grueling work. But all had their part in the grand campaign, and all served Pyre as best they were able.

After a short burst of work, Elliott gave his arm a rest, fastening his gaze on another circling crow. It appeared as if the bird swam in a sea of blood. The reddish tint wasn't as red as it was said to have been in years past—during the Days of Blood—but it still lingered. Before the Year of Night it was said the skies were a deep blue filled with white clouds. All Elliott's generation knew was a reddish hue that darkened at sunset. The clouds had lightened over the years but still held crimson lines and shadows.

He doubted he'd ever see the sky as it had been in Salbrin's youth. Of course, these were all minor matters, since everything would be destroyed by the coming flames. The purified world to come would be perfect, and Elliott would get to enjoy it with all the others found worthy. It was a fitting reward for which he was eager to serve.

"Looking for omens, are we?" Sir Pillum's voice woke Elliott from his reverie.

"No, sir." Elliott leapt to his feet, keeping the shield in hand as he did so. "Just resting my arm."

Sir Pillum glanced down at the shield. "Well done, Elliott. You already cleaned up the armor, and the shield looks more than presentable for Selection."

"Thank you, sir." He took a quick glance across the half-plate suit Sir Pillum wore, making sure there wasn't a stain or spot anywhere. He didn't see anything. He knew the sword strapped to Sir Pillum's side was in good condition and extra sharp so took careful stock of the open-faced helmet resting under his master's arm instead.

The nose guard had given Elliott's fingers a good battle; it was often crusted with blood that refused to leave no matter how hard he scrubbed. It was almost as bad as the scale mail section attached to the helmet's back lip, protecting Sir Pillum's neck from attack. He didn't see anything out of place.

"I think you've earned a bit of a break." Sir Pillum nodded toward the various rags and containers holding the polishing balm and other cleaning oils and supplies beside Elliott. "Get that put away and you can accompany me into the town."

"Yes, sir." Elliott did his best to keep from showing too much of his excitement as he hurriedly picked up the materials and put them into Sir Pillum's tent. He hadn't been able to attend too many Selections thus far and was particularly interested in this one. "They do you a great honor, in letting you present the choice."

"Yes, they do." It was clear Sir Pillum was pleased with his part in the process. It was a way for those who served Pyre with honor to be honored in turn. Elliott could think of none more deserving. "I'm most thankful for Commander Calix and Milec allowing me the privilege."

"Do you think many will step forth?" Elliott came running back out of the tent, straightening his own attire as he did. Selection was an important event. He needed to make sure he represented Sir Pillum and Pyre well. Though he wore only a simple tunic and pants, he made sure they were kept clean and in good repair.

Sir Pillum nodded his approval of Elliott's appearance. His master had never found fault with it before, but there could always be a first time—and especially today, when more eyes would be upon him than usual.

"These Laromi are weak," said Sir Pillum, taking his shield and affixing it to his left forearm. "I doubt there will be many found worthy, but we still need to honor Pyre by giving them a choice."

He ran a hand through his black hair before donning his helmet. Like all the Salamandrine, Sir Pillum kept it cut short and his face clean shaven. "Let's go. I don't want to dishonor the commander with any tardiness," he said, spinning on his heel and making for the town's partially demolished walls.

Elliott was fast at his heels.

"If things go like they have been," Sir Pillum continued, "we might even have time for some more lessons this evening."

"I've been practicing in my free time."

"It shows." Sir Pillum peered over his shoulder with a hint of a smile in his brilliant gray eyes. "Keep it up and you'll make all of us proud."

"Yes, sir," Elliott cheerfully replied.

For the remainder of their walk, he couldn't help but envision himself fighting alongside his master and the rest of the Salamandrine. Soon enough such daydreams could very well become a reality.

It was the custom that survivors from any conflict were presented inside the main courtyard of what remained of their town or village. Here, parts of the walls had been breached in sections and the smoke from the fires still lingered. There was no need to extinguish the flames. They'd have plenty of company soon enough.

The courtyard was ideal for holding large groups of people and easy to defend and secure should anyone try something foolish. Few did, but there were always some you had to watch. While not all would embrace Pyre's mercy, some would actively oppose it. Those had to be made examples of lest Pyre's great name become tarnished through leniency.

Most of the squires and the bulk of the infantry were kept back to mind the camp while the priests and the Salamandrine were given the privilege and responsibility of Selection. Neither took it lightly. Elliott was included today as a form of honor for Sir Pillum, and he was eager to witness his master's part in the rite. He found himself wishing they could just rush though the preamble and get into the meat of things but checked his rising lack of discipline. There was a process, and he would keep to it. Salbrin had been given it from Pyre himself. It should and would be honored. If Elliott couldn't do that, then he wasn't fit for the ranks of the Salamandrine . . . or service to Pyre in general. Willing himself calm, he occupied his mind by studying the Laromi.

Like all on Annulis, the Laromi possessed olive skin and a mixture of hair and eye colors.

Those gathered were mostly women and children, with a much reduced number of men. All stood silently before the priests, doing their best to look brave. Elliott had seen it before and heard of it more times than that. The arrogant ones who refused to embrace Pyre's mercy were all alike, seeking comfort in their own stubbornness rather than humbly embracing the truth.

The difference, besides their choice of gods, was in their clothing. Elliott had never seen anyone else on Annulis share the same appearance. Laromic men dressed exactly alike: brown or black pants with off-white or white shirts, plain belts, and boots. They all were clean shaven and short haired. The women wore similar attire, with brown or black skirts and off-white or white blouses. Their hair was longer than the men's, but even so they wore it in similar styles. Why anyone would want to look just like another was beyond him. But so were most of the ways of those outside Pyre's mercy.

The infantry closed off the back and sides of the square, with the Salamandrine in front, blocking the main gate. Each soldier wore leather brigandine armor. All of it had been polished, along with their swords, maces, and daggers. The archers among them made sure their bows were strung over their shoulders opposite their full quivers of red- and yellow-fletched arrows. All wore open-faced helms and carried round wooden shields marked with the crest of the great city of Pyrus and its god.

A line of standards spread out among the frontline of knights keeping a respectful distance behind the priests. The white banners flapped in the early evening breeze, making the flaming bird they displayed appear to be fluttering in flight. Above these banners, on top of each wooden pole from which the white cloth was draped, perched a bronze bird. Seemingly composed of living flame, its spread wings caught the light and shimmered with a radiant glow.

"Submit or be slain," Milec, the head priest of Pyre, informed the Laromi gathered before him. "These are the words of Pyre and Salbrin, his herald." He, like the rest of the priests, was dressed in white robes. Over these he wore a scale mail shirt. On top of this was a red tabard with the same blazing bird found on all the Pyric shields. Unlike on the shields, though, the crest sewn over the priest's chest was made of golden thread.

"Praise be to Pyre," Milec continued, holding his blaze rod firmly in hand. The device was carried by all priests of Pyre. The slender metal staff was a wonder of the age and another clear sign of Pyre's supremacy over all the other so-called gods. It was made of polished steel and contrasted with the golden circlet on each priest's head, crowning them as servants of the great god of Pyrus.

"Praise be to Pyre and his herald, Salbrin," Elliott joined the army in shouting with one voice. A certain sense of pride rose within him. How could it not, when you knew you were one of the chosen who'd see the world to come. He allowed himself a fleeting glance at the toppled statue of the Laromi's supposed goddess.

Laroma's remains were scattered around the pedestal on which she had stood. With a prominent place in the center of the courtyard, she had welcomed and reminded all of their corruption from the truth. The statue had been sculpted from solid stone and painted in an attempt to resemble a living woman. It was foolishness, of course, for no stone statue could ever be a god. But it was a common thing among the people outside Pyrus.

She had worn a black dress and crow feathers, but the rest was lost in her now-fragmented form. The sound of some nearby movement turned Elliott's attention to his left. Sir Pillum was carefully shifting his weight between his feet. Elliott grinned at the notion of his master being nervous but could understand his concern.

"The time has come to select your fate," Milec bellowed at the Laromi. His naturally deep voice made his words even more impressive, as was evident from the reactions Elliott saw flash across some of the Laromi's faces. "You have no other choice."

"Sir Pillum, please approach." Milec turned and motioned for him to step forward.

Elliott's chest swelled with pride as Sir Pillum squared his shoulders and strode through the space between the Salamandrine and the priests. When he arrived at Milec's side, he took a small breath, then addressed the Laromi with a strong, loud voice.

"There is coming a judgment to this world—a great fire that will burn across all Annulis. But Pyre in his mercy has allowed an escape."

"There is only Pyre," said Sir Pillum. "Great is he and single in power!"

"Great is Pyre!" Elliott joined in with the rest of the army's shout.

"You have before you a choice." Sir Pillum pointed out the scattered stony bits of their fallen goddess. "You see the fate of your false god. She, like the rest, cannot save you. But it is not so with Pyre." He turned around and grabbed one of the standards a nearby knight was holding. In one smooth motion he spun back around, lifting it overhead. It was a clever and dramatic flourish of which Milec and the other priests heartily approved. "There is only Pyre and his people!"

"There is only Pyre and his people!" The great shout arose from Elliott and the rest of the Pyri, who repeated it about half a dozen times. Each time it was chanted, the unease among the Laromi increased. Some even started inching backward, as if they could actually flee from the truth confronting them. When the shouting subsided, Sir Pillum lowered the banner, but not his voice.

"Those who wish to be purged from this world's corruption and look forward to the Great Conflagration with joy instead of fear, step forward. Pyre is not one to deny you a choice. He desires loyal followers ready to carry out his commands. You are free to choose whom you will. Today you can step forward and submit to Pyre, the true god, or you can remain as you are and in the end face the cleansing to follow."

Now Milec faced the Laromi, lifting his blaze rod overhead. "Those who submit to Pyre, step forward."

The air was thick with tension. The silence was near deafening. Even the crackling of the scattered fires couldn't break its hold over the area. None of the inhabitants dared look at each other. Each kept their eyes anchored on the ground, mothers guiding children's faces into their skirts. This continued for what seemed like hours, until finally two older men sheepishly stepped forward.

"Only two?" Elliott whispered. It was the lowest number he'd ever seen. Didn't they know what Pyre was looking to save them from? How he would reward those who submitted to his mercy?

"Will no more heed Pyre's call?" Milec calmly asked, but it was clear he shared Elliott's sense of disappointment. When no one else ventured forward, his face became like stone. "Then so be it. Selection has ended. Your fate has been sealed."

A tongue of yellow flame leapt to life atop Milec's blaze rod. The rest of the priests followed in igniting theirs. The whooshing sound of the flames coming to life nearly in unison still sent a shiver up Elliott's spine.

"Come forward and kneel," Milec commanded the two Laromi who'd been selected. They did so with cautious steps, keeping their heads down and eyes far from meeting anyone's gaze. "You will not be appointed unto Pyre's displeasure but in the Great Conflagration will enter into his favor. But these," he said, directing his blaze rod at the others behind the two supplicants, "will share the fate of all who refuse submission to the great Pyre. Let the purging begin!"

Sir Pillum stepped forward, drawing his sword. This action was repeated by all the army save the squires. They were to refrain from such an honor until brought into the ranks of the Salamandrine. The infantry would keep the perimeter, making sure none could escape. With keen precision, the knights slaughtered those who hadn't stepped forward. Some Laromi tried to run in the panic that followed, but those who managed to flee the knights' blades found the infantry's blades ready to catch them.

There was no escape.

Elliott watched as the shield he'd so painstakingly cleaned was quickly splattered with blood yet again. Sir Pillum, like all of the Salamandrine, was ruthless. There was no room for mercy now that Selection had been made. These Laromi had chosen their fate and were sealed in it. Pyre had shown his mercy. They had rejected it, and now bore the brunt of that rejection.

As one who had seen such a thing before, the sights and sounds didn't trouble Elliott in the least. In the beginning there had been a small twinge, but over time it faded. It helped to remind himself of how Salbrin compared the matter to weeding a garden. The undesirable weeds were removed so the ground was made suitable for the righteous plants to grow.

All during the purging the two supplicants knelt and sobbed. Their actions weren't lost on Milec. Seeing such a display soured his features into a disapproving scowl. "Take them to the camp," he instructed a nearby soldier. "Once they have been properly introduced to Pyre, we'll see where they might be placed."

The soldier yanked the two up by their arms and led them outside the town. Once the two had been removed, Milec lifted his hand and blaze rod as Elliott, the other squires, and the priests lowered their heads in reverence. "Oh Pyre, we offer you this sacrifice. May it hasten your day."

"Praise be to Pyre the Purifier," said Milec with his deep, powerful voice.

"Praise be to Pyre." All gathered spoke in unison.

"Now, my brothers, let this filth be cleansed." All the priests raised their blaze rods as the knights departed the square that had taken on all the trappings of a fresh battlefield. As one, the priests directed their blaze rods at the slain Laromi, shooting out a line of fire onto their bodies. In short order a fire was kindled among them, and thick, oily smoke began darkening the heavens.

"Praised be Pyre," said Milec.

"Praised be Pyre!" went up the refrain as Selection came to a close.

Everyone quickly went about their appointed tasks, working in tight uniformity, allowing no waste of time as fire pots were brought in and what remained of the town was set alight. The stone walls were even set ablaze with a powerful concoction able to bring forth such intense flames that even stone was consumed.

Before night had fallen, the town had been transformed into a pile of charcoal. The mounds of the fallen Laromi outside the walls would follow. Each would be set ablaze and left to burn throughout the night. When the fires cooled the next day, only ashes would remain. The land would then be cleansed, and Pyre would be glorified.

CHAPTER TWO

The Hanging Girl. The Silent Village.

S arah watched the small girl's body gently rock in the breeze. The dead oak branch from which it hung creaked and groaned but held true, suspending the body a good four feet off the dry earth below. Though little more than a collection of skin-wrapped bones, she was close to her own fifteen years, Sarah figured. All that covered her skeletal frame was a brown skirt and baggy white blouse. Her feet were naked. A worn gray placard hung around her neck. The bold block script written in black paint simply read: THIEF.

Stray flaxen strands of hair fluttered about her head but didn't keep the two crows perched on either shoulder from pecking into her once-innocent face. Their frenzied consumption had only recently begun. The cheeks and skin about her eyes and nose were freshly torn. Soon enough, the muscle and bone would begin peeking through. The crows, swallowing pink ribbons of flesh as fast as they could tear it free, cared little for the audience of one hundred below them.

Sarah wondered if the girl's parents had been present during the hanging. She even found herself wondering if they might have been forced to do it themselves. Though still half a year from claiming her kerchief and dagger and stepping into full adulthood, she knew quite well what their customs decreed.

No matter how much something might unsettle her, it wasn't her place to interfere. The girl was a Dweller. She may have had the same olive complexion and resembled the other girls in the congregation, but that had nothing to do with it. There were Dwellers and there were Sojourners. That was the real and most important difference. She knew Dwellers were harsh at times, especially toward each other—and had grown even more so since the Days of Blood. What was before her mattered little. What had been done was done.

"No more than two days ago, I reckon," said James. He was a broad-shouldered young man she'd been watching grow up since she was old enough to notice him.

She had always enjoyed his thick curly brown hair and soft blue eyes. She didn't always get to see his hair these days, since he'd taken his cowl two years prior, but she saw glimpses now and then whenever the congregation found a chance to bathe. Like all the men in the congregation, his face was mostly clean shaven, with a beard sprouting under his chin and jawline. James had been slow in growing it, finally getting it started earlier this year. At first she'd found it too scraggly, but as it had filled in, she thought it looked rather nice and respectable.

"That looks about right," Caleb, another young man who joined James near the hanging girl, agreed.

Both had taken the lead, leaving the rest of the congregation a few yards behind. Sarah was the farthest forward of the women and children, allowing her to hear them better. The other women and younger children kept to the small assortment of carts and livestock in the back, while the rest of the cowled men in the congregation kept watch over them.

She glanced to her side, seeing if her father would let her keep her place. He had always given her more freedom than what was common for girls but had also become more protective following her mother's death. Though the face returning her gaze was stoic, she focused on his brown eyes. They told her all she needed to know. She could stay for the time being. Sarah braved a step forward and concentrated. She always had good hearing and didn't want to miss a single word.

Even as Caleb and James approached, the crows continued pecking and rending. When one finally plucked out the girl's eyeball, a muffled cry arose from the women and children. Mothers rapidly turned their children's gaze away, focusing instead on the dead forest flanking the right side of the dirt road they'd been traveling.

"You would be wise to avert your eyes too." Her father's strong timbre pulled her gaze his way. "Such sights are not pleasant to keep in your mind."

"I have seen so much death already, Father," she reminded him. "One more body will not change that now." Sarah shared his same brown eyes but had inherited her mother's light blond hair, which she kept in a tight ponytail, like all the girls and women of their congregation.

"Still"—her father's hand found rest on her shoulder—"it is best to avoid what you can when you can. The less you have to contend with, the better. Such thoughts have a way of haunting the mind and chasing away any peace you might find."

"The forest is dead," said another of the men as Bram, the patriarch, joined Caleb and James.

"Dead wood still burns," Bram replied without turning his head from his two assistants still studying the swaying girl. Like all the men, Bram wore his brown cowl and off-white long-sleeved tunic with black cuffs and collar. His brown pants were a little tattered, the black cuffs perhaps most of all. His shoes were the most travel worn, though—even more so than his brown cloak that was at least Sarah's age, if not older.

"We will gather what we can," he continued. Like all the men in the congregation, Bram used a walking staff, but unlike them he used his for staying upright as much as for moving forward.

White haired and bearded, the patriarch had a youthful nature to his eyes that helped soften the lines on his face. This helped him appear younger than the ninety-five years he'd endured wandering Annulis. His bushy eyebrows still made Sarah smile. She'd never fully gotten used to them since first sighting them in her youth.

"Should we leave her?" she heard James ask. He had finished walking around the girl's position, obviously noticing nothing out of the ordinary.

"You should know the answer by now." Bram's rebuke was mild. Even so, she could see the muted embarrassment flash across James's cheeks.

"Yes." He gave a nod, taking sight of Sarah in the process. She couldn't help blushing. But if James thought anything of it, he didn't give any sign.

"Compassion is a worthy trait," Bram continued. "It was what urged the Sovereign to send the heralds, after all. But we have our own customs and must see to them. They have served to help guide us in such dark times and will continue for as long as we hold to them.

"And so the body stays." Bram considered the darkening sky, wrinkled face scrunching in displeasure. Raising his voice, the patriarch addressed the others, saying, "The night will soon be upon us. We must be quick about our work. We follow the road until dusk and then make camp."

This said, Bram made his way past the body, plodding onward at a respectable pace. The rest of the congregation waited for a moment longer, then followed their patriarch. With their movement came a cacophony of sounds from the back of the group as the children, carts, and animals were prodded into action. The animals they had with them—some chickens, cows, geese, and even a few goats and sheep—didn't seem that perturbed by the dead girl as they walked beneath the body, each keeping to themselves. The geese and chickens to their cages, the cows calmly pulling carts, the goats and sheep beside the ones who held their leashes. Even the children were placid.

Sarah found herself wondering how quickly she'd become accustomed to such things—how young she must have been. Things had changed after her mother's death, true, but had she been so accepting of such familiar sights before that? She dared one final view of the girl as she passed, her father keeping much of the sight from her by taking to her side. Yet even so she thought how quickly the innocence must have fled the girl's face. It was as if it had literally been only skin deep, like much of the world around them.

"That girl was not a promising sign if we seek their favor," said Caleb to Bram.

Of the two assistants, Caleb was of a more serious nature. While only twenty-five, he behaved, thought, and even spoke like someone twice his age. Bram often wondered how he'd be when he grew into an elder. He didn't have any gray in his black hair and beard, but there were some strong lines deepening across his face. It was important to keep a level head, but if there was never any joy, either, then what was life?

"It is not our place to judge, Brother," Bram replied. He still kept the lead, an assistant at each side: Caleb to his left, James to his right. "Youth does not always equate with innocence. If anything, it is a sign we are close to a village or maybe a town. And since we are in need of supplies, our paths cross at a good juncture."

He kept his eyes on the dirt-packed road meandering through what once had been a healthy, thriving forest but now was thinned by axe, fire, and death. Not many of the trees still lived. Those that did were spindly and sickly, using all their strength to push out anemic leaves from their weak branches.

While they'd been passing through more grasslands and fields of late, forests were not unusual. But the harshness of the terrain, the sheer sense of life itself slowly surrendering to its demise, was growing more common these days, increasingly so the farther they went.

Things had seemed so much better in his youth. When he'd been James's age, it wouldn't have been uncommon to come across clumps of woods still thriving, even wild crops of which they could partake. Water had been more readily found, and the people they came across more inclined to help and trade. Such times were little more than memory now. All the more proof of the heralds' truth and their need to continue seeking the Veiled City while they still drew breath.

"What if they will not barter?" James asked.

"Then we will move on. The Dwellers owe us nothing, and the Sovereign keeps watch, do not forget." Bram knew James didn't lack faith, but it was good for all to hear the truth spoken now and again. It was easy to forget if one grew too focused on what was around them.

"Just stay alert," Caleb advised. "A sharp eye and sound mind can make a great difference in any situation."

"That they can." Bram's words conjured a silence among the trio as they regarded the road weaving closer to some walls rising in the distance.

He was careful in his step, mindful that an even pace was needed to make sure those who followed didn't fall behind. They needed to keep a decent rate for the children too. The youngest rode in the carts with the animals and supplies. Those who could walk did so for as long as they could. The faster they grew in strength, the better it was for the congregation.

Bram listened for any signs of life. It wasn't entirely unusual to come across an empty area near a town or city but as one neared, there would be sounds of habitation or the smell of smoke. So far he smelled and heard nothing.

Sojourners had been taught that the cities were to be avoided whenever possible. Called out from them centuries before by the heralds' decree, they had but one city they sought, forsaking all others. Their intention was to keep on the path and stay as self-sufficient as possible. Not an easy thing these days, but Bram wanted to honor the tradition for as long as he could.

As they drew closer, the dying daylight outlined the chipped and worn fieldstone walls of what was clearly a village: not a large one but not too small either. That should be good. Perhaps it was just the right size to have a small excess of goods. He wasn't hoping for much, but they did need to refresh what they had soon if they wanted to continue comfortably. But while this was a nice thought, he didn't put too much trust in it. These were still Dwellers, and if what he'd seen of the world during these last few years was true, their love could be even colder than usual.

"No smoke." Caleb declared what was clearly seen now by the entire congregation. Nothing was rising above the tall walls and thick double doors serving as the village gate.

A closed gate.

"And no people," added James darkly. "I do not even hear a dog."

Bram came to a stop about twenty yards from the gate, raising his staff high as a signal for the others behind him to stop. He made a final inspection of the walls, then proceeded as custom decreed.

"Hello," he shouted.

Nothing.

"Hello," he repeated, this time with more effort.

By now a watchman should have sighted them and reported them to the leaders inside. A parley would have been arranged, and then, if they were willing, some form of bartering might take place. They, like many Sojourners, carried some coin, but since they had little use for it and the price of things fluctuated wildly from place to place and even day to day, bartering was the more dominant and reliable form of exchange.

Bram peered up at the reddening sky with a sigh. It often deepened at sunset. Though it wasn't as dark a shade as it had been after the Year of Night, the sky still reminded him of a great open wound, with dirty brownish-red clouds mingling with a few sickly white streaks, like strands of tattered, dirty wool bandages.

"Check the gate, Brother Caleb." They needed some resolution before night was upon them.

"What are they doing?" asked Sarah.

"I do not know, but it must be something important." Her father, like the others, spoke in hushed tones as Caleb cautiously approached the gate's tired gray oaken panels. They watched him knock on the wood. In the process the gate inched inward, allowing him a chance to peek inside.

"Brother Caleb looks rather excited," said her father as Caleb ran back to the patriarch with some obvious enthusiasm.

"Where are the Dwellers?" She found it a little unsettling, coming across what appeared to be a silent village. It wasn't as uncommon these days, but still rare enough for an icy twinge to race up her spine. The hanging girl's death was recent, and if she came from the village—if it was done by the village—there should still be some villagers present.

"We will soon find out."

"What are they doing?" Nathan, an older man behind Sarah and her father, spoke as James and Caleb rushed to the gate. "There was no parley. We have no right." He wasn't yet an elder but was getting closer every year.

"The patriarch is not about to break custom, Brother Nathan," came the even older voice of Elder Milton as Sarah watched James and Caleb open the gate together. "Trust in his wisdom and the Sovereign guiding our way."

Murmuring arose when Caleb and James moved inside the gate. Sarah held her breath, waiting for their return. Thankfully, they did a moment later, allowing her a chance to take in some fresh air. The action wasn't lost on her father, who raised his eyebrow in response.

Once Caleb and James had conferred with the patriarch, he turned and addressed the congregation, saying, "The village is deserted. You have nothing to fear. As has been our custom whenever we come across unclaimed items in the wilderness, we lay claim to them. I propose we do the same with anything of use we find inside this village."

"A wise decision," said Elder Milton.

"I have decided we also will make camp tonight behind the walls," the patriarch continued.

"*What?*" Nathan was beside himself. "That is not right. We do not dwell with the Dwellers." He wasn't alone in his surprise. The congregation were murmuring among themselves.

Bram raised his hands. "It is only for one night, and the village is deserted. And if there is anyone out there looking to do us harm, as that hanging child might indicate, then I would feel better with some walls around us."

"Unusual, but not outside the norm," Elder Milton thoughtfully concurred.

"You cannot be serious?" said Nathan. "You *agree* with him?"

"It makes sense," Sarah heard the elder reply. "We do not know what else might be out there or why the village was abandoned. And it is for only one night. And there are no Dwellers. I do not see the harm." There arose some more mutterings, but these were short lived. It was growing late, and none wanted to be left making their bed in the dark.

As one the congregation stepped forward, moving for the gates as the sun continued bleeding across the horizon. Behind the gray stone walls was what would have been an active courtyard common to the places Dwellers called home. Instead, what greeted them was an empty, echoing space, silence spilling out from nearby shops and abandoned carts and continuing down the main roadway into the village.

"Not a soul in sight," her father observed.

"Do you think it was Marauders?" asked Sarah. Thankfully, she had never seen a Marauder but had heard enough tales to understand the threat they posed. They might even have been the ones who hanged the girl.

"No," her father confidently replied. "They would not leave anything behind if they could help it. And they would have been sure to topple that." He pointed to a statue near the center of the courtyard.

About as tall as a person and standing on a pedestal of the same height, the statue was obviously made of stone but had been painted to seem like a living woman watching all below. Clothed in a black dress, she also wore a strange crown resembling spiked circles that interconnected at intervals. In one of her hands she held aloft a clear glass globe, as if offering it to those below as a gift.

"Another goddess?" Sarah had seen a handful of them as they had continued their sojourn. Not all—for there was said to be one for every city and people across Annulis—but she'd encountered enough that she was able to spot the similarities.

When she'd first seen one, she'd thought it a rather funny sight. Raised on the truth of the Sovereign, she didn't understand why one would worship something their own hands had made. For how great could something be if it could not have existed without a human forming it? Over the years the more often she came across one, the more saddened she became. It was a clear sign of how far from the truth so many had fallen and how corrupted Annulis and its people had grown. Truly, it was all the more reason to stay to the path and find the Veiled City.

"Laroma," said her father, "the supposed protector of the Laromi. You can identify her by that crow-feather cape." Her father, like many of the congregation, had learned of the stories and people across Annulis through their journeys. Bram even had said there were times when he was young that other congregations would cross their path and swap tales and knowledge. She'd never experienced such a thing herself. The older she got, the stronger her fear they might be the only congregation left. It was a foolish thought, she knew. There had to be others somewhere. But it still rose to harass her every so often.

"They seem to enjoy crows," she said, pointing out the crest carved into the pedestal on which the statue stood. The overall design was simple but hard to miss: a silhouette of a crow with raised wings. It appeared as if it was going to leap into the air at any moment. Behind its head was a circular nimbus. The only other detail was the single narrowed eye on its profiled head. Sarah thought it lent a sinister air to the overall image, like it was sizing her up for something less than pleasant.

"The crest of Larom," said her father. "We must be in their lands now."

"Is that good?"

"We will see. I do not remember hearing much of them. We tended to keep to the West more growing up. Much of the East is still new to me."

Sarah, having been born along the way—as most Sojourners were in these generations—didn't know much about anything that had come before she was old enough to register what she was passing. And even then her memories were still faint and dream-like at times. Annulis was a large place, making it quite possible to wander its confines for lifetimes and still not see the end of it. And many had already before her . . . hopefully, she would not join their number . . .

A lone crow alighted at Laroma's feet. It turned her thoughts back to the young girl still swaying from the tree. The crows must have come close to tearing off her cheeks by now, if not her entire face. She wondered if anyone else saw the irony in her death given what these Dwellers apparently worshiped. She wondered if her mother would have. She didn't think of her as often as she used to, but when the thoughts came, they still possessed enough of an edge to cause her stomach to clench.

Her mother had died of a fever six years ago, though sometimes it seemed even longer. Disease and wild beasts were just as feared as Marauders or some Dweller's treachery. If one didn't get you, the other probably would, according to what the men said from time to time around the fires. In truth, as she got older, it became harder for her to imagine what her mother might think. She was seeing the world in a new way—a way that didn't mesh as well as it once did with her mother's memory. One night she'd realized that the older she got, the less of her mother's memory remained, and the less good she could draw from it. This had troubled her for a while, but she was slowly coming to accept it.

The Sojourners had a saying: "Let the dead bury the dead." And now, on the cusp of womanhood, she could see the truth in that more than when she'd first heard it. There were some things best left to the past; the future and present needed command of your full attention. Constantly seeking something that was gone wasn't a way to help anyone. It was fine to remember the fond memories but not to get lost in them and miss her way in the present. Life wasn't easy, and the older she got, the harder it seemed. She'd be wise to keep her focus where it was needed.

"Come on." Her father took hold of Sarah's hand. "We should set up camp with the others before it gets too dark, and there is still the communal hearth to tend to."

"I still feel a little strange about this," she confessed. "I do not think we have ever had a night behind walls."

"We never have, to my knowledge. But if it seems right to the patriarch, who am I to disagree?"

Sarah couldn't argue with such a statement. She had been taught to follow the elders and the patriarch especially. There was a reason they'd lived so many days while others had passed away. And it was that wisdom that should be heeded if they wanted their days on Annulis to be long and hoped to catch sight of the Veiled City before their end.

"At least we will not need the tents tonight," he said. "A dry night is a good night." This was another common phrase that had become a proverb among them.

Some of the men went to gather wood from the forest for the hearth and their own fires. Others would look for fodder for the animals. The rest took to their own tasks, just as she did to hers. It had become so ingrained in her that she didn't even think about it anymore, letting her mind and eyes wander to other matters . . . and persons.

More than once she spied James preparing the patriarch's bedroll, along with his own. He didn't see her, but that was okay. And yet she wasn't so enamored that she missed another young woman watching him with her clear blue eyes. And she *was* a woman.

Malena had received her dagger and kerchief a full year ago. Like all the other kerchiefs, it was a cream-colored cloth trimmed with black. What set it apart, however, was Malena's stunning red hair, which was further highlighted by the black leather strands all the girls and women used to bind their ponytails. And even though both of them wore the same brown dress with matching black cuffs, collar, and hem, Malena filled hers out in ways Sarah did not. The thought of Malena eyeing James knotted her gut and creased her brow.

"Sarah?" Her father's stern voice brought her back to her tasks. "How many times must I remind you about keeping your mind on your duties? This bedroll is a mess."

"I am sorry, Father," she replied, turning her back on Malena and noticing just how askew her bed really was.

"It is well you were not sent to fetch the wood, else we might have had no hearth tonight."

Embarrassment flooded her cheeks and neck. That reckless disregard wasn't her way—wasn't the way of the congregation. Each had their duty and was expected to perform it—and perform it well. With renewed concentration and vigor she tended her bed while the final logs of the communal hearth were laid in place at the center of their camp. And soon enough, it, along with the rest of the cookfires, was lit.

Each ate their meal in silence and gratitude. Another meal meant one more day of life.

The simple bread, broth, and dried goods weren't as great as some of the fare she'd heard the Dwellers used to eat, but it was sufficient for her needs, and that was all that was important. Once the evening meal was finished, the gates closed, and the carts and animals secured for the night, Bram found his seat near the blazing flames of the communal hearth. The women and children sat closest to the hearth with the men behind them.

While Sarah found some memories fading, there were others etched deep into her mind and life. The communal hearth was one of them. Each night was the same. When darkness fell, the congregation would circle the hearth. Most often this would take place in the open wilderness. It was strange gathering at the side of a statue of the Dwellers' goddess, but it would make for a special memory. Other than this, the ritual proceeded as it had from the time the first Sojourners had heeded the heralds' call.

It was one of the few ties that kept them connected to their past. That was what her father had said years ago when asked why they repeated the same thing night after night. For unlike the Dwellers, who had places to call their own, the Sojourner was as the sparrow, finding rest where they could. In such a life there was nothing but rituals threading the centuries and generations together. Without such things they'd be little more than wandering vagabonds, as the Dwellers often thought them.

Seeing all were seated in reverential silence and everything was completed for the day, Bram began the ceremony. "It is important we not lose sight of the hope which we seek. Such hope is the light to our path and our refuge in these places where we now find ourselves sojourning. For without this hope we truly are lost wanderers forsaken by and forgotten to time and man, as others would have us believe. But we know the truth to our journey, and though we have not yet arrived, each day we get closer than we were before.

"And what is our hope?" The question, when asked, always shook Sarah's bones. There was just something about it that inspired her. She wouldn't be surprised if others in the congregation didn't ask themselves the same question from time to time when things were wearing upon them.

"The Veiled City," the congregation answered as one.

"So spoke the heralds, and so we have believed," Bram continued. "For we know the truth." The patriarch gave some of the burning branches and logs a slap with his staff.

Crackling sparks burst into the air. These were supposed to mimic the night sky as it had been in the beginning of all things: awash with stars. "The Sovereign created Annulis to sit among the stars. And he placed upon it the city of Mundus and a steward to watch over it and teach the people the ways in which they should live. And there was peace for a season."

"And there was peace for a season," Sarah and the others recited in unison.

"And from the mighty city arose stewards to tend to one hundred more, which sprang up across Annulis like great trees across the plains. Each had a steward descended from the first. And so the Mundi spread across the world and stayed true to the Sovereign and his teachings."

"May it be so with us," the congregation recited.

"But in time the people looked to their own ways and thoughts, turning aside from that which they had known to be good and true for what they desired instead. And so there came strife, division, and unrest. City rose up against city. Each coveted the other, seeking enrichment and empowerment of themselves by diminishing others. But one cannot make his candle burn brighter by snuffing out another's. And while there were some who sought to hold back and still the divisions and discord, what had been released would not be contained. Rebellion had taken root and was now affixed firmly in the hearts of many."

"Sovereign watch over those who yet remain true," came the reply.

"Each of the cities tore into the other, raising up a new goddess to guide their way. In their pride and delusion they cast away the truth, holding to a lie with all their strength."

"Sovereign watch over those who yet remain true," the congregation repeated.

"Even in Mundus they could not hide how far they had fallen. Though they still pretended their love for the Sovereign was as it was in the days of old, it was not. For the stewards were no more in the city, instead following after Maraud's example, becoming emperors instead.

"But then came the heralds." Here the patriarch paused, letting the weight of the silence peppered with the crackling of the fire rest upon all present. It was meant to be a time of inward introspection as well as outward reflection. Her mother had said it was fitting to examine oneself during that moment and see if they really did still hold true to the heralds and Sovereign or were veering in the way of the Dwellers in their heart. Sarah was pleased to discern she was still true to the path.

"Blessed be the heralds and the one who sent them."

"Blessed indeed," Sarah and the others recited.

"To all who would listen, they delivered their message faithfully. They condemned the cities and towns, the villages and people, for having fallen away from the Sovereign and the ways he imparted through his first steward. They spoke against the goddesses and strife, and condemned the emperors as nothing more than petty tyrants, having lost their place and right as steward long ago. But they also spoke of a war. A terrible war that was looming on the horizon."

"Let he who has ears hear," said the congregation.

"For those who would be kept safe from the dark times and free from the corruption of the rebellious should seek out the Veiled City, whose builder is the Sovereign himself. The first city built before all others."

"Let he who has ears hear," the others repeated.

"Those who heeded the heralds began their sojourn, as do we who follow in their footsteps. And those who stayed behind dwelled in their old lives, as they still do today. And though the others mocked the ones who first set out, their days grew darker and the terrible war came upon them. But those who sojourned were kept safe.

"When peace returned to Annulis, the Dwellers thought the worst had passed, but those who held to the heralds' message knew better. For while all were welcoming peace and brighter days, there arose sudden and terrible destruction."

Taking a nearby stone, Bram cast it into the midst of the hearth. A great swell of snapping sparks rose from the flames. It was a meager thing compared to what it was supposed to represent, but Sarah had seen it enough times to imagine the dreadful event it mimicked quite vividly in her mind's eye. So vividly, in fact, that some nights she shivered at the work of her imagination.

"Fire rained upon the world." Bram's voice had taken on a more growling rage after his previous calm timbre. "It fell upon all Annulis in a burning cascade. The cities that remained were toppled, and great Mundus—that would-be empire of Annulis—was crushed into dust and ash and given the sea as a shroud."

"Let he who has eyes see." Sarah joined the others in speaking.

Bram continued more energized than before. "For three whole days the fire fell. And on the fourth day there was darkness, which lasted a year."

"The Year of Night," said the others.

Sarah often tried imagining what such a thing might have been like. She couldn't fathom how anyone or anything could survive such a fate. The sun, moon, and stars all hidden from sight for a whole year at a time? She'd take red skies and a bloody moon over total darkness any day.

"But that was not the end," said the patriarch. "For whenever it would rain, blood fell from the skies and added to the land's woe. Crops failed, people perished, and animals died. But we Sojourners were kept safe as the Dwellers continued to suffer. Even after the sun once more dared shine and the rains continued their days of blood."

"But the Veiled City still stands." All of the congregation spoke with a passion.

"And it is the only hope for all who wish to escape from this wounded, dying world. For what the heralds have spoken shall come to pass." Bram lifted his arms and began pacing around the fire. "There is only it and nothing else. Everything has proven false and will soon fade away, but to those who find the Veiled City, peace and life are their reward."

Sarah watched Bram lower his head and arms as if contemplating the flames once more. Though she had heard what followed many times, she never failed to get a twinge of sadness in her chest. "Should I not find the city before my years grow full, recall all I have spoken this night. Pass it on to others who have taken the journey with you. Keep the truth before you and let it guide you onward."

"We shall," said the congregation, bringing the ritual to a close.

She watched the patriarch take his former seat as the others went to their beds. Once more the sadness took hold of her as she again pondered the patriarch's future. He had seen the days before these dark times. He had journeyed for years after and still might not find the city before his death. If he might not make it, then what hope was there for any of them?

It wasn't a question she constantly wrestled with, but it had been popping up more frequently—this last year in particular. As before, she pushed the thought aside and let her eyes fix themselves on James.

He seldom even came close to glancing her way. He was focused too often on helping Bram to notice anything else. She didn't mind. She was content enough to end the evening with a few moments of his figure filling her gaze. But any enjoyment in her own nightly ritual was dampened when she noticed Malena doing the same. There was a flash of anger followed by a strange sense of loss that washed over her. The anger she could understand, but the sensation of loss startled her. She couldn't place its purpose or reason. Instead, the more she sought an answer, the greater her frustration when none came. Finally, she sighed and returned to the rest of her nightly chores and rituals.

"Best get some sleep," her father reminded her while unlacing his shoes. The others in the congregation were doing the same. Her countenance and heart lightened with another part of the evening she enjoyed. No matter the day, she always welcomed freeing her feet from her shoes and socks so they could get some fresh air.

And so ended another night. A night similar to ones that had come before. And in the morning, as with every other before it, they would arise and continue their journey. So it had been, was now, and would be for the foreseeable future . . . until they found the Veiled City.

Sovereign hasten the day.

CHAPTER THREE

A Disturbing Find. Too Many Questions.

"What happened here?" Sarah asked her father.

"I do not know," he replied, carefully studying all around him, "but stay close."

They were standing in the midst of an empty street lined with deserted houses. The dirt roads were hard packed. The houses were strong and had the look of being occupied until fairly recently, but there was no sign of an attack. So where were the people and animals?

Like most of the men and some of the women, they had begun to scour the village, searching for anything that might be of use. But if what they had come across so far was any indication of what remained, there wouldn't be much to gain. The remaining men were collecting and chopping firewood. The other women and children would see to the animals' needs. It was a basic pattern they had adhered to for so long, she doubted if any even questioned it, instead simply following along without a thought.

"Let us check those houses and then be on our way," he said, moving for the nearest one on his right. Sarah followed, looking over her shoulder at every strange sound, made all the more noticeable in the unsettling quiet around them.

Behind the thick pine door was a simple room. In it resided a cold stone hearth, a bed, and a few barrels and chests, but nothing else. It also didn't smell like anyone had been here for a while. Living outside towns and cities had given Sarah a sense of such things. Most Dwellers grew accustomed to the odors of people living in small confines for many days and weeks. Sojourners were free from such familiarity.

"Check those barrels," said her father as he went for the chest at the corner of the room.

Sarah did as ordered, pulling up the lid on one of them and peering inside. A faint dusting of what appeared to be flour coated the bottom of the barrel. Not even enough to do anything but tempt the hungry with a hint of what could have been. In the other barrel she discovered a small white mound piled on the bottom.

"This one still has some salt."

"We will need all we can get when autumn comes," said her father. "Assuming we come across some game," he added, squatting before the chest in front of him. It, like most of the things in the village, was very plain, not even possessing a lock. He lifted the lid, peered inside, and then promptly closed it.

"Anything?" Sarah drew near.

"Nothing we can use," he said, springing back to his full height.

"The chest looks strong enough," she continued. "And it is always wise to have an extra one on hand should—"

"Not this one." He took her hand and pulled her out of the house with him. "Come. We should check those other houses."

"But we have not looked at everything here."

"We have seen enough," he said, moving back out the door with Sarah still in hand. She watched him carefully as he led her from the first house and into the second.

"Is everything all right?"

"It will be fine, Sarah. For now we need to keep up our search."

"Given what we have found so far, I do not think we will find much else," she said.

"We will not know until we have finished looking."

Inside the second house was a scene similar to the previous one, save this time the barrels were both empty, as was the chest. Though they did find a ball of twine hidden under the bed that was good enough for future use.

"Be quick but thorough," advised her father as both entered the third house. This one was larger than the first two, possessing two rooms. The second was behind a closed door across from where Sarah and her father stood.

There were some barrels that yielded nothing, but two chests held cloaks and lengths of wool. These could be made into tents or new clothing, which were always hard to come by. Still not the food she'd been hoping they'd discover, but it was better than nothing. Once the first room had been searched, Sarah followed her father to the door into the second room. This door, like all the others they'd seen so far, didn't have any locks, only a partially corroded bronze handle.

The door gave a small squeal as it opened into the darkened room beyond, letting what light was present puncture the darkness. She could make out the outlines of what she supposed was a small private bedroom given the bed in its center. Windowless and without anything else of value, it didn't seem too important. That was, until both she and her father glanced at the walls and noticed the words scrawled by dagger point across the planks lining the room.

While all on Annulis shared the same language, not all were able to read. However, because it was deemed important to know what was around them and beneficial in seeking out clues about the Veiled City, all in Sarah's congregation were taught to read at what most Dwellers would consider a competent level. But knowing how to read something and comprehending it are often two different things. Such was the case with what they had found.

It was a simple rhyme carved deep into the wood over and over again. In fact, it appeared to get deeper the closer the phrase was to the floor. But the words didn't stop at the walls. They flowed down and onto the floor. The whole room was a mess of the same phrase snaking all about. If the silence of the place had been unsettling before, this frenzied display set the hair on her neck on end.

The crows have come to rip and tear, to take us all into their snare.

"What does it mean?" she asked in a low voice.

"Hopefully the patriarch will know," came her father's equally subdued reply.

"This is not right," James commented as he, Bram, and Caleb stood in the courtyard, watching some of the congregation returning from their searching. Most were empty handed. Those that weren't had found meager things: some bed sheets, cloth, a few fair pairs of shoes, but nothing truly monumental.

As to why and where the whole contents of a town—people and all—could have gone, Bram hadn't a clue. And that was what was souring his stomach. Mysteries of this sort weren't good to leave unsolved. The journey was hard enough without things such as this making it worse. It could have been as simple as people leaving because of a lack of food. He'd seen some villages do the same over the years, but it also could be much more serious. And not knowing was a dangerous place to be.

"Why would they leave without a trace?" James continued, echoing Bram's thoughts. "These walls are solid enough."

"The gates were a bit weak," Caleb offered.

"Yes, they have taken some abuse," mused Bram.

That was an understatement. They had taken a great deal of damage from both the elements and what looked like external challenges—but those had been across the years. There was nothing recent, as far as he could tell. "But it would be hard to find anything that has not taken a beating these days," he continued.

"Do you think it might be Marauders?" Caleb watched Sister Susanna, a middle-aged woman in the congregation, place a bundle of bedding into an open cart. It could make a workable tent, he supposed, or maybe be used for a bedroll or blanket when they made camp.

"If it was, then there would be more damage, bodies, and blood," said Bram. "No, this was something else."

"No livestock or crops," Caleb continued. "Maybe they just left for better lands."

"So they became Sojourners, then?" James shot Caleb a grin.

Bram could see the humor implied by the question—the absurdity of a Dweller actually becoming a Sojourner—but left it alone. Caleb wasn't amused, of course, remaining as serious as ever. The two of them were thinking along the same lines he was and soon enough would turn to him for clarity on what to do next, and the whole congregation after that. Having something worthwhile to share would call for a miracle at this point.

"Whatever their fate, it is not any of our concern," he said as he strode closer to the statue of Laroma. While he hadn't seen all the goddesses across Annulis, he was amused by how they all shared the same form. It seemed all had a certain idea of how a goddess should look and didn't deviate from it. "As long as they remain Dwellers, their fate is sealed. In the very least we can gain some things without having to part with coin or goods—"

He was interrupted by an excited shout from Brother Desmond, who was racing their way.

"Sarah and I have found something you should see!" Desmond managed to get out between breaths. Their excitement wasn't encouraging. Nor was it upsetting. Bram had learned long ago to not be moved by anything. An even keel in one's disposition was best for all.

"And what is that?" Bram made sure the exchange wasn't attracting too much notice from the others. While *he* managed to keep calm, not everyone else did.

"It is better you see it for yourself," said Desmond in a lower, more serious tone.

"Then lead the way, Brother." Taking Caleb and James with him, he followed Desmond and Sarah at a steady pace as they led them down a couple of streets until they came to a cluster of rather ordinary houses.

"In here." Desmond guided all into one of them. Leading them deeper inside, he directed their attention to the open door of a second room beyond the one they presently occupied. So far Bram hadn't seen anything warranting a second look, but once his eyes adjusted to the room beyond, that changed.

"Crows setting snares?" Caleb asked James beside him. Both men were inside the room and close enough to trace their fingers over the deeply gouged text. "What does it mean? Something tied to their religion, perhaps?"

"Nothing good, from the sound of it," said James before prodding the bed with his staff, bringing up the sheets and rough straw.

"But why carve it over and over again?" Caleb looked to Bram. That was another good question. But he had no answers. All he kept getting were more and more questions that continued to sour his stomach.

"Is this the only place you found something like this?" Bram asked Desmond as he looked up and down the room. It was everywhere. The same phrase was carved over and over. It was like the litany of some madman. But what did it mean? And why just this room? No one else had made mention of any other discoveries in the rest of the village.

"Yes," said Desmond, "none of the other houses had writing." He paused. "But there was something else."

"What?" Bram saw Desmond glance at Sarah before facing the patriarch with a stoic expression even Caleb couldn't match.

"Skulls," he flatly announced.

"*Skulls?*" Sarah was just as surprised as the rest of them. "I did not see any . . ." Revelation dawned across the girl's face. "*That* was what was in the chest."

"Yes." Desmond sighed. "But there is something else about them."

"And what is that?" Bram cautiously inquired.

"I-I wanted to be sure, but it appears they might have been—well, you best have a look for yourself."

Desmond led them to another house and to a chest within it. Bram followed, watching Desmond carefully lean over and open the lid. Taking a step closer, Bram joined the rest in peering inside. There were three skulls in the chest. They all were small, making him think they belonged to children. This in itself wasn't so macabre. Death wasn't new to him or any other inhabitant of Annulis. Rather, what troubled them was what was clear to anyone with two eyes when they peered closer at the bone.

"Are those cut marks?" James's voice was small.

"I believe so." Bram noted the cruel lines slashing here and there along the bone—right where key junctions of muscle would join. It was similar to what was done to any beast when carving meat from bone. Except this wasn't some common animal but a human being.

"Sovereign, have mercy." Caleb took a breath and exhaled slowly through pinched lips.

"I did not want Sarah to see it"—the love for his daughter was clear in Desmond's face and voice—"but after seeing that other room, I knew it had to be told."

"Sadly, you did right." Bram did his best to keep his eyes from drifting back to the chest and the skulls still holding Caleb's and James's fascination. "It would have been better to have gone on not knowing such things, but in the light of truth, we are able to see still more truth." The old proverb never seemed more apt than now. For truly in light of such insight they now had a greater understanding of what might have happened here and quite possibly what might be awaiting them in other villages and towns along the way.

"I am sorry you had to see all this, Sister Sarah. If you wish, there is no harm in taking to some more pleasant place."

"I believe I shall remain," said Sarah, much to Bram's surprise, "if that is all right." He watched her eyes drift James's way. The young man didn't pay it much mind, but Bram had lived long enough to understand the meaning.

"Of course." He succeeded in suppressing a small knowing smile from his lips.

Bram had known Sarah her whole life. In some respects, she wasn't like the other young girls. Most endeavored to shelter themselves from the darker aspects of the world. That in itself wasn't too strange—it was even logical in many ways. But the way in which not even the bleakest things affected her was a curious matter. Had some members of the younger generation grown so calloused to dark deeds that nothing truly unsettled them? If so, what did that bode for the future of the congregation and their chances of finding the Veiled City? If they became too much like the rest of the world they sojourned through, they ran the risk of rejoining it instead of staying on the path.

"I am just as curious as you are, I am sure, about what this all might mean." She was supposed to be speaking to Bram but kept her eyes on James the whole time.

"Nothing good, I reckon." Caleb tossed the skull back into the chest with a thud.

"Not if we can believe our eyes," he replied. "But truth does not often come by sight. Still, we would be wise to move on from here as quickly as we can. Have you finished searching the rest of your area, Brother Desmond?"

"Yes."

"Then take anything else you have found and join the others in the courtyard. Once we have assembled, we will make an inventory and depart."

"Come on, Sarah," Desmond said, taking hold of his daughter's hand and making his way out of the room. There was a flash of disappointment in her eyes, but she quickly recovered.

"You are not joining us, Patriarch?" she asked from over her shoulder.

"I wish to take a second look at these skulls and that room," he said. "We will join you and the rest of the congregation shortly."

"Sarah." Another tug of Desmond's arm brought her to the door.

"Brother Desmond?" Bram called out, stopping Desmond on the threshold.

"Yes?"

"If you could keep what you found to yourself and Sister Sarah for the time being, I would appreciate it."

"Of course."

Bram nodded his thanks, and the two left. "I trust you two will do the same?"

"It would only cause worry to share it now," said Caleb.

"Exactly," he agreed.

"So what does this all mean?" Caleb continued.

"That we should be more cautious in the days ahead," answered Bram, "but little else."

"But the skulls." Caleb pointed to them again, as if Bram had forgotten their sneering smiles and cut-marked surfaces.

"Are they not proof enough of the Dwellers' inhumane treatment toward each other? Is that not what the heralds said would be the case in the times to come? More darkness and wickedness among those who continue to forsake the path to the Veiled City?" True words, but Bram still had no answers to give, only dark questions leading him to ponder even darker possibilities.

"Then what of the message?" James finally pulled himself away from the chest.

That wasn't something he could easily explain. "Perhaps it is best you and Caleb return to the others." Noticing their concerned looks, he added, "I will be fine. I plan to have one more look and rejoin you shortly."

Bram watched the two depart, thankful at least that he didn't have to deal with their questions. That just left him with his own, which were more than enough. Picking up one of the skulls, he studied again the cut lines across the bone, turning it this way and that and making sure he wasn't seeing things. The longer he examined it, the more convinced he became. This child had been at the very least skinned and at the worst . . . He prayed they were already dead when it occurred. But it was as he'd said: one should not be surprised by the wickedness Dwellers worked upon their own.

But as gruesome as it was, the discovery didn't shed light on what happened to the village's inhabitants. In the best-case scenario they'd taken what they could and departed en masse. But to where and for what purpose? Might James actually have been onto something with his jesting? Had they suddenly come to their senses and become Sojourners? He doubted it. A handful, perhaps, but not the whole village. Even when the heralds first appeared and stirred their hearers with their message, only small portions of villages, towns, and cities took up cowl and cloak. It would be no different here, if any heard the truth.

He gently returned the skull to the chest, closed it, and made his way to the other house and room. Once there he stood amid the mad scrawling and found himself just as lost as he was before. It could *be* anything, *mean* anything. And it could equally be just meaningless musings from a truly troubled mind. But as patriarch it was his duty to keep those in his care safe as well as help them on their journey.

Crows . . . The birds were carrion eaters, of course, and they fit the idea of coming to tear flesh and such—like they all had seen firsthand with that hanging child yesterday—but was that all? Was there instead some hidden meaning, and if not, why scrawl it over and over again? Of course the one who did it could have been insane. Perhaps insanity had led him or her to kill those whose skulls were in the chest. And then again, it could be something much more . . . Too many questions.

He knew from stories the Laromi favored the crow; it was part of their city's emblem and had something to do with their goddess. Could that be part of it? Seeing he wasn't going to get any more answers, Bram departed for the courtyard. He'd have to find something to say eventually, as the congregation would wonder about why the city was deserted, and while he didn't think Desmond would say anything, it was possible that Sarah, Caleb, or James might let something slip in passing—and thus rouse even more unrest among the congregation.

They were at their best when united and free of strife and fears. A single mind focused on a single purpose. Division was the birthplace of confusion and strife, and with it came every sort of evil temptation. And so Bram pondered what to say and do next, wondering if any other patriarchs or matriarchs before him had dealt with such a quandary. He sought every corner of his mind for a simple remedy but kept coming up empty. Since it was clearly beyond him, he offered up a simple prayer.

"Sovereign, grant me wisdom."

CHAPTER FOUR

A Funerary Rite. A Pilfering of Goods.

Dawn swelled across the sky as Elliott packed the last of his master's belongings into his saddlebags. They'd be making their way east for the Brachin Hills. It was between them, the Ashen Hills, and the Kondis Mountains where the city of Larom resided. The town behind them and the Laromi who had called it home were no more. The walls, like the bodies inside them, were now nothing but fading memory. Soon the same fate would befall Larom, and Annulis would be one step closer to the Great Conflagration, and those loyal to Pyre that much closer to their reward.

Elliott, like many of the other squires, was eager to see the blessed day come in his lifetime. Though he'd only been on campaign for these last three years, it seemed as if they'd never see an end of it. Annulis was truly massive. When he thought about how he'd left Pyrus three years ago and had only seen about a third of the continent thus far, he was amazed. Of course, they hadn't been making a straight line in their travels, instead methodically clearing out all areas they could find, combing them carefully lest they miss a single town or village.

Salbrin had made clear Pyre wanted all to hear of his mercy before the end. And while it took some effort—and plenty of time—it would be worth it. He and all the rest who were on campaign with him would be able to have a clear conscience when the end finally did arrive or they drew their last breath, whichever came first.

But thankfully, they weren't alone in the effort. There were other armies in the field, others being raised up after them, who would continue the mission as long as necessary. It took Salbrin over twenty-five years to bring about the reforms in and around Pyrus. And that was just one part of the world. The other armies had helped since then, but off the shores of the continent, Elliott knew about islands yet to be explored, and then there could be so much more still waiting for discovery.

Sir Pillum was strong, but even he wouldn't be the same in ten years, let alone twenty. And then there was Elliott, who, though young, wouldn't be able to go on forever. So he, like so many of the other squires and knights, prayed for Pyre's favor in speeding the process along. And the farther he traveled from Pyrus, the more earnest and fervent those prayers became.

For while those back in Pyrus might only have heard Salbrin's fiery sermons on how fallen the world had become, Elliott was seeing it firsthand every day. There wasn't anything that hadn't been tainted following the Burning Cascade. If anything, Pyre had used this first sign to make the dross float to the surface. Now it fell to them to scrape it away and reveal the pure reality underneath.

"Everything packed?" Sir Pillum emerged from his pavilion. He was dressed in full armor and appeared eager to head out. Elliott had learned it wasn't so much Selection but all that led up to it that held his master's interest the most. It was more about the press and challenge to get to it rather than the end result. Now that it had passed, he was eager to begin the press anew for the next Selection.

"All but the tent," said Elliott.

It would be the last of the things struck before the army moved on. The soldiers kept simpler accommodations, which were always struck first. The Salamandrine had the privilege of being last to leave their tents but first to lead the army. There was a reason for this, of course. In wartime the infantry saw to the final preparations of any fallen Pyri. The knights' taller pavilions also provided a convenient cover for the horses corralled in the pens peppering the Salamandrine camp. Striking them last made more strategic sense.

"Leave it until after the rite," he replied, looking Elliott over in approval. "Come on then, they'll be waiting."

Together they made their way to what was now mostly a large empty field. It had been their camp, but with all the infantry's and camp workers' tents removed, it was restored to its former state. Most of the knights were already there or making their way with the rest of the army to the center of the field, where the bodies of the slain Pyri had been assembled yesterday.

The tent that had covered the area, keeping them safe from the crows, had been removed. The fallen infantry had been piled into two small mounds, and another pile of about the same size contained the fallen Salamandrine. Each pile sat upon and was outlined with a thick layer of kindling and wood. They had suffered fewer losses than the Laromi, but it was still more than just a handful of men.

This, when added to the casualties of previous battles, meant they weren't as large a force as they had been upon setting out from Pyrus. If not for the occasional reinforcements, they might have been half their former number by now. Thankfully, with those reinforcements their numbers had remained relatively even. The occasional addition from Selection was helpful too, but most of these never saw combat, only serving in support roles for a short while until they were sent back to Pyrus for the completion of their perfection in Pyre's mercy.

"How much longer until we reach Larom?" Elliott asked as he and Sir Pillum joined the growing throng around the mounds.

"If we keep this pace and the weather holds, no more than a few days. Of course, if we encounter any villages or towns between now and then, it'll be longer." Elliott noticed the subdued tone in the last part of his master's comment.

It was clear he hungered for the larger prize that was Larom. He didn't blame him. Not if what they had been encountering so far with the towns and villages was any sign of future results. If they kept putting forth all this time, blood, and sweat for only two converts—and not even the best to join their ranks—he could understand the temptation to view it all as drudgery. But if it was Pyre's will, then it would be done.

"Sir Pillum." Calix, the commander of the Salamandrine, greeted Elliott and his master. "A fine job on Selection last night."

"Thank you, sir."

"Nice touch with using the banner. I hear Milec rather enjoyed it." Calix was probably one of the oldest men in the Salamandrine. He kept his black hair extra short, which accentuated his widow's peak. His graying temples, like the silver threading his eyebrows, lent a mature, confident look that no doubt helped with his command.

"I only wish we could have gotten more than we did," his master lamented.

"We can only do our part. Pyre sees to the rest. If they want to despise his mercy, then so be it. We're innocent of their blood, as is Pyre." Calix turned his weathered face back to the priests conversing among the three piles of corpses. "But we'll keep extending his mercy as long as there are people who haven't heard the message."

"Still," said Sir Pillum, "for only two men. It hardly seems worth even offering them mercy."

"To you and me both," said Calix, "but we must obey Pyre's will."

Elliott observed the two Laromi who'd been selected. They stood at the front of the gathering, where they would have a clean view of what would soon unfold. Silent and despondent, they resembled many of the people he'd seen selected. It could be a challenge for some to let go of the past. The taint in the world was a hard thing to shake free of for many, but in time they'd be shown their place.

The priests would decide where they'd serve Pyre, and that would be their place to grow and thrive. Until their place was decided, uncertainty could always be found, providing a foothold for fear. But unlike others Elliott had seen, these two seemed different. He couldn't decide what it was exactly, but there was a shadow of something lifeless about them. Something that made him think he was viewing two dead men rather than depressed converts.

"May Pyre's wings ever enfold us," said Milec, addressing the assembly.

Elliott immediately snapped to attention. The rite had begun.

Milec stood in the open space between the crowd and the piles of dead men, dressed as he was the night before but projecting a more somber air.

"And may his herald always lead us true," all gathered replied.

"As has been our custom since the first days of Pyre's herald," continued Milec, "we look to honor those who have fallen in Pyre's service. Free from this corrupt, dying world, they're now awaiting the coming of the Purifier, eager for a world reborn."

"May he come quickly," said Elliott along with the gathered throng.

"As Salbrin has said, all will be purified, even our flesh. And so we lay Pyre's kiss beneath his fallen warriors. May it burn as a beacon of hope for all who yet walk Annulis and serve as a pleasing sacrifice to our god, who has received these—his precious ones—to his breast."

Silence returned to the gathering as three groups of priests formed around the piles of dead. Once in place, they unleashed lines of flame from their blaze rods at the kindling and wood, setting it aflame.

"There is but one god," Milec roared above the crackling fire.

"Pyre!" All shouted their conviction.

"There is but one herald." Again Milec's deep voice boomed.

"Salbrin is his name!" There was always a jolt of excitement whenever Elliott made the confession. It raced from his brain to his feet like lightning, straightening his spine and lifting his head. It was the core of what they all believed and were fighting for. It was the basis of the truth they brought to all, who'd either receive it and be embraced or reject it and be purged.

He watched the flames lick the fallen bodies as smoke began filling the sky. The bodies had been stripped of their weapons and armor, which were saved for the reinforcements to come. Only their flesh and clothing would be burnt, which was both a way of preserving the dignity of the dead as well as a practical matter, as bloodstained and torn attire was easier to replace than to clean and repair.

As the flames grew stronger, Elliott knew the unmistakable smell of burning human flesh would soon waft his way. Of all the things he'd encountered, it was perhaps the least tolerable. Thankfully, there was no wind to blow any directly toward him, but you couldn't escape it, not as long as you were required to stand in memorial by the blaze.

"Larom will fall." Calix kept his deep blue eyes on the fires. The priests were retreating as the heat and flames increased. Soon everyone would take a few steps back, until the full force of the bonfires' blaze had passed. "Their corrupted city will be toppled alongside their goddess, and all who refuse Pyre's mercy will burn."

"There's some talk of their weapons," Sir Pillum said. "Something new and potentially quite deadly. There's even been some debating about it among the army."

Calix looked Sir Pillum full in the face. "But not in the Salamandrine."

"No, sir. We know nothing can stand before us. Not with Pyre on our side."

"These Laromi are nothing special. Everyone else we've encountered has fallen before Pyre's might. Have you ever seen one of them gain the better of us in any battle?"

"No, sir." Sir Pillum was rapid in reply.

"Larom is nothing," Calix continued. "Their weapons—real or imagined—are nothing. We'll be upon them soon enough. And they will fall, as did the rest who failed to receive Pyre's mercy. And then we'll continue to the next people and place. As long as Pyre is with us, we shall never fail." This said, he resumed the vigil over the dead, Sir Pillum mirroring him.

As Elliott's eyes drifted across the field, they passed again over the two Laromi who'd made it through Selection. He thought he could see them exchanging a few short words but wasn't sure, since they kept their heads low. They also seemed more nervous than when last he saw them. There was an excited energy about them twitching across their frames. One moment their eyes were fixed on the burning mounds, the next on those around them. Back and forth it went, until, like a bolt, both men dashed into the circle, making a mad run for one of the fires.

Before Elliott or anyone else knew what was happening, the two men had leapt into the ravenous flames with a horrid scream. Instantly, their clothes were alight and skin was bubbling and burning.

Some of the soldiers rushed in, with a couple of priests beside them. Using their swords, they tried peeling the two Laromi from the bonfire. Amazingly, the men resisted their attempts, instead howling in defiant rage and using what strength remained to keep themselves fixed in place until the fire had finished its grisly work.

When it was over, both dropped like toppled logs atop the rest of the dead. Nearby soldiers flung them free from the mounds as if prying a slab of bacon from a skillet. The Laromi flopped to the ground. One landed on his side, the other on his back. Both were dead and partially charred. Elliott could only make out the sockets and gaping mouths on their ruinous features. The small bit of fire that still lingered about their figures dwindled into greasy smoke.

"So they showed their true heart in the end," said Calix as casually as Elliott had ever heard him speak. No one else seemed unsettled by the development either. Only Elliott appeared surprised. That they had stepped forward to avoid death only to embrace it later—choosing a harsher end than they would have had last night—made no sense.

"A defiant town," added Sir Pillum as they watched the soldiers and the priests walk away, leaving the two Laromi where they lay.

"Which could give us a taste of what's to come in Larom." Calix sighed. "It would be a lot easier to take them if we weren't called to be so merciful."

"Yes." Sir Pillum begrudgingly nodded. "But we must be true to Pyre, no matter what we'd like to do instead."

"As soon as the fire's done, we'll strike the tents and push hard for Larom," Calix continued.

"Yes, sir."

A reverential air fell on all gathered as the army watched the fire do its work. As the day brightened, the wood crumbled into white ash, mingling with that of the bodies, leaving only some small assortments of charred bone. These would be pounded into pebbles by camp workers and infantry while the knights' tents were struck. At least that was how it should have been. Instead, when the Salamandrine and their squires returned to their horses and pavilions, they found much less awaiting them than had been there when they'd left for the rite.

"There's nothing left, sir." Elliott was referring to his master's saddlebags, but it applied equally to everything else. Sir Pillum scowled as he took in what was clear to anyone to see: a ransacked camp.

"They left the horses and took just enough to carry," his master growled. "We might have noticed the horse theft while observing the rite, but not this. Smart and bold. But still foolish if they think we won't respond."

"But who did this? Surely it wasn't the Laromi."

"If it was, they'd be doubly foolish."

A trumpet calling for the Salamandrine to assemble sounded over the camp.

"Strike the tent and pack up what remains. I want the horses ready to ride when I return."

Elliott watched Sir Pillum hurry off to Commander Calix's pavilion in the center of the Salamandrine encampment. As with the other knights' pavilions, his was a simple white, but on either side of the entrance flap waved banners emblazoned with Pyre's crest. The tent had more open space around it, allowing for a defensive line or a place for the knights to assemble, like now.

Knowing how short this conversation was bound to be, Elliott had to work double time. He didn't want to hold his master or anyone else back. Speed was of the essence. Thankfully, they had a few extra saddlebags he could use, recovered from the fallen knights. His fast thinking assured he got enough for his purposes. Those who came after him weren't so fortunate. He worked up a sweat repacking what had been pulled out of the bags before taking on the pavilion, which he'd tie up and attach to the back of his own horse.

The infantry carried their tents in wagons, which thankfully still remained. It would have been an added discomfort to turn the men into pack mules when they were already faced with such a long march. Elliott didn't know how so many of them managed to do it as it was and was thankful he'd been blessed with a horse. His wasn't as mighty as Sir Pillum's steed, Bakan, but it was still something to keep him from the long slogs, even letting him imagine at times he was already a knight.

Though he didn't indulge in such fantasies that often, it was still a pleasant pastime in which to engage when there was nothing but wilderness around them for miles on end.

He'd barely finished attaching the tent when he heard Sir Pillum behind him. "Calix is taking the Salamandrine to find these thieves while the rest of the army marches for Larom. On horseback we're better suited to recover the stolen goods, then catch up to the infantry and resupply them before nightfall." He made a quick inspection of the horses and then turned to Elliott. "Are you ready?"

"Yes, sir."

"Then mount up. We leave at once."

CHAPTER FIVE

A Respoiling of Goods. Retaliation in Kind.

T he pounding hooves had passed into the background of Elliott's thoughts. He kept his horse at the side and rear of Sir Pillum's. Like the other squires, he endeavored to be on hand if needed while not being so close as to risk hindering his master from any sudden action.

Calix kept to the rear of the Salamandrine, all five hundred of them. Normally he'd be at the front, but this time the scouts took the lead, guiding them on mile by mile. They'd alternated between a rapid trot and a full gallop for the past couple of hours, stopping now and then to take their bearings.

The tracks left at their camp had alternated between definite shapes and faint whispers. The rocky patches in the terrain they encountered obscured their path, slowing their progress and forcing the scouts to stop more often than he and the rest of the Salamandrine would have liked. Because such efforts ate into so much of their time, Calix tried making it up with these bursts of speed.

It was clear early on the thieves had started on foot but soon changed to horseback. That would explain why they didn't take any of the knights' horses. It also explained why their group hadn't run into them after pressing the horses hard in pursuit. But loaded down as the thieves were, they wouldn't be able to outrun the Salamandrine much longer. And then there was the question of how many there were and just who they were. Elliott didn't think it could be more Laromi. He'd never seen them with horses. He wondered if they even knew how to ride.

"There!" Sir Pillum pointed out a shape in the distance.

Squinting confirmed the mass ahead was a group of horses galloping at top speed. They didn't look like Laromi, but it was hard to tell from this far back. However, it was clear they numbered around a hundred. He spied bulging backpacks and full saddlebags. They must have stuffed everything they could into them until the bags were just short of bursting.

"Forward!" Calix ordered, pushing his horse harder. The others parted, allowing him a smooth path into the lead.

As the knights' horses devoured the distance between them and the thieves, Elliott could make out finer details. He could see scale mail shirts, brigandine leather pants, and scale mail coifs under horned helmets. While none carried a standard, each had a familiar crest painted on their kite shields. The black falcon with spread wings over a red background was hard to miss—even harder with a three-pointed golden crown in the yellow sun behind the falcon's right-turned head.

"Marauders." He heard Sir Pillum curse over the rumbling hooves.

It couldn't have been easy keeping such a rapid pace. It spoke of their determination . . . and desperation. But that seemed their nature in a nutshell, which colored their reputation and the tales of their encounters that preceded them. Even though Marauders had an ordinary appearance, there was something else—something setting them apart from the common rank and file. It was one of the few things Marauders and non-Marauders agreed on.

Elliott was as versed as any on Annulis in the tales of these landless people said to roam the world scavenging supplies and finding comfort where they could. It was said they were once part of the most revered and feared army of the Mundian Empire, now fallen after its destruction during the Burning Cascade. This time, they'd made a foolish mistake trying to steal from Pyre's army. Such disrespect could only be met with one response.

"Circle around them!" Calix shouted.

The Salamandrine formed two wings, spreading out to the left and right as they came alongside and then passed the Marauders. Elliott joined Sir Pillum in the left wing, pushing his horse hard as they joined the other flank, completing the circle and thereby stopping the Marauders in their tracks.

The squires went to the outside of the circle, allowing the knights in front room to maneuver. Though in back, Elliott could still see everything clearly. The Marauders drew their short swords and lifted their shields, bringing the ancient crest of their fallen empire front and center.

The Marauders' horses whinnied and neighed, but none tried closing the gap between them and the Salamandrine. Instead, they moved into their own formation, drawing their horses around to face their foes in a tightly formed circle. Their helmets helped add to the show of strength. Each covered half their face and was crafted into a grotesque visage topped with horns. One could imagine them as some sort of monster. It was an obvious tactic used for generating fear in their foes, but it wouldn't work against the Salamandrine.

"I believe we'll take what's ours," Calix told the Marauders. Yet even with chins and jowls slick with sweat and chests heaving under their scale mail shirts, none would back down nor seek any quarter.

"You're welcome to try," said the one who Elliott assumed was their leader.

"You're more than outnumbered," Calix said, stating the obvious. "Just surrender."

The Marauders' leader spouted mocking laughter. "And what then?" He jabbed his sword at a nearby knight's shield. "You try and convert us to follow after that crazed god of yours?"

"It would be an act of mercy," countered Calix. "Both by Pyre and us."

"Mercy from those who kill and destroy whole towns and villages? We've done many things over the years—some better than others—but we're not butchering zealots. If you want to try and take what you think is yours, then you're welcome to it."

Elliott could feel the tension thickening in the air. This was going to be close-quarter fighting, and he would get a firsthand viewing. His exposure to actual combat in the field was limited. While he was still being trained he got to watch a few encounters, but nothing like this. He'd get to be almost side by side with Sir Pillum and the rest of the Salamandrine. It would be like he was an actual knight. Such a thing was beyond words but not without a flood of emotions.

"So be it." Calix drew his sword. The rest of the Salamandrine followed his lead. The sound of the near-unison action gave Elliott goose bumps.

Neither side moved, only stared at the other.

"No quarter!" Calix shouted and drove his horse for the clump of Marauders.

A riotous shout arose from all gathered as swords clashed with bodies and clanged off shields. An eyeblink later, all were locked in bloody melee.

Elliott did his best to keep from the brunt of the attack, but it was hard to avoid when it was all around him. The discipline of both sides held through the conflict. The Marauders kept their circle, and the Salamandrine were unable to break it.

"For the glory of Pyre!"

"Cut these infidels down!"

"Now!" the Marauders' leader shouted over the fray.

They all reared their horses and chopped down with their swords. The combined effect pushed many knights back, surrendering ground.

"Half-moon!" came the next command.

The large circle split into two equal clumps, which raced through the space created by the previous maneuver. The Marauders slid through, slashing knights at will.

One by one they trickled out of the melee, racing through their foes and into their squires behind them. Elliott barely breathed as a handful shoved their way through only a few feet from him.

Hallin, another squire, tried putting up a fight but was quickly rebuffed with a sword through the chest. Other Marauders rumbled through on his right.

Fear gripped Elliott's heart and troubled his stomach. He kept his horse steady, watching the Marauders draw a line behind them while also retrieving the bows attached to their saddles. Elliott hadn't noticed these weapons before, nor the arrows they were hurriedly nocking.

They let the arrows fly at will. At such close range many of the missiles found their mark, drawing blood from horse and rider alike. It was by the grace of Pyre he didn't take any himself. Instead, he endured his fellow squires' cries when shafts dug into their shoulders and sides.

"Take down those archers!" demanded Calix.

Sir Pillum wasn't going to wait for a second command. He raced through the enemy, swinging at any Marauder still inside the Salamandrine's crumbling circle. When he was free, he reared Bakan. Two Marauders under him lifted their shields but couldn't stop the horse's full weight from crashing upon them. They fell from their saddles with curses. Sir Pillum brought down his horse and trampled them.

"Kill him!" In a rage, the Marauders' leader pointed to Sir Pillum.

A few arrows were loosed his way, but Elliott watched in utter amazement as his master stopped them with his shield. Before any more could be released, scores of knights were galloping for the archers. This finally broke their unified front. Each focused on their own defense, proving a poor match for the knights.

The Marauders were picked off and cut down from all sides. Half their number fell in the first few moments. The rest held their own for a short while, but the eventual onslaught of so many and their previous hard ride took a toll.

Slow blocks allowed for armor-penetrating cuts and thrusts. Weak retaliatory responses also did little good, leaving them open for still more slashes and jabs. Finally, the last of the Marauders toppled to the earth, battered, beaten, or dead.

"Take what you can," said Calix, dismounting. "Both what they took and what they have. We can leave it on their horses. And see to those as well. Take only the strong. We'll have to ride hard if we're going to meet the rest of the army by nightfall. Leave the bodies for the crows."

As the rest dismounted and began sifting through the fallen, Sir Pillum came up alongside Elliott. "Are you hurt?"

"No, sir. They rode right past."

"It looks like you got more than a taste of combat today."

"Less than others got." His eyes found Hallin's body slumped over his saddle. Sir Pillum noted the dead squire with a somber expression.

"I'll see how best to comfort Sir Andrew. He was looking forward to Hallin's knighting next year."

"And Hallin was looking forward to being knighted," added Elliott, solemnly.

"And now he has a greater reward," Sir Pillum returned, looking his own squire over carefully. "Not a scratch on you. This will make quite the tale."

"Not as good as what you did today, sir. You were incredible."

"A knight does what has to be done, Elliott." Sir Pillum dismounted. "The Salamandrine are expected to get results, and that means whatever has to be done is what needs to be done. A good lesson to remember if you're ever going to pull your weight."

"I'll remember it," Elliott assured himself and his master alike.

Sir Pillum turned back to Elliott with a hint of a smile across his lips. "That isn't to say I didn't enjoy any part of it. Now help me gather the spoils."

While the Salamandrine had been off chasing their thieves, the rest of the Pyric army had been marching hard through the Ashen Fields. The now-lifeless prairie was named for the pale grasses that once dominated it. But the name became more apropos after much of the terrain had been burnt to ash during the Burning Cascade. What managed to grow back were more or less sickly stalks mixed with a raggedy carpet of stunted sward. While far from inspiring, it made it easier to gauge their progress. The taller peaks of the Kondis Mountains in the distance also helped in that effort. Should they keep their pace, they might even be able to see the hints of the lower hills ascending to those forbidding peaks by nightfall.

As was the case with so much of Western Annulis following the Burning Cascade, what remained wasn't the vibrant, living landscape that had been before. This was true for people and animals as well. Most clung to villages and towns, both for safety and for the concentration of labor that made it easier to raise livestock, farm, and do the other things necessary to keep a people and community going. As a result, what had once been seen as an area open to conquest and expansion was now a no man's land littered with faint echoes of what had been decades and even centuries before.

The only life in the area was the column of Pyric infantry, followed by the priests, and then the rest of the camp workers behind them, marching through the grass. Stray mounds of tumbled rock were left like cairns across the swaying, waist-high stalks. Even the derelict farms and rotting carcasses of houses they passed were ignored, each serving as silent testimony to the slow death hanging over everything.

Drenn, the commander of the infantry, was at the head of the column. As second in command of the army under Calix, he knew the limits of what was possible even in strange, hostile territory. And from what he could see so far, things were going exactly to plan. While not having to march faster because of the Salamandrine's occasional impatience, the men were making good time. With the knights away, they could keep a speed that would work for them until setting camp. And he wasn't worried about any attacks. At twenty-five hundred men, they were a more than capable force.

Even if the Salamandrine sometimes doubted them, the infantry could hold their own. While some might consider them the weakest link, Drenn knew they were really the backbone. And not just of *this* army, but the whole Pyric army. Without them there wouldn't be much of anything to speak of. He didn't hold any ill will toward his fellow warriors. Knights and infantry both were brothers in the same fight and honoring and being honored by the same god. In the end they would all get their rewards, and everything would be as it should. For now they fought and served as long as they had breath, hopeful the next day would bring them closer to the end of this cursed, doomed world.

"When do you think the Salamandrine will return?" asked Arthur, Drenn's second. The middle-aged warrior was already worn from battle, giving him a hard-looking exterior. It was a contrast to Drenn's baby face. He hadn't been able to shed it even in his thirtieth year, giving him a constantly youthful appearance he'd finally learned to accept.

"When they do," said Drenn, "we'll hear them long before we see them."

"Hopefully, they'll recover everything," said Arthur. "I'm not looking forward to calming grumbling soldiers upset over some missing meals."

"I don't think it'll be that bad," Drenn returned. "These are strong men, not fresh recruits."

"You're right." Arthur grinned darkly. "Those tend to die first."

"The training is getting better in Pyrus," he replied. "They've learned to only send the best options our way, leaving the rest back in the city."

"Which could explain why we haven't seen any new recruits for some time."

"Rather fewer but better-trained men than scores who don't know which end of a sword is which."

Arthur stopped, cocking his head to one side. "You hear that?"

Drenn also stopped and looked around. "They couldn't be back this early." He didn't see anything, nor did he really hear anything around them.

"I thought—"

Arthur was cut short by a crossbow bolt through his neck. He could do little but surrender a gurgle and collapse into the grass.

Suddenly, scores of men appeared. How they had kept themselves hidden, Drenn didn't know. That wasn't important now. The men had formed a good line on either side, hundreds of people in each.

They were Laromi. But unlike the Laromi they'd faced in the towns and villages, these were soldiers. Each wore a chain mail shirt over brigandine leather pants. Fluted steel greaves and bracers covered their legs and forearms, while open-faced helmets with nose guards crowned their heads.

A low growling sound mingled with something akin to a clanking chain drew Drenn's eyes to their shields. They were round and painted white on the front with a black crow in profile. Its raised wings and glaring white eye were meant to intimidate, but the sharp blades around the shield's lip did a much better job.

These were the source of the noise. The blades rapidly rotated around the shield lip in a constant, hungry motion. He'd never seen anything like it. There had been talk circulating among some of the men about a new type of weapon used by the Laromi. He hadn't put much stock in the rumors, but now here it was ready to cut into him and his men.

Rushing into the fray with short swords drawn, the Laromi were accompanied by a frenzied flurry of crossbow bolts. These tore into the frontline of Pyric defenders with gruesome results.

"Stand your ground!" Drenn shouted.

The Laromi had a couple hundred on each flank. But the Pyri had the advantage in numbers. If they kept their discipline, they'd be able to cut them down before much harm was done.

And then he saw another line rise behind the first. These had been hidden in the grass, but they weren't attacking. Instead, they stood and waited, weapons ready.

Drenn knew the men could weather the crossbows. There was still time to get into defensive positions. But those shields with their rotating blades were another matter. Men screamed as the shields were brought down on hands and bodies—even necks. The sharp spinning edges were keener than any sword, sawing into the exposed parts of their victims with one motion. Blood sprayed and limbs and heads fell as a new volley of crossbow bolts flew into the infantry like angry wasps. These too found their targets, puncturing shields and armor.

What made the attacks even deadlier was that each crossbow was firing five bolts in succession without any reloading. Instead, when the five bolts had been expended, the bowman simply reached to their belt, took a new clip of five fresh bolts, and snapped it in place. The design allowed for self-cocking and loading of the next bolt with a deadly mechanical efficiency.

Even so, they wouldn't be cowed by these infidels. To a man they pressed back as hard as their opponents gave, not wasting a single opportunity. Soon enough they'd managed to stop the vise from closing any further.

"Let them feel the wrath of Pyre!" Drenn could hear Milec's loud voice from where he marched with the priests in the back.

Blaze rods burst into life, spewing out flame on the unsuspecting Laromi. While groups skittered back from the fire, others wildly sought to extinguish the flames tightly gripping their frames.

More bolts were returned in rebuke.

"Take the fight to them!" Drenn commanded.

The Pyri split into two groups and swelled forward, slashing and shoving everything crossing their path. They still had the numbers. It was clearer now the enemy numbered about five hundred—split between each flank. It wasn't as serious a threat as he first thought, just something meant to slow them down and force some losses.

Some were shoved back, but others squeezed through the Laromic ranks, forming a fissure through which more could stream in and unleash their anger. This was the case with both sides of the fighting, and for a short while the Pyri were pleased at the seeming turn of fortunes. But only for that short while . . .

With renewed zeal the Laromi found their second wind, hacking and slicing with a brutal determination. The blades on their shields had ceased whirring, but even in their stationary position, the metal-toothed outlines were quite a fearsome—and effective—display.

The Pyri were pushed back against each other, allowing the Laromi to close in once again. Both sides had lost men, but the Pyri had suffered more. And while the priests' blaze rods still flashed and flared here and there, they were unable to stand before the constant barrage of crossbow fire that was now renewed with greater intensity.

"Second wave, move in," came the command from the Laromic ranks. Their frontline melted away, letting the fresh troops take their place.

The familiar whirring sound began anew as these Laromi entered the fight. Eager to make their mark, each brought their terrible shields up against the Pyri, and once more the pattern of carnage resumed.

So much for ending this quickly.

"Stand and fight!" Drenn roared. "No mercy!"

"For the glory of Pyre," Milec added. "Hold your ground."

CHAPTER SIX

A Troubling Walk. The Citadel.

The sun was at its zenith as the congregation continued down the road. The endless stretch of rock-hard earth was lined by dry, waist-high grass, waving in the slight breeze. It was a common sight for any Sojourner. But whereas before Sarah might have eagerly played mental games as to what might lie a little further beyond them, now she wasn't so sure she was willing to speculate.

From what she understood, this area was called the Ashen Fields. It was said to have been named long ago, but the name became more fitting perhaps with all that followed the Burning Cascade. While they didn't use maps in their travels, most Sojourners gained a working idea of where they were through the collective memory of their elders, who passed on the stories of what had gone before and what was said to be ahead. These days, however, the memories were growing fainter, and new information was sparse.

Fewer interactions with other Sojourners and even Dwellers meant less insight into just what was really ahead. And that wasn't the best way to travel. But she wasn't an elder. She was hardly even ready to take the mantle of matriarch and would gladly leave such concerns to them. She had plenty of her own to contend with as it was. But the Sovereign, she was sure, would see to all in time.

The flat, empty road appeared to go on forever. It was said the ancient Mundi had built roads all across Annulis with the intention of connecting their empire with every city, town, and village. From what she had seen so far in her travels, she believed it. Of course, with no one to maintain them, many of these roads had slowly been swallowed by the earth, the ancient imprint of their design still haunting the scenes of their previous glory.

Sarah had noticed that the better the condition of a road, the more likely it was they would come across people nearby. The constant traffic of feet, hooves, and carts helped to maintain the roads. But now she wasn't so sure that was the case. Not after what she had experienced this morning . . .

As always, Bram led the way for the congregation, with James and Caleb at his side. The adults followed after them, with the children in the middle, and then the carts and animals after that. A few men kept to the rear for added protection or to help with the animals, but it was a fairly uniform pattern Sarah had learned and fell into even without thinking. The older she got, however, the more fluid her place became, allowing her to move between the adults and children without hearing any comments or concern. In just a few weeks, she could cross over completely and remain in the adult company permanently.

And while at any other time such a thought would have cheered her mind, along with the fineness of a day that was far brighter than most she'd experienced in her young life, such contentment wasn't reflected in her thinking. She couldn't stop pondering what they'd experienced in the village, hopeful of getting some sort of understanding.

Yet the more she tried, the more her mind clouded over with what had befallen the Dwellers. She couldn't help wondering what would drive someone to do such a thing. And why others would allow such things to happen in the first place. Had the whole world truly finally gone mad?

"What is troubling you?" Tabitha asked from beside her.

"Just thinking."

"It must be hard work," Tabitha continued. "You seem to be very engaged in it." Sarah shot her a smile. "That looks better," she said, returning the grin.

While over half the congregation were older adults, there weren't that many younger people Sarah could befriend. There were five children under the age of five, and ten more from five to ten years old. Sarah fell within the group of twenty-five who were between twelve and twenty years old. She wasn't above talking with those younger than her, but she couldn't have the same sort of conversations with a twelve-year-old that she could with someone closer to her own age. That meant her options for deep friendships were rather limited, which is why she was so thankful for Tabitha.

Tabitha was a year younger than Sarah but in some ways acted much older. She was about the same size as Sarah but with a slightly shorter brown ponytail and green eyes. She also had a tendency to seek more independence than did most of the women and girls in the congregation. Of course, so did Sarah, which had been what made them such quick friends.

"Did you find anything in your searching?" she asked.

Sarah paused. "Nothing worth sharing." It wasn't a lie, but it also wasn't telling Tabitha anything about what the patriarch had said to keep to herself.

"We did not find anything either," Tabitha returned. "Father thinks it will be like that from here on out, but Mother still hopes for something more."

"My father is the same way," said Sarah. "He wants to expect the best, even when the patriarch had us stay in that village instead of camping outside."

"I do not think too many of the elders were happy with that."

"He is patriarch, though," offered Sarah. "It is his right to do what he thinks best."

"It was strange sleeping behind those walls. It felt like I was trapped in some cage." Sarah hadn't thought of that before but could see the comparison. "Of course, their goddess was the most unsettling."

"Yes, that was strange," she agreed. "Having the hearth near it seemed very odd too. I am surprised the elders allowed that."

Tabitha started laughing.

"What?"

"Listen to us. We are like a couple of gray-haired elders ourselves. All this talk about what is and is not proper."

"What else would you talk about?"

"You and James."

Sarah blushed. "There is nothing to say."

"I know. Which is something we have to fix."

"*We?*"

"Have you spoken to him yet?" Tabitha's curious eyes unsettled her.

"No."

"Then it looks like you could use some help."

"And what would you do?" Sarah wasn't sure if she liked the idea of Tabitha stepping into her private affairs to such an extent. It was fine to have someone to confide in, but to get them involved in something that was so very personal . . . .

A mischievous glint appeared in Tabitha's eyes. "I will think of something." Tabitha's confidence only increased Sarah's unease.

"I would not feel right letting you help me if I could not help you in return." Sarah found a way to change course, taking some of the discomfort out of their discussion. "You and Joshua are still not speaking to each other."

It was Tabitha's turn to blush at the mention of the young man who had caught her eye the year before. "We have some time," she replied. "He *is* only thirteen, after all."

"Still, why risk him setting his sights on another?" Sarah continued her ribbing. It felt much better having the attention directed elsewhere.

"All right. Fun is fun. We each have our own excuses to overcome. Let us just leave it at that."

"At least no one is looking at Joshua yet," said Sarah. "I am beginning to think Malena has set her heart on James."

"Malena?" Tabitha looked over her shoulder in an attempt to locate the young woman behind them.

"Stop it. She might see you." While Sarah was sure Malena was out of earshot, that didn't mean she'd be out of sight.

Tabitha spun her head back around. "Are you sure about her liking James?"

"I have caught her looking at him a few times now."

"That could be anything. You might just be imagining things."

"No." Sarah shook her head. "I did not imagine the look in her eyes when she saw him."

Tabitha paused. "Then you better speak with James soon."

"I know." Sarah sighed. "But I never seem to have a chance. If he is not with the patriarch, he is with Caleb or someone else. And then . . . and then I do not know what I would even say if I *did* get a chance to speak with him alone."

"What?" Tabitha's eyes went wide.

"I . . . I just worry about him not liking me the way I do him. I am sure I could endure it if we were alone, but if I had to discuss my feelings for him in front of others . . ."

Tabitha rested a hand on Sarah's shoulder. "I know. I have started wondering the same thing about Joshua—when he is a little older, of course. But still, I sometimes wonder what he will say when I do bring it up. It is not like we have many options to choose from."

"No, we do not," Sarah agreed. "Unless we wait on the young ones' coming of age."

"That could only take a decade." Tabitha laughed. "But maybe we will have found the Veiled City before then."

"Maybe." Sarah's levity faded.

"What?" Tabitha inquired.

"Just thinking again," she returned.

Tabitha nodded. "I suppose I better get back to my parents. They have been testing me on how much I know about our history."

Sarah could relate. Her father did the same, though not as often. It was the duty of the older generation to instruct and inform the younger. The communal hearth was one thing, but there were other parts of their history and family lines that if not passed on would fade like so much of Annulis's past. It was both a duty and an honor, she knew, but other times it seemed more like a chore and work.

"I still cannot make much sense of some of those sayings," Tabitha confessed. "'A sparrow's song shall help move you along' I can see in some ways, but what does 'At the highest point all answers shall be given' mean?"

"My father has said it refers to looking at the larger picture of things—getting a view from higher up. Though I do not believe anyone really knows." Sarah made sure she kept her answer just between them. It wouldn't do to speak too loudly about such matters. She didn't want it getting around that she wasn't as clear on all the ways and customs of her people as she should be. Though, as she just confided, she didn't think anyone in the congregation fully knew everything—with the exception of the elders and the patriarch, of course.

"Well, take care," Tabitha said. "It is a bright day; if only we had some better scenery to enjoy. But we do not get much of a choice on that matter, do we?"

"'No map shall guide the way, only the words the heralds say,'" Tabitha and Sarah quoted in unison. The saying was probably one of the first things all Sojourners learned when they were old enough to understand anything.

Tabitha's face beamed with her mischievous grin. "That one at least makes sense."

Tabitha gave a nod and moved further up the line, taking a place beside her parents, leaving Sarah alone once more with her thoughts. After a short while her father came up alongside her.

"You thirsty?" He extended a canteen her way. Sarah took it gladly.

They had found some small stores of potable water in the deserted town, which was good. Between the congregation and the animals they needed a good share of it, and finding fresh sources wasn't always easy. When she'd finished wetting her throat, she handed the canteen back to her father.

"You and Tabitha have a nice chat?"

"It was fair enough."

"You did not share anything about what we found, did you?"

She turned his way, letting the seriousness of her face speak volumes over her words. "Of course not." She was surprised he'd asked.

"Good. I did not think so but still had to ask. I know it can be hard not saying anything, but until the patriarch deems it right, we must keep it to ourselves."

Sarah focused her eyes back on the road. "And what if we find the same or even worse in the next village?"

He paused, seemingly tasting his words before they left his lips. "I do not know. But what I do know is that we should not let it bother us."

She found that hard to do. Not when the image of those skulls kept bobbing to the surface of her mind like pieces of wood in a pond. That and the poem. "Something had to happen to the Dwellers in that village, and I do not believe it was something pleasant."

Her father's features sobered. They often did when he was looking to teach her a lesson. And the more important the lesson, the more seriousness would line his face. "We are not living in a pleasant world, Sarah. And what the Dwellers do to each other is bad enough. Why do we need to immerse ourselves in it more than we have to?"

"Because it is all around us."

"It may be around us, but we do not need to become ensnared by it. We walk through this world but do not look to become part of it." It was a well-ingrained principle she, like all of her congregation, had heard since their youth. It had served them well and was true, but it wasn't always easy to maintain.

"But I cannot help but recall what I have seen."

"Do you remember what I told you when you saw that hanging girl?" Surprisingly, Sarah had forgotten about the matter after the more recent discoveries. "Sometimes it is wise to not even look in the first place."

"I just cannot help thinking about who would do such a thing to those children. Is it really as you and the patriarch said? Had the flesh been cut from them?"

Desmond sighed and shifted his focus back to the road.

"And why has the patriarch not told the others?" Sarah made sure she kept her voice low. While it felt better to discuss the matter with her father, she didn't want anyone to overhear. "Surely they should know as well."

"For what? To have them be as troubled as you?"

"Are you not troubled by what you have seen?"

Desmond gave another sigh as he faced his daughter with all-too-knowing eyes. In them she could see far more than anything he would say. She knew he and her mother had been through some difficult things before, but never had she understood how much it still weighed upon him.

"I have seen more than I would have liked and try and forget what I can. You would be wise to do likewise. The Veiled City is what should hold our focus. The Veiled City and nothing else. For nothing else truly matters, Sarah. Not in this world. And we must have faith in the patriarch to guide us. He knows what is best. He is the oldest of our elders and the wisest among them. He will make plain what should be known soon enough. For now we need to trust him and keep our minds on our path."

Sarah gave a nod and let her face slide back to contemplating the road.

"You are very much like your mother." Her father's voice was small but still warm. "It took much to unsettle her, and she was always asking questions."

"And what would she have said about what we saw?" Sarah cautiously inquired. It wasn't often she dared such a question, but it felt right given the situation.

"That you need to listen to your father. We will be getting close to more villages and towns soon. If there are any answers to be had, they will be there."

Sarah knew it was time to put the matter to rest, though she was certainly still free to think about it. And while she might have dwelled on it more, she turned to another topic that had occupied her thoughts from time to time as they traveled. As faithful as she was in refraining from mentioning the village again, she wasn't able to stop the next thought from spilling out of her mouth.

"Do you think we will find the Veiled City before we die?"

"We will if we keep faithfully seeking it." Her father didn't even hesitate in his reply.

"But so many others have come and gone, and none of them have found it."

"And how do you know they have not?"

Sarah stopped for a moment and considered her response. "If they did, then we would have heard about it. They would have come back and told us."

"Like the heralds? If the Dwellers did not believe the heralds, they would not listen to anyone else, even someone who had been to the Veiled City and returned to tell of it." He gave her a curious look. "Besides, why would you want to leave after finally arriving?"

"To tell others how to get there," she blurted. Immediately hearing the flaw in her thinking, she added, "Like the heralds."

"And those who would listen have already heard the way." This was another refrain common among the Sojourners.

"As the sparrow flies," said Sarah, returning the next part of the refrain.

"As the sparrow flies," Desmond repeated with satisfaction. "Now let us have no more talk of what is behind us."

Bram was silent throughout much of the day. Flanked by James and Caleb at the head of the congregation, he led them forward as he had done for countless days prior. However, this day he was also joined by the congregation's four elders—three men and one woman, among whose number he'd once belonged before his elevation as the current patriarch. As the eldest elder, this was his right and responsibility. They all made sure they were far enough ahead to keep from being heard and kept their voices low for good measure. Such was the way of many of their councils—whether on foot or seated around a fire.

And there was plenty to discuss. For while he had told Sarah and Brothers Desmond, Caleb, and James to refrain from speaking about what they'd found in the town that morning, the rest of the council had been discussing it for a good hour at least.

"I disagree," said Milton, one of the oldest of the elders, whose bald head, when uncovered, helped emphasize his thick eyebrows and beard. "I see something unnatural in all this. No one—not even a Dweller—would leave their village or town as we have seen. There is something else afoot."

"The crows?" This was Anna, the youngest of the elders, but still a woman well seasoned in years. Her silver ponytail sparkled in the daylight.

"Perhaps," said Milton, "but there could be much more we do not yet see."

"And how will we see it?" asked Thomas, another elder. "They left no trace of anything save rambling poems."

"And skulls." Bram's reminder of the grisly details left all silent for a spell.

They had been discussing the facts again and again, debating what was possible, knowable, and discernible. For none of them wanted to lead the congregation into danger or further troubling scenes. But the more they discussed the matter, the less they found any answers. They had gone in circles with little to show for it save spent time. Thankfully, they were walking while they talked and could thus make some sort of progress.

"So the question is did *they* do it or was it done by someone else?" Milton asked.

"Why would they keep them?" Anna was understandingly troubled by the thought. "For burial?"

"Dwellers normally bury their dead," said Bram.

"I think we know the answer to this," said Thomas. "Only we do not wish to speak it."

Yes, Bram had been musing over that terrible possibility since Brother Desmond had first shown him what he'd discovered. It was just too horrible to contemplate. There were some things that should never be done, even in the darkest of times . . . but as the world continually darkened around them . . .

"The only question is why?" asked the wizened Mathias, the last of the elders, in his raspy voice. He was the next oldest after Bram and thus the most likely successor after Bram's passing.

"And if it will meet us any further along our path," Thomas added. "We *are* in the lands of the Laromi now. Them and their crow goddess."

"Crows . . ." Bram muttered. Was that poem connected to their false goddess?

"It might be wise to just avoid all settlements altogether," counseled Mathias. "Make sure our paths never cross—for the safety of all."

The other elders muttered among themselves. There was a wisdom in Mathias's words, but it was up to Bram to decide what was the right path. If the way to the Veiled City took them by villages and towns and even the city of Larom itself, then so be it. Wisdom and the asking for grace were required to keep clear in his heart the way he was meant to follow. And a heart full of fear could muddy any waters.

"We will continue to travel as the sparrow flies, Brother." Bram's words did little to change the others' mood. If anything it made them more withdrawn and somber. Never a good combination when one sought counsel. Still, he couldn't blame them. He'd been one of them until the matriarch before him had passed only seven years prior. With such elevation came an expectation, which was also a weight always resting rather heavily upon him—especially in times like now.

Looking up, he spied a crow sailing through an ever-darkening heaven. Whether it was an omen was unclear. What was certain was the sight of dark red clouds gathering in the southwest. They were moving their way. They would need to find shelter soon if they wanted to be removed from the worst of it. It had the look of being an especially bloody one.

"It looks like we have more pressing matters for the time being. A blood rain will soon be upon us."

"I will inform the others," said Thomas. "I was praying we would find some clean water for bathing. Looks like we are going to need it now more than ever. It takes me days to get all that grime off me."

"All the more reason we need to keep our eyes open for a decent site," said Bram.

"I know the process," said Thomas, moving back into the line of people behind him. "You just keep up your searching. The sooner we find something, the better for all."

"And we should try to stay clear of any dwellings," added Anna. "Camping outside them could be fine—if they were empty. Staying outside could keep any more unfortunate discoveries from being known."

"I agree," said Mathias. "The fewer who explore any town or village—if it is empty—the better."

"Wise counsel," Bram concurred. "A practical solution we can explore for now, but we will not be able to keep it forever. At some point the congregation will be exposed to the whole matter."

"And we should not lie to them." Anna was adamant.

"Of course not," Milton assured them. "But hopefully, it will be well behind us by then," he offered. "We will pass through the Laromic lands soon enough."

"Maybe not soon enough," muttered Bram.

Thunder boomed overhead. The clouds that had been thickening all day had finally swelled to their limit. Sarah had seen rain before, but blood rain wasn't as common as it was when her father was her age. The rain that had fallen after the Year of Night was dark red in color and often tainted with a metallic, earthy aspect. If one used their imagination it wasn't hard to envision the heavens actually raining blood. After falling for some time the water turned brackish in places, and some crops were said to have suffered horribly. Those that survived watched it subside, and now a blood rain was an uncommon event in the parts of Annulis where the congregation traveled.

"We should be setting camp soon," said her father, adjusting his cowl and cloak as he spoke. It was at times like this she wished she had a kerchief of her own. While it wouldn't keep her dry for long, it would at least offer some protection. Blood rain left an unpleasant residue on one's body and hair, drying like sand or salt and finding its way into all sorts of nooks and crannies besides being a general nuisance. "It looks to be a strong storm."

As if to prove her father's point, a gust of wind bellowed across the shifting grass on either side of the road, startling the cows, goats, and other animals. This was followed by a wicked crackle of lightning that lit up the dark skies cluttered with burnt-red clouds. The echoing thunder that followed rattled Sarah's teeth and joints. The women murmured as the small children were loaded into what space they had in the carts. Then the rain started to fall. There were tiny droplets at first—like flicks of spittle sailing about the air—but enough to start freckling her face.

"There," came a shout from the front. Sarah assumed it was one of the brothers near Bram and the elders. He was pointing off in the distance at what appeared to be the walls of a town. "Make for the walls!"

It wasn't going to be easy. The structure was still about a mile away by her reckoning. Not close enough to get to before the rain fully fell, but if they—

"Run!" came the shout as all the congregation made a dash for their new destination.

Those with the carts did their best to hurry the animals on, but the cows and goats moved at their own pace. She was more thankful than ever that she didn't have that responsibility. There were still some benefits to not yet taking her kerchief.

As she ran, Sarah lifted her skirt to move faster. But it was the rain itself that impeded her. The faint droplets increased in size and found purchase in the corners of her eyes, stinging and bringing forth tears. She knew her face appeared splattered with blood, just like the others she caught glimpses of as she ran.

Her father appeared as if he'd been in a hard battle: crimson streams ran down his nose and cheeks. Even the children pumping their legs as hard as they could resembled victims of beatings taken to the extreme. Not to mention the matted and reddened hair and kerchiefs of the women and other children racing beside her.

She didn't know if she could keep her pace for the whole distance but dared to try, spurred on by new flashes of lightning and claps of thunder. The clouds finally burst a moment later, covering all in a mighty downpour.

The spurt of speed had fallen into a light jog before they even caught full sight of the dead gray walls. Sarah was drenched like all the rest in a thin layer of red. Cloaks, kerchiefs, dresses, and cowls clung to all. Hair and beards were horrid-looking things, but the worst would come when the rain stopped and the water dried.

"Looks to be a citadel," said Brother David, one of the men beside her and her father. She had always thought well of him over the years. He was a kindly man, which always showed in his face.

"We must be getting close to a city." Her father ran a hand down his face, wiping away some of the rain.

Sarah had never seen a citadel. Towns and villages, yes, but never something like the thing looming ahead of them. It was like one single curtain of stone was wrapped around three squat buildings. She wasn't sure what purpose these buildings served, but it was clear they were important. The most impressive sight were the two large doors at the opening of the wall. They were rectangular and made of solid wooden planks with strips of black iron nailed into them. This was something unlike the normal village and town gates. It gave the impression of being more secure—more solid—which is probably just what those who built it wanted to convey.

"It looks deserted," she heard Brother David say.

"Looks can be deceiving," said her father.

"Take a look inside," Bram directed Caleb and James. His white beard had turned a brownish red, and his eyebrows resembled two plump caterpillars. "But be careful."

Both hurried to their assigned posts, inspecting the doors with careful eyes, noting nothing out of the ordinary. They were solid and sure, unlike the doors of the last village. Caleb asked James to join him in opening the left door just a crack for closer inspection.

It opened smoothly under their effort.

"Just like the village," said James, noting the open, empty area the two could make out through the crack between the doors. Both were thoroughly soaked. Their faces and chins were dripping red, but neither would be rushed.

"No," said Caleb. "This is not a village, but a place of war."

James grew worried at the thought. "Maybe we should move on."

"Not without taking a look," said Caleb. "It would be irresponsible to not know what we would be leaving behind us. Help me get a wider opening."

Together they applied their brawn until the doors had parted far enough for Caleb to squeeze inside. James followed. Behind the walls was a fairly utilitarian design. There were the three buildings they could see from outside but also a couple of smaller ones nestled between them. Apart from the two main cobblestone roads striping the dying sward, there was nothing else of note.

"Looks like it has been empty for a while." James crept around the immediate area, prodding places with his staff as if they might hide pits or traps hungry for his feet.

"So it does," said Caleb. "Let us take a quick look to be sure and then report back to Bram. Maybe there is some water we can use for washing after this storm."

"The animals will need something fresh too," added James. It wasn't uncommon for any water source left uncovered to be tainted for a few days to a week after a blood rain. "I do not see any goddess about," James continued. "Maybe it is unclaimed by any Dwellers."

"It might be too old for them." Caleb pointed out a faded carving on the wall behind them. There, on a cornerstone overlooking the gate, was the crest of ancient Mundus. Though it had been worn down by the years, in its day all would have honored the Sovereign. The crest was supposed to show his favor to the people he created. The crown resting in the sun above and behind the falcon depicted that favor.

A crash of thunder rocked the earth about them.

"Come on," urged Caleb. "A quick search around the buildings, and we should know the rest."

It was about an hour later when they emerged from behind the gate. The others had been waiting anxiously, eyeing the sky from time to time and making sure the fading clouds were indeed done for the day. This left the scarlet-tinted heavens to darken as evening crept in.

"Nothing is inside," Caleb informed Bram upon their return. "No people or animals, nor anything of real value anywhere."

"What of the buildings?" asked Bram.

"They are solid enough, but hold nothing—apart from some beds."

"Beds?" Bram raised an eyebrow. "How many?"

"A good number," said James, "but they were all empty. They were stacked on top of each other, but did not look like they had been slept in for a while."

"But nothing else except those beds?"

"No," answered Caleb, "it was empty of just about everything."

"What about water?"

"There was a well," offered James, "but it has long been dry."

Bram nodded. "It should be safe, then, for the night. We will camp outside the walls. Have the animals graze where they can. We made a hard press already before the rain. Some rest will do us all good. And the less we have to do with that citadel, the better."

CHAPTER SEVEN

Bonfires and Rest.

T he bonfires were already burning when Elliott and the Salamandrine rejoined the army. The ride back had been slower going than he'd thought possible. The extra horses and provisions slowed them more than they'd have liked.

Calix had ordered them to gallop when he could, but the horses could only take so much. As it was, they lost two along the way. The time spent reclaiming their property—as well as collecting that of the Marauders— also ate into their schedule. Of course, with the army moving away from them all this time, Elliott figured when they finally rejoined the others it would probably be night. What neither he nor the rest of the Salamandrine could have expected was the sight of so many burning mounds of dead bodies.

"What happened?" Elliott slowed his horse to a trot, mimicking his master beside him, along with the rest of the knights.

"Laromi." Calix's voice was low. He was still at the head, where he had remained since vanquishing the Marauders.

"Thank Pyre you've returned." Drenn jogged to Calix's horse. He was clearly tired, and his armor showed signs of having been in a conflict. And a fairly good-sized one from what Elliott could surmise.

"How many have you lost?" Calix brought his steed to a halt, the other knights following his lead.

"Three hundred, with about one hundred more wounded," Drenn replied soberly.

"Three hundred?" Elliott heard the words before he knew he'd spoken them. He quickly blushed when he saw Sir Pillum's disapproving glance. It wasn't his place to speak when Calix was talking with other commanders.

He knew there were a good many bonfires ablaze but hadn't counted them all. Even as he tried, he quickly came to the conclusion it was better to just stop and let the matter be. There were more than enough dead to contend with—a great blow to their overall strength against Larom.

"Five priests were killed and some of the camp workers," Drenn continued. "But most were infantry. Arthur was killed too. He was the first to fall. They were waiting for us. We held our own and took most of them with us, but the cowards retreated once the tide turned against them."

"How many?" Calix turned his eyes to the trampled field of sickly grass. Bodies of the fallen Laromi were still strewn here and there, but most had been pushed into random piles. From what Elliott could see of the aftermath, he was amazed the infantry didn't suffer any more losses than they did. Pyre clearly was watching over his chosen.

"Five hundred. They kept behind their shields and pelted us with bolts until we brought the fight to them."

"Do you think the Marauders were in league with them?" Sir Pillum asked Calix. "Maybe it was a ploy to separate our forces—"

"No." Calix shook his head. "The Marauders are loyal to no city or people other than their own."

"We would have done better," said Drenn, "but they used some new weapons against us. Their crossbows could fire five bolts before most men could fire one arrow in response. And then their shields . . . We weren't expecting them, and that gave them the opening they needed. We recovered, but it wasn't the best we could have done. I'll see about drilling the men more on the fundamentals. If we're facing a city filled with these warriors, we need to be better prepared."

"Agreed," said Calix. "They've also showed us their hand, letting us know how they fight and something about their forces. We'll study their weapons and tactics once we've added the final bodies to the fires. The next time we meet, things will be much different."

"It seems you fared better with the Marauders." Drenn motioned to the extra horses among the knights' numbers.

"It wasn't without our own loss," said Calix. "A few horses were killed, but we gained more from our would-be thieves. We even gained some more supplies thanks to what they were carrying. But we lost five good knights and three squires."

"*Squires* were fighting?" Drenn's pale green eyes flashed in surprise.

"Not by choice, but I can fill you in on the details once we've laid them all to rest."

"I'll have the men tend to them," said Drenn.

"Once you do, have them strengthen the perimeter. If there are any more out there waiting for us, they'll have seen our fires. We'll have to double the watch and make sure things are secure from all sides." Calix dismounted effortlessly. Elliott was always amazed at how fluid the older man's movements were. Not even the hardest of battles had ever seemed to break him down. "Once that's done, meet me in my tent. We have much to discuss." Drenn gave a nod and hurried off into the infantry's camp.

Calix turned to Sir Pillum. "See that the supplies get back to where they belong and the Salamandrine camp is secured."

"Yes, sir." Sir Pillum straightened in his saddle.

Elliott watched Calix walk to where some of the Laromi had been piled, obviously interested in making a closer inspection.

"You heard the commander," Sir Pillum shouted to the rest of the knights. "Half of you tend to the supplies, the rest see to setting up and strengthening the camp." The knights and squires divided themselves into two groups, eager to enact what had been commanded. Sir Pillum dismounted, prompting Elliott to do the same.

"You think they'll come back," he said as he and Sir Pillum made their way into the midst of the knights taking care of the recaptured goods.

"Not unless they have reinforcements. They lost too many to try anything again now that we've returned. I'll need you to set up the pavilion while I deal with some other things."

"I'll have it ready well before you return." Elliott was quick in reply. It brought a small turn to the corner of Sir Pillum's lips. Elliott welcomed it after the look he'd been given in response to his earlier outburst in front of Calix. He allowed himself a small sense of peace knowing all was as it should be again.

"No need to rush things; just make sure it's ready and the area around it secure. We've all earned our rest today." Elliott couldn't agree more. "Well?" Sir Pillum shot him a curious gaze. "Off with you, lad. It's not going to get any lighter."

"Yes, sir."

He took the reins of both his horse and his master's, leading them toward the infantry's camp. It was impossible to miss the burning mounds as he went. There were just too many of them. He'd seen dead Pyri before but never in such numbers. Only handfuls had fallen previously—scores at most—but this was something almost impossible to imagine. And it was just one encounter. True, it was a surprise attack, and it was against the infantry, but it still gave him pause.

His eyes fell upon a shield resting near some of the dead Laromi on his left. But it wasn't just a shield. No, it was a weapon as well. Curious, he stopped and moved closer for an inspection. Unlike Sir Pillum's shield, this one inspired a vivid mental reenactment of how such a device worked, made all the more real by the dried blood coating the cruel blades outlining the shield's circular lip.

Freeing his right hand from the reins allowed him to pick one of the shields up. It was heavy. Heavier than a shield should be. He attributed some of the weight to the blades, but there was something else. The shield was thicker in the middle than normal. And there was something that looked like a handle for a winch to the left of two metal bands meant to keep your arm affixed to the shield. The winch was small and made of solid brass and was kept as flush to the back of the shield as possible.

Curious, Elliott gave it a crank to the right. There was a clanking sound from inside the shield. He gave it a few more turns, feeling something grinding inside like wheels or maybe even the tumblers of a lock. The more he turned it, the tighter the handle felt, as if the gears inside were pulling against him.

About three fingers above where he figured the wearer's thumb might be was a small brass knob. You'd have to stretch a little to reach it, but it was possible. Wanting to try it for himself, Elliott slid his left arm inside the metal bands, then attempted to reach for the knob.

With the slightest touch the knob depressed slightly into the shield. When it did, something unlocked with a loud click. Suddenly, the blades started slowly circling the shield's lip. Between this and the grinding emanating from inside the shield, it made for an awful racket. This certainly wasn't something you'd be able to use if you wanted to sneak up on your opponent.

The blades marched around the shield. It wasn't a snail's pace, but it wasn't that rapid either. Even so, they managed to get in a full rotation before stopping. He figured if he'd worked the winch more times, it might have kept the blades spinning, and faster at that. So it only had a limited window wherein it was its deadliest. That could be helpful to remember.

Content for now, and mindful of his duties, Elliott returned the shield to where he'd found it. He imagined the sight of five hundred warriors wielding them—and the carnage they could unleash. It was a miracle the infantry hadn't suffered more losses. And yet it was possible a whole army still awaited them, outfitted in such gear . . .

He wondered if he was really ready for what was before him . . . if any of them were. In a few days they'd finally take Larom. But they wouldn't be fighting alone. Pyre would be with them. Just as he had been with them before. He might not have understood why things happened as they did, but he could trust Pyre's will was being done and any losses would turn into great gain soon enough. Once more focused on the brighter day to come, Elliott shifted his full attention to setting up Sir Pillum's pavilion. He wasn't alone in his task. Other squires had joined him, either tending their masters' horses or raising up their pavilions.

By the time night was full upon them, he'd set up the pavilion and had tended to the horses. He decided to take a rest, lying on his side just outside the pavilion. Best to relax while he could. Once Sir Pillum returned, he'd have to see to his armor.

Eventually the bonfires faded. Only a few charred piles of bone and bodies remained, on which the weak flames did little but nip and nibble. The army enjoyed some food and water, finally settling down to rest after the long day. A perimeter had been established, but most were unsure if any more incursions were coming. The general wisdom was the enemy had been beaten so badly they lacked the courage for another assault. Some even foolishly spoke of the Laromi having lost most of their forces and said the skeletal force that remained would be easily crushed even with the Pyri's depleted numbers.

Elliott was wiser than that. His master had taught him that you never underestimate your enemy. You shouldn't live in fear of them, but you shouldn't discount them out of hand either. The moment you start to do so is the moment they make use of the opening your pride allows them. No, it was good to hold to the truth: the Pyri were the victors over all before them, but also wise in understanding that victory was not assured to those who wouldn't soberly battle to attain it.

"Now here's a well-set-up camp." Sir Pillum's voice woke Elliott from his light nap.

"Thank you, sir." Elliott leapt to his feet.

"The men will rest tonight and march at first light for Larom," Sir Pillum continued, undoing some of the belts and other fixtures across his armor. "Did you eat yet?"

"No, sir."

"Then get to it. I can deal with my armor for one night." He started for the tent. "Might as well start getting used to it, since before you know it, I'll be short one squire but richer a brother in arms." He stopped short of the flap, turning back to Elliott with a smile. "You're going to make a fine knight, Elliott, and do us all proud."

"I'll do my best, sir."

"That's all Pyre asks of us," said his master before entering the pavilion.

With the praise still fresh in his mind, Elliott began seeing to a simple meal. His head was in the clouds. If he continued to do well, he could soon enough stand beside Sir Pillum as an equal—a brother in arms. He'd still have to prove himself for a little while longer, but if he proved true, Sir Pillum had already spoken of how he'd vote for his acceptance into the order.

It wasn't until he had nearly finished his dry bread and thin slices of smoked meat that Elliott's head descended from those clouds. He finally understood the way forward might be harder than he'd first imagined it. Up until today things had been pretty consistent—pretty easy. Though he never participated in any of the actual fighting, what he did see didn't take too much from the army. The Salamandrine especially weren't under much pressure in any conflict. They'd taken a few cities in the last three years, but all were skeletal things long past their former glory.

What if Larom was different? It was a troubling thought. He really didn't enjoy contemplating it, but it was something worth considering. None of the other cities that opposed them had come after them like the Laromi had. The attack could have been born of desperation, but what if it wasn't? What if there was more coming—and soon? Elliott stopped himself, shaking his head to clear it. Thinking things through was one thing, getting lost in wild speculation another. If he'd learned anything in his service, it was that speculations ate away at a solid foundation.

"You still up?" Sir Pillum poked his head out of his pavilion, startling him.

"I was just finishing my meal."

"Well, you still need some rest. From here on out we're going to have to be doubly vigilant. Another attack could come at any time—especially the closer we get to Larom."

"So how big of a force do you think we're facing, sir?"

"Large enough for them to take comfort in, but not so large as to stand before the might of Pyre or his warriors." As if reading Elliott's thoughts, he added, "You've seen what they're capable of, but they were still beaten back, and that was without the full force of the Salamandrine behind them."

"But with just five hundred men, they took a fairly large slice."

"They have nothing, Elliott," Sir Pillum continued, "only a stone idol they foolishly call a goddess. We have Pyre. And his will shall be accomplished all across Annulis."

"Yes, sir." Elliott gave a knowing nod, feeling his convictions solidify the truth he'd just received. It was one thing to know something, but when another came along and confirmed it, there was nothing else like it in all the world.

"Now, get some sleep." Sir Pillum's head ducked back into his pavilion.

Now that his work was completed and his stomach filled, it sounded the best course of action. Elliott took to his bedroll beside his master's pavilion. Though there was room inside, squires weren't meant to share their master's pavilion unless there was rain or other hard weather. Sleeping outside was thought to toughen up the young men and prepare them for the rigors of the knightly life ahead.

He'd become so used to it he didn't even give it a second thought, nor did he harbor any ill will against his master for getting such comfort while he suffered. Some squires had complained in times past, citing the tents the infantry were allowed, but never Elliott. From the beginning he understood Sir Pillum had done the same as a squire and so there was a certain sense of equality and aspiration in it. If his master could endure it when he was young, rising to the knight he was today, then so could Elliott. It might even do him some good.

Closing his eyes, he focused on getting some rest and not the list of duties and chores awaiting him at first light. Not surprisingly, after such a rigorous day, he didn't have to focus long.

CHAPTER EIGHT

A Rude Awakening. A Feast of Spoils.

The congregation made camp a short distance from the citadel's walls. Not too close but not too far away either. The standard process was adopted, which saw them pitching tents around the communal hearth for another night. The recent rain made many wary of the weather.

These tents, like so much of their garb and gear, were simple affairs. A length of brown cloth was erected over a bedroll by means of slender, short wooden stakes, forming a low-rising triangle. There was little privacy allowed the sleeper, since the lone section of cloth draped over the sticks left the front and back of the tent open. This allowed the wind to blow through, but if one knew where to pitch the tent and how to do it right, most of the worst could be avoided.

All had tried cleaning their faces and hands of the blood rain's residue as best they could before joining in the communal hearth. They had plenty of wood, but the top layer in their cart had been soaked in the rain and would have to dry over the next couple of days. Thankfully, the bottom layer was still dry enough for cook fires and hearth. Once more, the meal was a simple affair but pleasant. When it was finished, each took to their tent.

Sarah slumbered near her father. She had been old enough for her own tent for years, but families tended to keep together at night. But while the others were already fast asleep, she couldn't find any for herself. It wasn't that she wasn't tired, for she was quite worn out from the sprint, on top of a normal day's travel. It was just no matter how hard she tried, sleep ran through her fingers like sand. She had tried all she could think of, but it just wouldn't come.

She eventually found herself with her head outside the tent counting stars. It was easier these days, she'd been told, since many were still masked following the Year of Night. None knew when or if they'd ever return to their former glory. But even if they were smaller in number, they were something on which she could focus her eyes.

She had no clue how long she had lain there before she felt something was wrong. At first it was just a mild sense of unease. Then her ears started playing tricks on her, making her think she heard sounds outside the encampment. She knew there was nothing out there, but the more she tried denying it, the more her mind had her imagining something slinking just outside the camp. Worse still was the thought that the sounds were growing closer.

Closing her eyes, she expelled such fears from her mind. She was safe. The congregation was safe. There wasn't anything around here for at least a mile. And then a strong hand wrapped around her throat. Before she knew what was happening, she was on her naked feet with her arms held behind her back, mouth covered with another strong hand. It was so large it almost kept her from breathing through her nose.

"Shhh." The low growl of a man's voice breathed into her ear. "You keep quiet and all will be well."

Once she had her bearings, she could make out a group of armored men encircling the camp. At least she hoped they were men. In the night it seemed as if they all had horns and terrible faces. There had to be close to a hundred of them.

"This your whole camp?" The question was accompanied with a strong pull backward against what Sarah could now feel was a chest covered in scale mail. She imagined he also wore a matching coif and leather brigandine pants, the same as the rest of the men creeping among the others' tents. She wondered if he had horns too.

When she didn't answer fast enough, there came a sharp jerk to her head and neck. "I can just as easily snap your neck. Is this your whole camp?"

Sarah rapidly nodded.

"They armed?" The hand thankfully left her mouth.

"Just daggers," she replied weakly. "All the adults have them."

Suddenly, she was turned and tossed on the ground. As she lay face down on the earth, her hands were yanked back and bound by rough rope.

"Bind them," said the same voice, now in a louder tone.

There arose a great commotion as all in the camp were rounded up and had their hands tied behind their backs. Those who resisted were beaten into submission. Their daggers were taken, as were the axes and other tools in the carts. The men even took down their tents for good measure.

"Take them inside," said the one who'd first spoken to Sarah. She could see now both his and the others' horns were part of a helmet covering half their face with a gruesome steel visage. What she could discern of his actual face was unshaven, giving him an even rougher appearance.

"What is the meaning of this?" Bram finally was able to speak once a form of order had returned to the situation. He, like all the others of the congregation, was barefoot, following their nightly ritual of doffing shoes and socks.

"Security," said the other. "We come back and we find you sleeping outside our door."

"We mean you no harm," Bram continued. "We have no quarrel with any Marauders. We were planning to move on in the morning."

"Where to?"

"As we are led." Bram's reply caused snorting and muted laughter from some of the other Marauders.

"And where might you be *led*?"

"As the sparrow flies."

"If I wasn't so tired, I might actually find this all amusing." The lead Marauder faced another of his comrades close at hand. "Take them inside," he instructed. "Lock them in the barracks until morning."

"What about their livestock?"

"Sojourners are supposed to be humble people." The lead Marauder's smirk appeared positively frightening coming out of his horrid helm. "I'm sure they won't mind sharing some of their bounty with us. They *did* say they didn't have anything against us, after all."

"You have no right!" Brother Bidon, a middle-aged man among their company, grew hot with wrath. But such flames were quickly extinguished by a punch to the face from a nearby Marauder.

"Be quick about it." Their leader headed for the citadel's gates. "The sooner they're locked up, the sooner we eat."

Bram could hear the Marauders from inside the barracks. The building served as a place of rest for the Sojourners, but it was also a prison. There was really no other word for it, for they had no means to leave on their own. The door was watched from the outside, and the windows in two of the walls were thin and narrow, allowing in only fresh air and some light but not much else. Even a child would have a hard time forcing their way through. And then there were the ropes still binding their wrists.

All of this seemed overly cautious. Their daggers and staves had been taken, and they didn't have access to any of their tools. Neither did they wear armor, but that apparently didn't matter to their captors. They'd even forbidden them to don their shoes, their captors taking those as well for their own. Thankfully the weather was still mild. Had they been forced to remain barefoot in the cold, their present situation would have been much worse. Though not knowing what yet awaited them, that was only a small comfort.

While they'd had their hands tied behind their backs, it was quickly discovered they could maneuver their hands forward and then step over them. This brought their hands to the front, which at the very least afforded a small level of relief from their discomfort. The rough rope, though, was already rubbing their wrists raw.

And while Bram had beaten himself up for not keeping the congregation safe, as he went over the last few hours, he realized how little could have been done. They'd had little chance to do anything but try to make sense of what was happening as they woke. Thankfully, the women and children hadn't been hurt or abused, but the night was young. He'd heard tales, as had the elders, of the great cruelty that was possible among those who gave themselves wholly to it. And Marauders were often known for their cruelty, if nothing else.

Trying to focus his thoughts on something more pleasant, he looked over those in the room. It was large enough to fit them all comfortably. This place must have been a fairly large outpost in the past. What it was defending, though, had long since faded along with the empire it once served.

There wasn't much talking among the congregation. Not knowing what was going to happen next, each took to their own families or friends for support. This was to be expected. Most had taken to sitting on the wooden bunk frames. They would have held straw-stuffed mattresses at one time but now were empty, solemn things.

"We could make a run for the door." James kept his voice low. "I am sure Caleb and I could subdue them." He sat across from the patriarch, Caleb at his side. The two meant well, but thus far their occasional suggestions did little to calm Bram's rising unease.

"With bound hands?" Bram's voice was equally hushed.

"We would have surprise on our side."

"Assuming the door is not locked," Bram added. "And even if you could, what then? They have a small army, and we have nothing."

"And wood *and* food," Caleb grumbled. "These men are little better than wild animals."

Bram wasn't going to argue. Marauders being true to their nature, the congregation wouldn't be left with anything apart from the clothes on their back—and even that was an uncertainty. From what he could smell of the cook fires, he doubted they'd have much in the way of livestock or foodstuffs left come morning. Whereas the congregation always rationed their meals, the Marauders would surely prove more gluttonous. And if the last village was any indication of what was ahead of them, then empty stomachs could be with them for a while.

In all his years he'd never heard of a patriarch leading his congregation into such a situation. Patriarchs and matriarchs were supposed to be wise and able to discern the right ways and paths—to know the good ways from the bad.

"We cannot do anything about that now," he advised, hating how lifeless his words and voice were. "What is dead and eaten is dead and eaten."

"So we are just to sit here and wait?" James was still far from pleased.

"If they wanted us dead, they would have already killed us. They could have easily done so while we slept."

"But if they have taken all we have, then we might very well soon be anyway," offered Caleb.

"The morning will bring us answers," said Bram, rising. "We should take what sleep we can." He then raised his voice, saying to the others, "The morning will be here soon enough, and we will need our strength for whatever might face us. Rest while we can and enjoy what peace we might. If they rob us of our possessions but leave us with our lives, we have not lost that much, as long as the Veiled City is still before us."

While he wanted to believe this, Bram found himself not entirely convinced by his own words. But if the others shared the same concerns, he couldn't tell.

He watched the congregation as they found room for their children and then themselves among the hard bed frames. It wouldn't be the best night they'd had, but if they endured, there would be better things on the other side. At least that was what Bram told himself. He prayed his faith wasn't misplaced, because at the moment he didn't see any way out of their situation.

"By the Sovereign, that smells good!" Kelvin, the Marauders' leader, stopped to savor the aroma wafting from the slab of beef turning on the makeshift spit in the citadel's courtyard. They'd repurposed some of the Sojourners' walking sticks for the task and were burning what was left of their firewood. The hearty smell rising off the flames was joined by the scent of a goose that was turning over another nearby cook fire.

Kelvin, like the rest of his men, had removed his helmet once their guests were safely put away. They'd leave on their armor. Most often slept in it these days. Experience had taught them that lesson the hard way in the earlier days of their new lives.

"A dead cow has never looked so good," said Caran, a middle-aged Marauder who couldn't keep his eyes from the slab of beef he was turning on the spit.

"I almost forgot what decent food even looked like," Kelvin agreed. "Must be a sign our luck is about to change. And these will help us get some more," he added, giving the full bag he carried a small shake. The contents inside clanked like stone hitting stone.

"I hope so," said Caran. "I just about worked my hands raw digging them up. Better be worth *something*."

"It will be, like I said. Just keep your eye on that spit. I don't want anything burned." Kelvin made his way from the cooking fire to a group of Marauders who had built another fire. They were sitting around it as they emptied out the contents of their sacks.

"A good haul." Kelvin plopped down next to the men, dumping out his own sack.

From the rough burlap fell a collection of shiny black oblong stones. Added to those already on the ground, it was quite an impressive mound. His men were making many similar piles around their fires. He figured there had to be at least thirty stones in every sack. He'd never seen anything like it in all his life.

"And all just waiting for us to find them." Kelvin had taken over as leader after their captain's death last year. He wouldn't call himself captain, though. He couldn't out of respect for the man who'd always hold that position in his mind. But the rest of the men knew that's what he was and treated him as such. And for the most part he had kept his men alive. That was about all one could hope for these days. And for that Kelvin was thankful. But now they had the chance for something greater.

"I'm surprised no one else tried digging for them already," said Nalgan, a balding man with a strong physique sitting across from Kelvin. "It's not like you can hide so large a crater that easily."

"Fortune favors the bold." Kelvin picked up one of the stones for a closer inspection. He watched the firelight dance across its surface in a rather attractive display. It was like staring at a perfectly polished oval of onyx. They must have hit a strong vein of something worthwhile. And anything worthwhile could be used to barter for something better: food, coins, supplies, and more.

"You really think they're worth something?" The grizzled Talan, another of his men, regarded the stones with a cautious eye.

"I wouldn't have us breaking our backs digging them up if I didn't."

They hadn't been digging for anything really. At first it was food— roots and such they might possibly find some use for. The citadel had been empty for months. They'd already burnt up most of the furniture and anything else they could spare and the horses had long ago been eaten. This forced them to forage farther and farther for resources. They'd been blessed with some wild crops and now and then with the odd animal, but it wasn't enough to keep them going.

The crater was a gamble. Kelvin had heard stories of intriguing discoveries in old craters. The stories ranged from diamonds to obsidian to other strange metals and rocks. He was hoping for something valuable. They'd have to start moving on from the citadel soon, and having something on hand to trade for better accommodations or food would be advantageous. And given what they'd discovered, it was looking like they could very well have hit the mother lode. Maybe it was even enough to purchase new horses and go further afield into better pastures.

"Larom isn't more than a couple days' march from here." Kelvin worked through his plan. "We dump these in their laps, and they'll be more than happy to give us whatever we need. Won't even have to raise a sword to get it either."

"Better be something nice after all that work," Vonn, another of his men, chimed in wearily. "A sword can get things faster than any shovel in my book."

"Not when we're outnumbered," countered Kelvin.

They already knew this, of course, but had been conditioned to the lifestyle the once-great imperial army now led. Since the loss of Mundus during the Burning Cascade, as things declined and the glory decreased, it had become about surviving by any means possible. But even that prospect was limited. Especially as fewer and fewer people remained, making it harder to get anything from them. So if they now had a means to change their tactics, Kelvin welcomed it.

"I figure we have enough to stock up before winter. Worst case, we even hole up here." The citadel had been a blessing. They had been wanderers for too long. Having a secure place to call their own was a real morale booster for the men, Kelvin included. And the fact it was an old Mundian fort made it even better. Not that they were even close to the glory of the once-mighty empire, but it felt good to just rest in its faded shadow and pretend the world wasn't as it was.

"So what about those Sojourners?" Marlin, Kelvin's second in command, joined the others around the fire. Blue eyed with black hair, he was perhaps the youngest looking of the lot, which wasn't saying much. Their hard living had set its claws deeper into them than they would have cared to admit.

"What about them?" asked Kelvin.

"We've taken what they have. Why keep them around?"

" 'Cause they might be worth something," Kelvin explained.

"Slaves?" Marlin raised an eyebrow.

"Not for us, but maybe for others. I'm sure the Laromi would be happy to get some cheap labor. And in the meantime, we can see if they might have come across anything else we might want to look into. Sojourners can travel quite a ways. I'm curious to learn what they've seen."

"Like having some scouts." Talan's amused grin revealed the missing tooth on his bottom jaw.

"I guess," Kelvin agreed.

"It'll make for a longer march," added Marlin, "but if the payoff is worth it—"

"Oh, it will be worth it." Kelvin picked up another of the polished stones. "I'm sure of that."

Sarah had taken to a bunk, but she didn't feel much like sleeping. She'd heard talk of Marauders—had even seen their work in times past—but never had run up against them until tonight. They were described as greedy crows picking clean every bone, even cracking into the marrow where they could. From what she had seen, heard, and now *smelled* from her bed, she was inclined to agree with the comparison.

"What do you think they will do with us?" she asked her father, who had taken the bunk across from her.

"Just get some rest." He followed his own advice, closing his eyes as he tried getting comfortable on the hard wood.

She let her hands rest on her lap, trying to ignore the compulsion to rub her wrists together because of the itching continually flaring around them. Her skin was already raw from previous efforts at freeing herself from the ropes. She didn't want to risk further injury.

"You think they will eat *all* our food?" she asked.

Her father remained silent.

"We were saving the cow until winter."

"And I was looking forward to giving you your mother's dagger with your kerchief," he returned. "But there is nothing we can do about it now." It felt like someone hit her in the gut. The trace of sorrow in her father's voice made it even worse.

Receiving your dagger was another sign of stepping up and being called upon to do more for yourself and the rest of the congregation. Most daggers stayed within families, getting passed from father to son, mother to daughter. Since they were harder to find these days, it wasn't uncommon for a dying person to leave theirs in the congregation's keeping until it was needed for someone who came of age. It was the last part of her mother she could actually hold and connect with, and it had been taken from her. And if things continued like this, there was going to be no way to get it back.

"Get some rest. I am sure we will need it soon enough. Have faith in the patriarch and in the Sovereign. If we are seeking his will and the Veiled City, he will see us through."

Sarah said nothing more. There was nothing more *to* say or think. None of it would help her. She couldn't change anything, only make the best of what had happened. And that meant at the moment there was nothing she could do but try to get some sleep.

She'd slept on hard earth for years, but the unforgiving wood beneath her was something else. There was just no way she could find a comfortable position. Her tied wrists further limited her options, forcing her into the unhappy situation of resting her spine on the wood, hoping at some point her eyelids would finally surrender and fall of their own accord.

She would wait for quite some time.

CHAPTER NINE

A Dark Surprise. The Black Swarm.
Sifting through Ruins.

As the night waxed long, Kelvin awoke from his slumber. Always a light sleeper, he sat up and took in the camp. All seemed right. The watch was alert and patrolling as he'd ordered, and the rest of the men slumbered around their low-burning fires. The Sojourners were still secured in one of the older barracks. Knowing dawn was about an hour away, he lay back down and closed his eyes.

It was then he heard the cracking.

It was so close to him he immediately opened his eyes. Sitting upright, he still saw nothing out of the ordinary. The cracking noise repeated itself. He was drawn to the black stones encircling the fire. Then he saw the oblong rock beside him move—a half roll from side to side.

Curious, he drew closer.

The stone rolled some more as the cracking sound grew louder. He watched fracture lines spread out across the smooth surface.

Instinctively, he leapt to his feet and took a few steps back. There were more sounds of cracking, and then the whole rocky shell flaked off. For that was what it was, he discovered—a cocoon of sorts housing a black locust about a finger's length long and two fingers wide.

The insect's dark body shone in the starlight as the creature waved its antennae and stretched its hind legs. The legs looked to have been dipped in red paint. A similar red was revealed on its wings when it gave them a test flutter. Instinct again had Kelvin reaching for his sword, only to discover he had removed it with his belt before he slept. Making an attempt to retrieve it, he was surprised when the locust leapt straight for him.

It landed on his scale mail shirt. As it climbed around and explored, he was able to lay hold of his sword and give the creature a small swat with the flat of the blade. While the action swiped the locust off, it also made it airborne. The insect circled to Kelvin's head. He felt a sharp pain in his ear as tiny teeth bit into it.

He growled, grabbed the insect, and ripped it free. This brought still more pain and fresh blood. He tried to squeeze the life out of the thing but was stopped when the locust turned itself around in his grip. He gave another growl of pain as he tried tossing the bug into the fire. His effort was unsuccessful, as it just went airborne again.

Examining his wounded hand, he cursed. It was missing a small piece of flesh between his thumb and index finger.

This was no ordinary locust.

By now the watch had been drawn to the event and saw Kelvin trying to slice the locust in half. It was too quick for him, darting and weaving before his blade could make contact. As if further mocking his feeble efforts, the locust landed on his sword, staring him down with its blood-red eyes.

"Get these eggs out of here!" Kelvin shouted and flung his sword and the locust on it into the fire.

"*Eggs?!*"

"Eggs." Kelvin motioned to the piles of obsidian objects amassed around the courtyard. "They're *all* eggs! We need to get these things out of here! Hurry!"

But even as everyone moved into action, an unsettling cracking filled the courtyard. It was too late. An instant later he finally grasped the full danger they were in: each of the eggs housed more than one locust . . .

The black swarm rose around the dying fires and elsewhere inside the camp. The low, droning hum was awful but not as dreadful as the sight of men set upon by scores of red-winged locusts. Most went for the face, but some decided to perch on armored shoulders or chests, burrowing their heads into the leather holding the scales together.

All was bedlam. The men were pushing aside whatever had landed on them while helping their fellows root out what they could. But it was a losing battle and a terrible fight. The locusts' skin was a kind of natural armor, hard to break without some effort. And all the while they continued munching.

"Protect what you can," Kelvin shouted, "but see to each other! Drive them off and take them down! We're not going to lose this fight!" But though his words sounded inspiring, Kelvin didn't know if he half believed them himself. And the more of his men he saw tumble to the ground in a cloud of fluttering locusts, the less confidence he had.

"Sovereign help us all," he muttered.

Sarah heard the screams from her bed: throaty, angry yelling and wailing. It sounded like a combination of pain, anger, and fear. She didn't know what it meant at first, but the longer it went on, the more she understood something was far from normal. Moments before it had been as still as could be with only the snoring of the others keeping her company. Now there was cacophony outside their makeshift prison.

For what seemed like endless moments she lay wide eyed on the hard boards of her bed. She didn't know what to do, and she wasn't even sure if there was something she could do. She had no weapons, and the door was surely still locked or guarded. Best to stay where she was for the time being. There was enough noise to stir others awake. Maybe they'd have a better idea of what needed doing.

While she waited she heard the soft flutter of wings. It was a low beating sound but quickly grew in volume into a droning buzz. And then she heard it fly through the windows. This was followed by cries of alarm from the congregation as all came face-to-face with the largest black locusts any had ever seen.

Women screamed along with their children. Some hopped from their bunks with hopes of fleeing the biting pests. Others rose with a growl, thrashing the insects with their closed and bound fists.

Sarah leapt to her feet with them, waving her tied hands, attempting to keep the locusts from landing on her face or hair. Even so, a couple alighted on her hands, scuttling around and nipping her skin around the rope. Her yelp of pain had her father beside her in an instant.

"Here." He knocked the locusts from her hands and wrapped her in his cloak.

"We need to get out of here!" someone shouted.

"Come on!" Her father hustled for the door while doing his best to shield her.

She could barely make out where they were going as she peeked through the small opening, but they were making progress. It was clear all had the same idea. She saw bloodied cheeks, hands, eyebrows, and necks and a never-ending stream of black bodies and red wings. The worst, she figured, was their naked feet, which proved tempting targets where several locusts could land. Sarah constantly kept an eye on her own lest she find the horrid things crawling and biting between her toes.

"It is still locked," said another brother before banging against the door as more locusts clambered over it, munching into the wood.

"All of us." She heard her father over the commotion. He motioned to the group of men gathered around it. "As one."

Taking Sarah by the shoulders, he stared firmly into her eyes. "Be still. The cloak should help keep out most of them." He too had streams of red dripping down his face and head and even more cuts and scrapes across his fingers and hands. Sensing her concern, he added, "I am fine. And you will be too."

An instant later, he joined James and Caleb in ramming their shoulders into the door. The loud pounding almost overcame the locusts' drone. Finally, there came a clank and then a creak and the door exploded outward.

"Hurry!" Bram shouted. "Keep moving. Out of the citadel. Get out of the citadel and away from here."

"You hurt?" Desmond took hold of Sarah once again. She lowered the cloak so she could see where she was going.

"No." It was then she saw the two dead Marauders who had been their guards. Well, what was left of them. They were slumped on either side of the broken door and covered in a carpet of locusts, who'd done a good job of skinning them and were working on clearing off the rest of their flesh.

Seeing what had caught her eye, her father took firm hold of her hand and dashed for the gates. All around them were the fallen Marauders and the ever-present plague of swarming death. From what they could see as they ran, it was apparent there was nothing left for them to salvage. All the animals who had managed to survive the Marauders had fallen prey to or were being assaulted by the swarm.

The wailing cries of the dying haunted Sarah as she ran.

"Keep running!" Bram urged with Caleb and James at his side.

Pressed with fear, the congregation weaved their way through the bodies and debris until they reached the gates. When all had finally made it through, Bram shouted: "Close the gates and run further afield!"

Desmond, Caleb, James, and some other brothers forced them shut.

"Keep low in the grass!" Bram continued. "Spread out and stay low."

Sarah threw herself onto the earth, gasping as she tried to get some sense of what was going on. She had been expecting the locusts to be right behind her, ready to pounce as soon as she stopped. Instead, it was quiet. But that didn't mean she was celebrating just yet.

"What *are* those things?" Sarah heard James ask Bram. Both he and the patriarch weren't too far from her and her father. The night air also helped amplify his voice, raising it above her pounding heart. Thankfully, James didn't appear to be gravely wounded. There were a few spots of blood and holes in his tunic and pants, but otherwise he was fine. It was one small consolation she allowed herself. "They are not like any locusts I have ever seen."

"No." Bram kept his eyes locked on the shut gates. "And now that whole citadel is full of them."

"Should we not be getting out of here while we can?" asked Caleb, who had crawled nearer the patriarch's position. Sarah had to admit she found some merit in the idea.

"And where could we go? It would be hard running in the dark with tied hands—and barefoot. And the swarm could be upon us no matter where we ran. Besides, we will need to salvage what remains. It would be foolish to remain empty handed on our journey."

"If they can do this to us in just a few moments there will not be much left of the livestock," James offered glumly.

"Perhaps, but there is little we can do about that now." Bram absent-mindedly wiped away some blood from a bite on the top of his hand. "But we cannot do much more until we have some daylight to make sense of what has befallen us."

"So we stay here for the rest of the night?" Caleb ran a hand through his beard, combing it smooth with his finger and no doubt making sure nothing was crawling around it.

"It is what I have decided," said Bram, "for the good of the congregation."

Sarah could see James clench his jaw at the idea, but he quickly swallowed whatever discontent had been brewing. "We will need a watch. I will see to it." James rose and selected a handful of men, Sarah's father among them.

"See if anyone has managed to salvage their dagger or a sword," the patriarch instructed Caleb. "We need to get these bindings off as soon as possible."

Caleb leapt to his feet and started making his own rounds. Eventually, he returned with two daggers someone had reclaimed as they ran. He kept one and shared the other with her father, who, after cutting his bindings free, went to Sarah.

"It will be okay," he said after loosing the rope around her wrists.

"It does not look like it will be," she replied.

"Wait until dawn. Things might look different then."

"And if they do not?"

She didn't like the flat look her father returned. "I have to see to the others." He made his way to the next person, helping set them free. Her attention returned to the citadel and its closed gates.

She would continue staring until dawn.

When morning finally arrived, Sarah and the rest of the congregation stood in the grass a stone's throw from the walls, no longer willing to remain on the ground. None really had slept since fleeing the citadel, instead keeping most, if not all, of their focus upon it.

Some murmured with each other, but most, like Sarah and her father beside her, didn't say much of anything. All kept their ears tuned for the dreadful hum, watching for the black cloud billowing out of the walls all knew for certain would arrive at any moment. But nothing had come. Even with the first light of dawn tracing its finger across the sky, all was still.

"Do you think they are still in there?" Sarah finally wondered aloud.

"Nothing left during the night," said her father.

"Have you ever encountered them before?"

He shook his head. "No, but I have not lived long enough to see everything." She followed his gaze toward the patriarch, who was conferring with the elders.

"You think the patriarch has heard of them before?"

"He might have, but even if he did not, we cannot let this keep us from our sojourn. The heralds said the way would not be easy, remember, but it would be worth it in the end."

"Still, it would be nice knowing—"

"Look!" An excited voice rose over the field.

All eyes locked on a swaying black cloud rising above the citadel. It was about that same time the wooden gates crashed to the ground with a sighing whine as what was left of them tumbled into splintered wood attached to worthless hunks of metal. The swarm spewed forth from the new opening.

"Take cover!" Another shout thundered over the frightful hum accompanying the insects.

Sarah dropped to the grass, closing her eyes and clamping her hands over her head. The next moment she felt the rush of air as the hundreds of locusts flew overhead. She imagined them landing on her hair and back, digging and biting into any and every part of her. She focused on keeping her mouth closed, lips tight, and jaws locked. She even found herself curling her toes for good measure. Thankfully, none made any landings. And then, just as suddenly as the whole ordeal began, the quiet returned.

"They have left!" A lone voice of praise rose from the congregation. Sarah and the others rose tentatively. "Sovereign be praised!"

As the people took to their feet, they were greeted with a surreal scene. Only the citadel stared back. The empty citadel. She searched for the black mass, scanning from horizon to horizon, but could not find them anywhere.

"Where did they go?" Sarah turned to her father, who was intently inspecting what remained of the gates from where he stood.

"Hopefully, far from here."

"Did they *eat* the gates?" She shivered at the sight. They resembled more the remains of rotten logs than the previously solid gate. Thankfully, the bodies of the animals and Marauders weren't visible from where she stood.

"It appears they eat just about anything."

Sarah again shivered.

Movement out of the corner of her eye pulled her attention toward James. He was walking up to the patriarch and the elders. He didn't notice her watching him but did happen to see Malena. She didn't hear what was said, but James gave a small nod and smile.

Sarah suddenly felt sick.

"Was anyone injured in their passing?" Bram inquired of the congregation. None were, for which Sarah again thanked the Sovereign. "Then let us go and see what can be salvaged. Retrieve what we can and then we need to depart. The sooner we put this place behind us, the better."

She couldn't have agreed more.

All followed the patriarch with quickened steps and troubled brows. That trouble only increased upon witnessing what the locusts left behind. Out of all the Marauders, not one was alive. Most of their bodies had been shredded, in some cases to the bone. Their armor and weapons had been useless against their attackers.

Given their armor and weapons remained intact, she surmised the locusts didn't eat metal. It was one small shaft of light peeking out of a dark sky. As to the congregation's provisions, all were gone. They had no more bread and grain—eaten by the locusts or the Marauders before them. The livestock that had survived the Marauders' feast shared the same fate as their captors.

Yet in the midst of this, their carts remained intact. So too did their bedrolls and tents. And most of their shoes and socks. The rest would have to be salvaged from the Marauders where possible. More than one among the congregation called it a miracle. Sarah was inclined to agree. Another sliver of light peeked through that dark canopy.

"Take what you can," said Bram. "Leave the animals."

"We could still save some of them," James protested.

"No." Bram was resolute. "We do not know if those locusts carried any diseases. It is wiser to leave them be."

"But we will not have any meat," James continued, amazed at the thought.

"Nor bread," added Caleb. "But it is better than falling ill and suffering a far worse fate."

"Trust in the Sovereign." Bram moved to end the conversation. "He will see to our way, as he has for us from the beginning. Now gather what you can. Put any fresh water in the carts."

Sarah lost herself in her work, wandering and pondering over what was still viable or could be salvaged. It seemed wasteful leaving anything with potential behind. They'd leave the swords and armor but reclaim their daggers and tools. The few tools the Marauders had—mostly shovels—were added to the carts. It wasn't much, but since they were missing the animals that had once filled them, they now had extra space.

"Nothing?" Sarah turned upon hearing Bram speaking with James.

"They had skins," said James, "but the locusts ate through them and the water was lost."

Sarah's heart sank at the news. She was hoping for at least some water. She was getting thirsty. She imagined it was even worse for the children.

"We will make what we have last," said Bram.

"How?" James wasn't as confident. "After this we have lost nearly everything."

"We have not lost everything." Sarah heard the voice of Malena, who had worked herself closer to James as he'd been talking. "We still have each other." The words caught his attention, making him blush. If she'd suffered under the locusts, Sarah didn't see it. Her face was still as smooth and lovely as ever. And those eyes—the way they sparkled upon catching sight of James . . . Sarah again felt sick but could do little more than stare at Malena with a growing sense of unease. But for the life of her, she didn't know what she could do *except* stare.

"Yes." Bram took up Malena's thought. "We still have our lives." He'd leaned on his regained staff as he hurried through the scattered remains. It was one of a handful of staves that remained that had been given to the elders and the next eldest of the men. "That is better than some have suffered this day." He continued surveying the scene while the rest rapidly finished gleaning anything that might have escaped their initial survey.

"Malena seems to have made the first move." Sarah turned and saw Tabitha at her side.

"More like the second or third." Sarah sighed. "I feel like I am getting too far behind."

"Maybe," said Tabitha. "But maybe you can find a way to work closer to him and—"

She stopped when both saw James join the ranks of the elders at the patriarch's side. "Or maybe you can keep waiting for your opening," she said instead.

"I thought you were supposed to encourage me."

"I am doing my best, but it is hard to steer a standing mule."

"I know." Sarah sighed again. "I have to be bolder if I want to get ahead of Malena."

"Or at least have James notice you," said Tabitha. "You *have* actually spoken to him at least once, right?" Sarah clamped her lips and turned away.

"Oh, Sarah." Tabitha's tone, while loving, didn't mellow the burning embarrassment coursing through her veins. "Let me see what more I can do. I will not speak to him for you, but if I find a way to point you both in the right direction, I will."

"Thank you." She felt safe sharing a small smile.

"I trust you were not hurt by those locusts?"

"Not really. And you?"

"I and my parents are well. Though Father did have one nibble on his big toe. He was able to kick it free, though, before it could sink its teeth in too deep."

"My father also fared well." Sarah cheered herself with the reminder of that bit of good news. "Most of us did, from what I hear."

"Another small blessing from the Sovereign, I am sure." Tabitha wiped some stray hairs back from her forehead. "I suppose I should get back to work. I just do not want to look at the bodies—the animals *or* the people. What I saw already is just awful. Much worse than that hanging girl the other day. Has your father ever seen those locusts before? Both my parents said they have never come across them in all their years."

"No, my father has not seen them either," she replied. "But I do not think they are a good sign of things to come."

"You think we might be getting close to the Veiled City? I heard some murmuring last night about the possibility of darker things before we reach it, and, well, you have to admit this was rather bleak."

"It would make sense if that were true, but if the patriarch has not said anything yet, I am still going to reserve my judgment." The conversation trailed off, and each returned to their work.

After some time had passed, Bram again entered the courtyard, flanked by the elders and James and Caleb. She could see the elders were discussing something with Bram. Whatever it was, he seemed inclined to it. At least from what she could see and surmise from where she stood.

Stopping, Bram raised his staff and his voice. "It is time to leave. We still have a long day ahead of us."

Sarah wanted to ask how they would be able to keep up such treks in the days ahead with no food and very little water but held her tongue. The others, she could tell, felt the same. It wasn't going to help the matter by asking when all knew the answer already. They had to keep their faith in something better before them while they endeavored to keep doing the only thing they'd known since they were born.

"As the sparrow flies." Bram lowered his staff and made his way for the gates.

CHAPTER TEN

A Gathering of Crows.

It was a few hours after dawn when a group of Laromi marched for Larom's slowly opening gates. Like all Laromi, they shared a very similar appearance. But unlike those behind the walls, these new arrivals were despondent to the point of resembling shuffling corpses.

Around this gloomy body of people was a circle of armed men. These too were Laromi, but that was where the similarity ended. Each soldier kept their short sword in hand as they pressed the others between them, directing them toward the gates. Their chain mail shirts, brigandine leather pants, and round shields would keep them from any harm, but none of their captives were bold enough to even try raising a fist. Like sheep silent before their approaching fate, they kept their heads hung low, eyes on the hard-packed road they traveled.

Corbin watched them enter the main courtyard. He wasn't alone. A smattering of other Laromi, dressed identically to these new arrivals, studied them closely. If they felt the extra eyes upon them, they didn't show it. Only when the great doors clanked shut behind them did some of them jolt their heads upward.

"This all you could find?" asked a gruff Laromic soldier named Martin. He briskly strode past Corbin as he made his way for the small company of newly arrived soldiers.

The captain of the city guard had become something of a leader of the army since Corbin had become princeps of the city. While Corbin was in command of the army—and everything else for that matter—it was nice to have some delegation, especially with these even darker days upon them.

"The pickings are getting slimmer all the time," answered the lead soldier.

Martin gave the newcomers a cursory inspection with his pale blue eyes. "Getting slimmer all the time." He sighed. "Take them to the cells. We'll coax as much out of them as possible." The other gave a nod and herded his prisoners through the thinly populated streets.

"Larom thanks you for your service." Corbin addressed the people as they passed.

Each soldier nodded, acknowledging Corbin's place as first among equals. Those they led said nothing, not even daring to look up at the man who was equal to but also a step above them.

Further aiding this distinction were the burgundy cape and black vest he wore over his white shirt and black pants. No one else would wear them but the princeps. "No doubt Laroma holds a special place for you all for willingly laying down so much for the greater good of your fellow citizens."

This was all a show, of course. None had volunteered for anything. No sane man or woman would. The old doctrine of equality—the maintenance of the status quo—had served Larom well for generations beyond memory. But it wouldn't hold as these days grew darker. All that kept it from cracking was this thin veneer.

The only reason they had any order was because of the hope that had been renewed by these recent excursions. As long as the other citizens saw the men returning with more people, order could be maintained. And part of maintaining that status quo was keeping up a good front for all who watched.

Corbin was no fool. He understood long ago that only the show of normalcy was needed, not normality itself. The illusion would conjure enough of a false impression to banish any questions. Questions were bad. They were bad before the present days and even worse now. If he could keep things moving, keep on an even keel, then the people would gladly continue deceiving themselves. And Corbin didn't blame them. The alternative was something he tried not to think about too much himself.

"I fear we've reached the top of the hill, sir," said Martin glumly. He'd returned to the princeps's side, observing the passing of the new arrivals with obvious disappointment.

"That's still about thirty good bodies." Corbin sought the positive. "Thin but still healthy from what I saw."

"Not enough to sustain the city," said Martin. "Not at that rate."

He was right. By sheer luck they'd been able to keep a population of about two and a half thousand alive. Most were in the army and therefore important. As much as he reminded everyone of their equal worth, the army was what was going to keep them alive. If not for the towns and villages, they would have been in a worse state. But there were only so many of those, as this new batch made clear yet again.

"Laroma will provide." Corbin smiled at his captain as the last of the people and soldiers flowed past. "She always has and always will."

"Until these dark days are over," Martin muttered.

"That's what we've been told," Corbin agreed.

"Let's hope they get brighter soon." The gruff soldier took in the statue of his goddess dominating the center of the main courtyard.

Larger than life and standing on a ten-foot pedestal, she let all below know who was the main power in Larom. They may have all been equal, but there was at least one above them all, presumably looking after their best interests. Corbin always envisioned himself in that place but did his best to nurture the idea of it being Laroma instead—especially when he was around any of her priestesses. It gave him some cover should anything he advocated turn out less than ideal.

But it wasn't just his own people he had to keep an eye on these days. There was another threat to the status quo coming from outside Larom—from non-Laromi—who were burning through towns and villages in a bloody swath that would eventually lead right to Larom's gates. That was bad for two reasons.

The first was the obvious threat to the city; the second was the loss of people outside the walls. Fewer people made the crows' job harder.

And their work was hard enough already. He had to prepare for the worst, though, even while hoping for something better. It was a pragmatic approach he'd use until he found a solution.

These zealots were a determined lot who didn't appear to have any real weaknesses, from what Corbin had heard from those who had managed to flee them over the previous weeks. He sought to keep news of the approaching threat as private as possible, of course—inviting those who shared such insights with him to help sustain their fellow citizens' morale and lives in other ways . . . But he wouldn't be able to stop this news from becoming known much longer—especially when a host of armed men arrived on the doorstep—and so had recently decided on a more measured release of such information, balancing it with a strong assurance of Larom's defenses, while taking more proactive measures with the army.

He'd sent the first contingent of men to scout out this new enemy and strike with surprise if they could, taking down some numbers in the process. And, from what the returning soldiers had shared, that was indeed the case, but it was far from the massive success he'd been hoping for. Still, it did help him gauge their abilities and provided a training exercise for the men, who could impart what they learned to the rest of the army. But that still didn't mean they didn't need to prepare as best they knew how.

"As long as you're here, I wanted to speak to you about our defenses." Corbin turned to Martin, keeping his voice low.

"I've looked them over as you ordered, and they're as good as they can be. Any minor repairs that were needed have been made."

"And the men?"

"I have the walls covered, sir. As you lead the army, I've left you to the planning of the rest."

That was all Corbin could hope for. "The battle will be on two fronts," he continued. "It's become clear to me these Pyri are little more than bloodthirsty zealots. So if they want a slaughter, we'll give it to them. They'll have a taste of our steel soon. I'm looking forward to giving them more than a bloody lip this time around, now that we know some of their tactics. If we can thin their numbers before they get any closer, we gain an advantage."

"And we need all we can get, sir." Martin was speaking the truth. For he, like Corbin, had heard the reports from those who'd faced off with the Pyri already. This wasn't going to be an easy fight, no matter how well they could prepare. But such things weren't good fodder for the people's mental digestion . . .

Corbin raised his voice to its normal volume, adding, "Larom will not be brought low and made subject to another. We are all equal and will not be made lesser nor forced to give up the adoration of our great goddess for some foolish flaming bird. Larom will stand—all of us will stand—as one. Just as we have lived."

The words had their desired effect, as evidenced by the renewed confidence on the faces of those within earshot. Now that there were fewer people on the streets, gossip spread much faster, and public sentiment was more subject to wild waverings. It was always wise to set the tone. If tongues were going to wag, they might as well do so in his favor.

Martin took his cue, responding in kind at equal volume. "The men on the walls will not let one of those fire worshipers get inside—not while they still have breath."

Corbin nodded approvingly. "From what I hear, they have a large force, enough to allow us quite the celebratory feast."

Martin's eyes sparkled at the thought. "Laroma provides."

"Yes, she certainly does," said Corbin. "I'll leave you to your rounds."

Martin nodded and left the princeps in the courtyard—a place that would have once been filled with all manner of life and activity but where now only whispers ventured. He hadn't been alive long enough to fully know of the greatness before the Burning Cascade, just enough years to understand something was missing—something had been lost, and there was no way to restore it.

And no matter what he'd just said, Corbin knew even if they should win against these fanatics, they wouldn't secure much of a victory. Their days—and lives—were numbered. The only consolation he took in the upcoming fight was that it would cause some of the soldiers to fall, leading to fewer mouths to feed. There was something deeply tempting in such a proposition . . . and they'd still be in service to the people in death. Yes, some definite advantages were to be had, but all at the cost of upsetting the status quo. And that, for the long term, was not good at all. Not if they wanted to keep drawing breath for another year . . .

Either way drastic action was called for. And either way there would be hard choices. Hard sacrifices. But if he was wise and took command of the situation before it got too far beyond him, he'd be better for it. And if he could safeguard any losses by extra precautionary measures, so much the better.

Turning to a passing soldier, he said, "Summon some more crows. I want them in the field as soon as possible." The guard bowed and quickened his steps for the barracks.

"Let's see what the crows brought us today," said Erlan, a hard-faced Laromic man, upon catching sight of the newly arrived citizens from some other village or town far outside Larom's walls.

They'd all been divided into five lines, six people deep. At the head and end of each line was a soldier. Just where they hailed from wasn't really the issue. None in the city cared for those outside its walls. Not anymore. All of Annulis had been condensed and packed between the great city's stone curtain. There was life in the city. Outside it was nothing but a slow death.

This was the hard truth all had to accept if they wanted to keep living. It wasn't easy for some, but those who had any trouble making the adjustment dwindled over time. This left only those who took hold of the hard reality with both hands, fearful to lose their grip. All they had was themselves and what they needed to keep their lives for another day. These new arrivals would soon learn this truth by serving it.

Erlan met them as he had all the previous arrivals: inside the circular room that served as the entrance to the dungeons. The open area had been created as a secure place to move in and out. The circular walls made it easy for the guards to put down any attempts at escape. It was the ideal place to sort things out without fear of revolt. Not that there were ever that many. Most, by the time they arrived, had given up on ever getting out alive.

Those who had been collected this time were a meager lot at best. He focused first on the elderly men and the few young children. They'd do for a short while. He didn't see too many kids anymore. He might be able to leave them for a time in hopes they'd grow some. But more than likely they'd be starving soon enough and lose any weight they did gain. This just left the remaining females and males—mostly middle aged, but suitable.

Of course, he didn't have much choice in the matter. And he wasn't about to take their place. He, like the rest of Larom, would take what he got. As long as the crows kept delivering their finds, the uneasy sense of normalcy could remain. He did his best not to think about what would happen the day they finally stopped delivering these finds. It was best to keep to the present and work yourself through it . . . day by day was the wisest way to live in these times.

"Not the best, but I suppose you'll do."

"For what?" asked one of the elderly men at the front of the group.

"You'll see soon enough," he replied. "Take him first," he pointed at the man who'd spoken.

At once the man was seized by two guards, each grasping an arm. It was probably a bit excessive, as the man was quite frail, but it was best to eliminate any opportunities as well as convey the right message to anyone else who might present a challenge.

"I've done nothing wrong," the man protested. "I'm a good citizen. I have broken no laws. I demand to see the princeps."

"Oh, you'll see him." Erlan shared a sardonic smile. "Sooner than you might think." The guards tugged him up to one of the cell doors behind Erlan that led into the dungeons proper. One of them opened it while the second shoved the man inside. Both soldiers followed, slamming the door behind them.

"Anyone else have anything they want to say?" Erlan eyed all the others in turn. The women and some of the men hung their heads in despair rather than face him eye to eye. It was normal and expected.

"Rest while you can," he continued, motioning to the guards. "It will make the time go faster."

The people were herded toward the same cell door the elderly man had been shoved through. As was custom, Erlan watched them flow through the doorway in single file. Each passed through without incident. Once they had passed he followed, closing the door behind him. But whereas they were directed to the left, he went to the right.

Following this torch-lit hallway into a series of others, he eventually found himself in an underground kitchen. But it was unlike any kitchen one might find in a common home. There were still large hearths for cooking, but these were joined by a selection of stone slabs spread across the room. Some lay flat, while others rested at an angle. All were bloody and stained from a great deal of use.

Chains hung from the ten-foot ceiling. At the end of each was a large, sharp hook. On a handful of these hooks were the remains of people, hacked and sliced like a side of beef. The headless torsos had long been stripped of skin, leaving the smoked or cooked muscle on the bone. There wasn't a lot of it left but enough for some to gain strength to see another day.

He had long ago forced himself to get used to the carnal stench of the place. There wasn't anything he could do about it. While it was strongest here, the smell permeated much of the dungeons, making it nearly impossible to ignore what was going on. Those above might be able to play games and hide from the truth, but those down here actually doing the work didn't have such a luxury. He long ago accepted the whole lot of it, forcing himself to just get whatever needed doing over with. Sentimentality was a weakness he couldn't afford anymore. Not if he wanted to keep his own corpse from joining the others dangling from these hooks and chains.

Looking past the hanging remains, Erlan saw two slender older men stirring a large cauldron over a fire in one of the hearths. Both had greasy hair and faces. Their white shirts and brown pants had been befouled by the messy nature of their work. Their soiled aprons had long ago failed in their duty.

A fresh trail of blood stretched from their location to another of the slabs. Erlan noted the body of the elderly man he'd sent here earlier resting on the stone. He was missing his head and arms. His naked torso was lean, but he was confident there was something there they could use—the organs at the very least could be made into some almost delectable fare.

"This one wasn't that bad," said Fallo, the older of the pair. "He was in good health. The organs should be good too."

"We've got a few more older ones," Erlan informed the men. "I'll send them when I can."

"This one should be fine for the evening meal," Gradin, the other tending the cauldron, replied. "But those outside the palace will need something more to hold them over—even with the rationing."

"Then I'll add some of the children. I wasn't sure how long they'd keep anyway."

"We'll make do with what we can." Fallo bent over to retrieve a large bloodied knife from an equally bloodstained table beside him. "We'll know more once we take a look inside." He made his way back to the slab and the headless corpse.

Leaving them to their work, Erlan made for the door. "I'll be back later with an updated inventory and options."

"No hurry," Fallo called after him. "We'll be busy for a while."

Erlan turned and retraced his steps, glad to be free of the stench of cooking human flesh. While he might have learned to stomach the actual eating of it, he wasn't yet accustomed to the smell of it being processed.

He ventured deeper into the dungeons, recalling the new arrivals. There was usually one or two who tended to stand out. It was always guesswork. Children were more susceptible to things than adults. But constant practice had given him the confidence needed to make the final selection. He had to do so quickly too. They preferred to cook everything at the same time, eliminating waste and making sure the right amount of food was available to make for the best rationing possible. It wouldn't do to have disorder and unrest in the streets. The status quo, no matter how illusionary, must be preserved.

CHAPTER ELEVEN

A Troubling Confrontation. Compliments and Praise.

I t was midday when the army sighted the town in the distance. Growing more cautious the closer they drew to Larom, they'd stopped and directed some scouts to investigate. After the quiet following their previous encounter with Laromic forces, Elliott had been ready to see hidden Laromi springing up at any moment. So far there had been nothing.

But they were much closer to Larom than before. And you couldn't expect them to not defend themselves—corrupted though they may be. Elliott had watched it play out time and time again. It was a natural instinct to protect yourself—your homeland and people. So it wasn't unusual to expect more soldiers hidden behind the walls of some seemingly simple town in the middle of supposedly empty fields.

And that was what he told himself. Not that he was actually worried about the absence of encounters. He realized it wasn't so much fear that was hounding his thoughts as the prospect of having to face such a large force at once. It was the idea that a massive force awaited them at the city, and they were moving headlong toward it.

Pyre would see they had the victory, of course, but in all of these last three years they'd never really seen a massive force marshaled against them. All the villages and the towns and even the handful of cities didn't have much more than a skeletal defense. And while no one said Larom would be any different, their previous encounter suggested something else. At least Elliott let himself imagine it did. After a while he realized most of his concern had been tied to what he'd seen upon returning with Sir Pillum to the fallen infantry. Seeing that many dead—the most who'd fallen in any battle during the campaign—stoked the flame, but witnessing the weaponry soon to be arrayed against them kept those embers of fear from dissipating.

He wouldn't share such concerns with Sir Pillum. He didn't want him to think any less of Elliott for what he knew were foolish thoughts. He would just have to work through it on his own, trusting he'd be able to do so before the next encounter was upon them. If he was to be a knight, it was the very minimum of what was required. A sound mind and strong sword arm were parts of the oath all knights swore when knighted. And Elliott would offer no less when he was given the oath.

"I don't see any livestock about." Elliott continued his study of the terrain as they waited, thinking it time to speak some and think less.

"They could have taken their animals inside the walls once they saw us coming." Sir Pillum kept his gaze fixed on the dirt road slithering to the base of the town's pitted stone walls. Elliott had noticed the roads improving in quality, giving rise to the notion that they were within the more populated and traversed part of the Laromic territory.

"But what about the crops?" Elliott was still confused about what he was seeing. "There should be some signs of whatever it is they are growing."

Sir Pillum gave a small nod. "There's that, but we'll soon get the truth when the scouts return."

"You think we might have driven them all back to Larom?" Elliott cautiously inquired, making it sound more like a casual question than anything else.

"Possibly. But I wouldn't put it past them to try something soon. We're close to the city and they're becoming cornered beasts. They know they can't stand before our might, nor Pyre, who favors us."

Elliott nodded. Astride his horse and beside Sir Pillum, he could do little else. He couldn't see anything more. The walls were too tall to peer over from horseback, and as he'd already informed his master, there was nothing around to hold any interest for bored eyes. Neither crops nor animals of any kind, nothing save those barren walls and the probably barren town behind it.

"Here they come now." The voice of a Salamandrine pulled Elliott's attention back to the gates.

The clump of men that emerged at first seemed familiar, but it didn't take long to notice these weren't the same scouts who'd been sent inside. These were men armed for battle but not in the Pyric manner. The round shields they carried, outlined in jagged metal teeth, made that clear enough. The severed heads swaying from makeshift straps in their free hands dispelled any lingering doubts.

"Hold your place." Calix's voice was firm. Both the Salamandrine and the infantry obeyed, even as the scouts' heads were tossed their way like so much garbage.

"They couldn't stand against our blades," shouted a Laromi who had taken the lead among the others. "Will you fare much better?"

"You have no idea what you're facing," Calix shouted back.

The Laromi smiled. "Nor do you." He raised his hand.

The action summoned a host of Laromic soldiers from all around the village. Some spilled out from the gate, others appeared on the walls, and still more sprung up from the empty fields and even along the road in places. Elliott couldn't get a decent count, but there were enough to put up a fight. For a moment he found himself wondering if this was what the infantry had faced earlier, before they'd—

A droning, buzzing sound suddenly filled the air. Everyone—Pyri and Laromi alike—lifted their heads as a thick cloud of black locusts came into view. Elliott had never heard such a thing before. The sound of so many insects was nearly deafening. None of the warriors moved, only kept their gaze on the swirling black swarm, trying to figure out if the other side was somehow in league with the phenomenon.

It quickly became clear neither was.

"Are those really locusts?" The closer they got, the more astonished he was. "I've never seen any so large before." He'd seen locusts before, but these had to be as long as a hand and at least two fingers wide. They were monstrous things—almost too amazing to fathom. And yet there they were flying toward them en masse.

"Neither have I," said Sir Pillum, drawing his sword as the cloud descended on the army.

"To arms!" A cry went up from the mass of men.

"Kill them!" A shout from the Laromic side rang over the din.

"A good time to test your skills, Elliott." Sir Pillum shot him a small grin. "Here." He tossed him a spare short sword he had strapped to his saddle. "I trust you know how to use it."

"Yes, sir." Elliott held the weapon tight.

The exhilaration of the moment mixed with the rising fear at the strange locusts' appearance made for quite a potent concoction flowing through his veins. It had finally come: his time for proving his worth as something more than a squire . . . of being worthy to be called a knight. If not for the pressing fight, he would have savored the moment as long as he could.

"Stick close if you can," Calix ordered. "The less space we allow them, the less we'll have to fight back. Two fronts. Half facing the locusts, the rest on the Laromi."

The horses whinnied and snorted as everyone hurried into their positions.

"Blaze rods level!" Elliott heard Milec command the priests.

"Archers, fire!"

A burst of arrows flew heavenward as the first of the locusts came into striking distance. Though released in a thick spread, the arrows did little to take down their foes. Only a handful of the plump insects were skewered with some well-placed shots. The rest continued onward, landing on horses, shields, and men.

"Now!" Bursts of flame erupted from the blaze rods scattered across the Pyric company. These tufts of flame cleared out portions of the infestation but made no real impact on the thick cloud hovering above them.

The continued buzzing was unnerving in and of itself, but to see the things face-to-face as he attempted to pry them from his frantic horse and himself was downright terrifying. Their black shells were like stone in places. It took all his strength to cut into them. When he did the sound reminded him of cracking eggshells. But just as soon as Elliott raised his sword, two more rushed in and took the previous one's place.

And then came the screams.

From the corner of his eye he could see some in the infantry struggling with the creatures as they skittered over their bodies, seeking any exposed area on which they could feast. And feast they did, biting into skin and muscle in wild frenzies. So deep were their bites they not only drew blood but removed chunks of flesh. Working together, the black swarm was swift in transforming their prey from strong warriors into helpless victims.

If there was any consolation, it was that the locusts showed no preference among their victims. The Laromi were equally as hampered as the Pyri. He could see some Laromi frantically ridding themselves of the threat with curses and hand swipes across faces and bodies. But even slowed, the soldiers continued their press forward, striking down any Pyri crossing their path.

"Salamandrine, charge!" came Calix's command. Half the knights and some of their squires galloped for the enemy. "No quarter! No mercy!"

Acting without thought, Elliott spurred his mount forward, ducking his head to his horse's neck as the nervous steed plowed through the locusts. He noticed some of them had landed on the creature and were feverishly satiating their hunger. He couldn't stop to scrape them off and hoped the horse would endure it.

His heart was galloping in its own right when he brought his sword down onto the nearest Laromi, who was too distracted by some locusts of his own to make any sort of defense.

Elliott had drawn first blood.

He'd managed to slice into the other's neck, releasing a small splash of crimson. A few drops of it got into his mouth, but he spat out what he could. Only a faint salty tang remained as he brought his sword down on another Laromi. This one had his shield ready and blocked the attack. He also had the blades spinning around it quite rapidly, which he stuck into the neck of Elliott's horse. The creature gave a powerful cry and stumbled backward on shaky legs.

Elliott could feel the horse weakening. Its legs had started quivering. He could feel its breathing becoming more erratic. Before he could dismount, the horse dropped to its knees and then its side, pinning Elliott's leg under its massive body. Thankfully, while held fast by the extra weight, he hadn't felt anything break.

Grunting with all his effort, he attempted sliding his leg free. A wide-eyed Laromi rushed forward, eager for an easy target. With a bestial grunt Elliott was able to pull himself free just as a clump of locusts rushed into the attacking Laromi's face.

Staggering back with a muffled scream, the man frantically attempted to rid himself of the churning black veil enveloping his head. Elliott didn't see much more. He jumped to his feet, making sure he avoided the black clump of insects that had settled on his dead horse. A quick inspection of the area didn't give him many options. Both sides were doing their best to keep back the locusts while crushing their enemy at the same time.

Retrieving his sword, he decided the best thing to do was to keep moving. He set his sights on the walls and began to run. No sooner had he done so than another Laromi leapt into his path. This one was fresh and free of any locusts.

He gave Elliott a passing slash with the whirling blades on his shield but Elliott dodged it with a sidestep. In return Elliott unleashed a few swings only to have them parried. This back-and-forth continued for a few more exchanges until Elliott heard the rumbling of hooves followed by a powerful downward strike.

A sword cleft through the Laromi's wrist. Instantly, the maimed soldier cried out, dropping to his knees.

"Elliott!" Sir Pillum stared at his squire. It wasn't a look of anger, just one of intense focus and dedication to the task at hand. He also appeared sound and whole—only a few scrapes and cuts here and there but otherwise healthy and strong.

"Get to the town!" he bellowed.

Elliott was pleased to hear he was at least thinking in line with a knight. It helped compensate for his less-than-effective job of emulating them in battle. He took off at top speed, dashing through the enemy host with a few brief exchanges but otherwise keeping himself free from the occasional burst of locusts. He could hear Sir Pillum close behind him, dealing out what death he could to any who foolishly crossed his path.

"Behind the walls!" Calix's command rose over the cacophony.

Elliott didn't have time to see who had obeyed or what was going on. His gaze was fixed on the open gates. The *nearing* open gates. A few heartbeats later he made his way behind them, as did Sir Pillum. Turning, he saw he wasn't alone. Scores of soldiers were making their way for them and the help they so seductively offered.

But they weren't the only ones seeking shelter behind the walls. Those Laromi who hadn't yet fled for their lives stood and vainly tried fending off the Pyric influx. Fueled by the chaos of battle and guided by their training and orders, the infantry, knights, and priests started making swift work of their opponents.

Elliott found himself pushed back from the fray, keeping company with a few other squires—their backs to the walls until the worst of the battle was finished. None of the Laromi surrendered, and no quarter was given. There'd be no Selection when they had finished, but that was all right, he supposed. He had a feeling these Laromi wouldn't be ones to surrender to Pyre anyway.

"You wounded?" asked Sir Pillum, riding up beside him. The knight was splattered with ichor—his shield now the bloodiest he'd ever seen it.

"No." Elliott shook his head. It was then he realized the skies above the town were relatively clear. Not a locust in sight. He wasn't sure why but at the moment didn't really care. Any change of fortune in their favor was a welcome one.

"We can't hope our luck holds." Sir Pillum read Elliott's thoughts. "We'll need a secure shelter for the wounded and those who can't fend for themselves should those things turn their attention our way."

"Keep moving inside," said Calix as he galloped around the small town square, trampling fallen Laromi in the process. There wasn't going to be enough room to house them all as it was—even if they all did as Calix ordered.

"How many?" Sir Pillum asked Calix.

"About twenty from the fighting here," the commander replied. "And I counted twenty outside the walls thus far—from the locusts mainly. Let's hope Drenn has better numbers, though I fear they'll be worse."

"What in Pyre's name is going on?" Sir Pillum glared back to the steady stream of infantry, knights, squires, and priests rushing behind the walls. Here the priests did their best at serving as rear guards, blasting the swarm and any Laromi still heading for the town with their blaze rods. Eventually the stream of men became a trickle and then nothing.

"Shut the gates!" Calix shouted.

The men nearest them did as ordered, even finding a fat wooden beam they could lodge into place for good measure. As soon as they were secured, all fell silent. Everyone scanned the heavens and tops of the walls for any sign of movement.

None appeared.

All held their breath.

For too long there was just the droning of the insects and the faint screams and moans of the dying. Then these too faded.

"Someone get on those walls for a look," ordered Calix. A quick-footed soldier hopped at the command, making his way up the battlement.

"Nothing," he shouted back. "The locusts have gone."

"And the others?" Calix returned.

"Fled or dead."

"Secure the gates and walls," Calix continued. "We'll camp here for the night." Immediately, men moved into action.

"You sure you're all right?" Sir Pillum gave Elliott a closer inspection from atop Bakan.

"Fine, sir." He was still trying to process everything, but it was good to know he and his master and most of the army were still alive and unharmed.

"You've got your first taste," Sir Pillum continued. "Sword and all. What did you think?"

He didn't really know if he had anything to say. It had all happened so quickly, and even now, after the events, he was finding it hard recalling things in detail. Everything was a blur. There was the fear and rushing around and just a whole mix of additional thoughts and emotions he didn't know one could think and experience all at once.

"It wasn't like I was expecting it to be." He figured this was as close as he could get to describing things at the moment.

Sir Pillum shared a knowing nod. "It never is. But you did well. In time you'll be able to do even better."

"Thank you, sir." Elliott let himself take some small comfort in the praise, even if he still was trying to get himself calm enough to take on the rest of his duties.

"Come on." Sir Pillum gave him a pat on the back. "We still have work to do." ·

After the town had been secured, Elliott returned to his normal tasks. Sir Pillum had joined the other knights in plotting their next steps with Calix. Drenn had his own meeting with the leaders of the infantry. This left the squires, priests, camp workers, and the rest to their normal business and routines.

The whole place had been searched for any sign of the enemy as well as anything of possible use. Nothing was found on either count. The place was stripped clean. It was clear the Laromi had wanted to turn the place into a trap. But with Pyre's mercy, the Pyri had been able to turn it around to bite them instead. Like Sir Pillum said, they must be getting desperate. And that, mingled with his own experience in combat, was enough to finally put his previous concerns and lingering fears to rest.

Most of the soldiers had gathered in the areas beyond the courtyard, which was left for the Salamandrine and their horses. The larger open area served as a stable of sorts where the squires and knights could care for their steeds. Even after the battle, they still needed to maintain order. Discipline was the heart of that order.

There would be no tents tonight. They would all sleep under the stars, which none grumbled about, but only accepted as the hardened soldiers they were. They were tightly packed inside as it was. Having tents and other matters to contend with would make securing the area more of a challenge. Not having tents to pack up would also allow them more time for a fast departure tomorrow, once the dead were sent on their way. Even now Elliott could see the odd soldier seeing to the fallen. He didn't have a clear view from where he was at the center of the courtyard with the other knights and their squires, but from what he could tell it was a good-sized number.

Elliott was tending to Bakan and was about to see to his armor when a crow caught his eye. The lone bird perched on a section of wall not too far from him. It just sat there silently observing Elliott with its dark, beady eyes. It showed no sign of fear—not of loud noises or human voices in the area. It simply stared as if keeping a careful record of all Elliott was doing.

"Calix isn't happy." Sir Pillum's voice shook him from his concentration.

"How many did we lose?"

"Too many—thirty knights and fifty more infantry. And a good many horses—thankfully, most were the ones we took from the Marauders."

Elliott couldn't believe it. He looked around for the same soldiers he'd seen earlier as a way of confirming such figures. "How many of the Laromi?"

"We don't know," he returned. "And no one is going to go check until daylight. I'm praying it's at least *triple* our losses. Between this and our last encounter they deserve it. All the wounded are still able to fight—a saving grace there—but it's still too high a number for our liking."

"You don't think they summoned the locusts somehow, do you?"

"If they did, then they didn't know what they were doing. They couldn't keep them off themselves any more than we could."

"So where did they come from? I've never seen or heard anything like them before."

"I have a feeling we're going to start seeing more unnatural and unsettling things the further we go about our duty," said Sir Pillum. "This is a corrupted world, and there are bound to be more twisted and wicked things rising from it. Especially as we near the Great Conflagration. I wouldn't let it trouble you. Just keep your faith in Pyre and your mind on your training, like you did today, and all will work out well in the end."

Elliott paused, not wanting to think it nor say it, but it had to be said, at least for his own sake. "Do you think those locusts will return?"

Sir Pillum sighed. "If so, there's not much more we can do. We'll get to Larom and complete our mission, no matter what's before us."

"Where are we going to set the bonfires?" Elliott took another look around the courtyard in case he might have missed something. He hadn't seen anyone making an effort toward that end.

"We'll pile the dead inside," said Sir Pillum. "Calix wants to send a message. We honor our dead and burn this place to the ground in the process."

"So we're going to need an early start, then." Elliott was already thinking ahead to what was needed. He stepped toward Bakan. "I'll see you have everything ready."

"I'm sure you will." His master joined Elliott in examining his steed, seemingly pleased with what he found. "You've yet to disappoint." The praise swelled Elliott's chest and straightened his spine.

He stopped and stared at Elliott with a curious eye. "You going to be all right?"

"I think he might need a new shoe in a week or so. It seems to be holding up well enough though, for now. But I wouldn't want to risk it for much longer."

"I asked about *you*, not the horse."

"I'm fine, sir."

"The excitement's worn off now from the battle. You might start seeing things or thinking about things you'd forgotten." He paused. "Some of those thoughts might be a bit rough."

"Rough, sir?"

"Maybe *raw* is a better word. That gets easier too the more you go through it. But that first time can be a little challenging. So, if you need to talk about anything . . ."

"Thank you, sir." Elliott was touched by the kind offer. It was just one more thing a fellow knight would offer another. "One thing I was surprised by was how fast everything was."

"Sometimes things can actually seem slower than normal. You can't really prepare too much for either, other than remembering your training and keeping faith in your cause and Pyre." Sir Pillum glanced at his armor gathered in a small pile to the side of the animal. "Looks like you won't have too much work to contend with tonight. The Laromi didn't get in too many hits."

"Something we're both thankful for." Elliott smiled.

"But the blood—well, that's to be expected, I guess."

"I'll manage, sir." And he would. It was expected of him, no matter what else might be going on around him. It was his duty—his mission—and he wouldn't come up short.

"It's too bad about the horses, though. We lost more from those locusts than anything else. If not for those extra ones, we might be hurting right about now. Some of our knights might have become unwilling infantry." He gave Bakan a gentle pat. "Thank Pyre you made it through, Bakan."

Bakan snorted.

"Were you scared in the fight?" Sir Pillum looked Elliott square in the face.

In truth Elliott had not given it much thought. He'd been so absorbed in his daily duties and routines, the matter had totally escaped him until just now. "I could feel the fear in me and around me."

"Palpable, wasn't it?" He saw a flash across his master's gray eyes, revealing he was quite intimate with the experience. "Almost like it was water you were swimming in, right?"

"Yes, sir." Elliott was amazed by so accurate a description.

"And then there's the gnawing in your gut too. That one comes and goes from time to time and battle to battle, but that thick sea of it is always there. You did well in pushing through, Elliott."

"Thank you, sir."

"You kept to your training. That's what overcomes it every time. You lose focus on your training, and you start sinking in the fear, and then you're not much help to anyone. How about when you killed someone?" Elliott's eyes widened at the question. "What did you feel then?"

"I don't think I actually killed anyone, sir. Not that I can recall. I know I took a slice at someone's neck, but that's about it."

"Well, slices on the neck tend to do most people in," said Sir Pillum. "Unless you just nicked him."

"No, I'm sure it was deeper than that." Instantly, he recalled the taste of the man's blood in his mouth, as some of it had splashed inside while he rode past.

"You sure you're okay?"

Elliott realized he had been lost in memory for longer than he realized.

"Fine, sir. It all happened so fast, like I said. I didn't really consider any of it."

"And he's still dead now, thanks to you." Pillum watched Elliott closely. "Now that it's sunk in some, anything troubling you?"

Again Elliott paused and collected his thoughts. "Nothing, sir. The man was an infidel, a corrupted enemy of Pyre and his truth. He needed to be removed for the greater good of all."

His master smiled. "Well said. I don't know how much more I need to teach you. You're very close to being found worthy. And after we complete this leg of the campaign and finally cleanse Larom, I'm going to put in my recommendation to Calix for you—see if I can accelerate the process a bit. Given our recent losses, we could use some more knights."

"Thank you, sir." Elliott was overwhelmed. "But if I've proven to be anything of note, it's due to your excellent instruction."

"Even the best teachers can have terrible pupils. But you're what every knight hopes to have in a squire. May you get another just like you to train under your wing."

Elliott bowed his head in gratitude.

"I'll leave you to the armor." Sir Pillum turned to leave. "When you're done, feel free to get some food and rest. You'll need all the sleep you can get—especially with us so close to Larom."

"Yes, sir."

Curious, Elliott sought out the crow he'd seen earlier. It was still in the same spot and held the same position. It didn't even look like it had breathed since he'd last set eyes on it. He found himself wondering if it had been watching him and Sir Pillum, observing their conversation. The bird cocked its head, gave a squawk, and then flew off into the thickening night. Mindful of his duties, Elliott picked up Sir Pillum's shield and gave it a careful inspection.

The blood had dried, caking the pointed corners as usual. But Elliott had learned a few tricks over the years and knew the best methods for scraping them clean and polishing the metal to a brilliant luster in record time. He might even find himself getting some extra rest if he pushed himself a little harder than usual. Something told him he would need the additional energy for the time ahead.

CHAPTER TWELVE

A Silent Journey. A Forgotten Shrine.

There wasn't much speaking among the congregation following their departure from the citadel. In truth, there wasn't much that needed saying. All knew the fate awaiting them if their circumstances didn't change. And with the previous encounter still fresh on their minds, it was with no small amount of trepidation they spied another set of stone walls rising from a series of hills under the late afternoon sky.

It wasn't a village and not quite a town, but something else altogether. It could have been another citadel, but as they neared, it was clear it wasn't that either. True, the walls ran across a rocky butte jutting from the earth and the hills around it with a tall tower rising up from the center of their square confines, but it wasn't a place made for soldiers. No, this was something different.

Bram liked none of it. He pined for more open areas free from Dweller encounters but knew the walls were also potentially beneficial if inhabited. If only they *were* inhabited. He wasn't enjoying the troubling pattern that was developing. What if there was nothing left in the East but bands of Marauders? If not for that lone hanging child they'd encountered, it could be a fairly accurate worldview. It was one he kept pushing down for as long as he could, hopeful and mindful of something better before them. If not today, maybe tomorrow. If they were following the path, the Sovereign would make their way prosperous. He had to keep faith in that—if not for himself, then for the rest of the congregation.

"Should we stop?" Caleb asked from beside Bram. The patriarch and his aides, as always, were at the congregation's head.

"Not yet," he said, eyeing the scene in a studious manner. "There seems to be no sign of life. No smoke or even movement on the walls."

"So it is deserted too?" James wasn't happy with the idea. "That is two places in just as many days."

"We will find out soon enough," said Bram. "The road passes right by it."

"You mean for us to go near it?" Caleb asked with slight concern. Given their last encounter, Bram couldn't blame him for it.

"Let us see what is there first," offered Bram. "If there is a suitable space, we might have to. For now we should just focus on getting there before dark."

The distant echo of thunder brought all eyes heavenward. From what he could see there were some dark clouds coming from the south. It wasn't a blood rain, thank the Sovereign, but a normal storm. That might actually work in their favor. They could all do with a decent washing after the last storm, and the severe rationing on water they were under didn't help. Maybe they could collect what fell if the downpour was strong.

"You and James go ahead with some other brothers. Do not take any risks," he warned. "Just make a basic inspection."

As they hurried to carry out his order, Bram turned and informed the congregation of his decision, telling them it was a good time to rest anyway. None would disagree with him there. While they were hardy, as all Sojourners were, hardships had a way of taking their toll in unforeseen and protracted ways. If they didn't have some good news to share soon, he feared things could get even more drawn out and darker for many.

"You are not going to stay inside the walls again, are you, Brother Bram?" Anna said, stepping his way. While she hid the disapproval from her voice, it couldn't be masked from her face.

"I will do what I think is right," he replied.

"And what is right is keeping to the proper customs," she countered rather firmly. "You have already violated them once."

"For obvious reasons," he calmly returned. "The area around the village was not suitable for a proper camp, and we did not know what else might have been lurking about. It was wise to be cautious. I will remind you of the command I gave at the citadel. We were not behind walls there, but outside them."

"Yes." Her tone was flat. "We should not have stayed there as we did."

"I did what I believed was best. All signs pointed to the place having been deserted. None of us knew there would be anyone returning. Not even you." He made sure to lock his eyes on hers on that last part.

Anna was a capable and wise elder but at times had bucked against Bram's lead. No doubt she wanted to be matriarch but would not reach it if everyone kept on living as they had. Bram didn't judge her. There was nothing *to* judge. She was just deeply concerned about the congregation and not losing their ways. He shared that concern and conviction and did what he thought was best. It was all any could do.

"I will continue to pray for you, Brother," said Anna in all sincerity.

"Thank you, Sister. We can all use as much help as we can get— especially in these days. I see the others are on their way." He motioned to the rest of the elders coming toward them. "We still have much to discuss. Those locusts still trouble me, and then there is, of course, what we found in that village."

"Yes." Anna nodded grimly. "That still troubles me as well."

"Let us hope we can find an answer to keep us free of any further trouble in the future. As it is we have more than enough with which to contend."

"That we do, Brother. That we do."

Sarah watched James, Caleb, and the other young men's progress with Tabitha at her side. Neither was sure what to make of things. They were probably half a mile away from the walls, which limited their view but did not prevent their speculations.

"Do you think it may be a city?" Tabitha was cautiously optimistic.

"I do not think so," said Sarah. "It looks more like a cross between a city and a town." She watched James and the others grow smaller as they jogged away from them. She wasn't sure how they could maintain such a pace after the long day of walking but was pleased they did so. The sooner they had answers, the better for everyone.

"So maybe a citadel again?"

"Maybe." Sarah paused. "Though I would like it to be something different."

"Me too. And I would welcome Dwellers over Marauders any day."

Sarah shared a weak grin. "You and me both." Though there was still much uncertainty around it, the sighting had brought a sliver of hope. And the increasing peals of thunder only added a sense of urgency.

"Do you think the patriarch will have us sleep inside again?"

"I do not know," said Sarah. "I would think not, but after the citadel it is hard to say."

She didn't know how much lowing cows, clucking chickens, and braying sheep had been such a comfort to her all this time until she walked a day in the silence of their absence. That silence was made even more dominant by the present stillness of the congregation. Before there had been free-spirited and comforting conversations with sounds of occasional laughter and goodwill. But since departing the citadel, a suffocating quiet had descended. Not even the children dared break free of its hold.

For Sarah with the silence came the creeping sensation of doubt and despair. She resisted it whenever she noticed herself sliding into its dark embrace by thinking of something that filled her with some flicker of hope. But the longer they traveled, the less she found to latch on to. Not only had the journey become bleaker, but she was finding fewer bright spots. It wouldn't take long for them to grow weary without food. And without water . . . She pushed her mind along with her eyes back to the walls.

"So, have you had any progress with James?" Tabitha, thankfully, changed the subject.

"No. Though I have had some ideas."

Tabitha perked up. "About how to talk to him?"

"Yes . . . But I have not been able to get much further than that—the idea part of the plan."

"I tried thinking up some ideas too, but nothing has come to me other than the most obvious of you just going up and speaking with him."

"I know." Sarah sighed. "I keep looking for a way, but then with what happened at the citadel—he was just so busy and distracted—"

"We all were. It has been a trying few days."

"Yes, it has." She didn't like how dreary the words sounded.

"Though, I think Sophie might have set her eye on Caleb."

"Sophie?" Sarah lowered her voice in case Sophie might hear, even though, since she was near the back of the congregation, it didn't seem likely. "Are you sure?"

"I have noticed when I have been watching James that she has been lingering near Caleb. Even more so of late."

"Caleb is a decent man."

"But Sophie is so . . ." Tabitha bit her lip to keep from saying any more.

"She can keep to herself at times." Sarah knew that was putting it mildly. Sophie, while between Sarah and Tabitha in age, tended to prefer her own company almost exclusively. She was polite enough and made mild attempts at conversation when called upon, but she wasn't one to initiate anything.

"That, and I would not have thought Caleb would even hold her attention—not that many things do, mind you."

"Tabitha." The rebuke was mild because it was true.

"Well, you have to admit they would make a rather interesting couple—Caleb so serious and Sophie so quiet."

"If what you say is true, then I am happy for her. Maybe she will even find some courage to reach out to Caleb in time."

"Maybe even before you," Tabitha teased.

Sarah sighed. "I have been trying—more so than before. If I just have the right opening to approach him."

"I know. And we will find it, Sarah."

"Or Malena will first, I fear."

"Looks like your father wants to speak with you." Tabitha's nod directed Sarah to her approaching father. "I will see you later tonight."

Tabitha departed.

"I did not mean to scare your friend away," said Desmond as he drew near. It was strange seeing him without his staff. He had always had one for as long as she could remember. She didn't know if she'd ever get used to its absence.

"You did not. We had just about finished speaking before you arrived."

"It is good seeing you with others your own age," he returned. "Sometimes we forget the simple joys of fellowship with our peers. Especially during trying times."

"And we have seen some of those," she agreed.

Desmond rested a hand on her shoulder. "Things will get better." It was meant to give comfort, but Sarah could take little from it.

Together both focused on the distant walls. James and the others were nowhere to be seen. No doubt they were already inside looking around.

"It looks empty. Why are there no people in these places?"

Desmond paused. "It looks old. Maybe it was abandoned long ago."

"Like the citadel?" Her father gave no reply. "It is going to be hard for the children if we do not get some food and water." Sarah stated the obvious in an attempt at reviving some form of communication.

"Your mother would be pleased to hear you concerned with the welfare of others," he said at last.

"I am glad you found her dagger." It was nothing short of a miracle that he did. After the mess the locusts had left, her father dug through and around just about everything in order to find it. Sarah had helped too but wasn't nearly as determined as he'd been.

"I am too." A strange look took over his eyes as he spoke. "And I am looking forward to giving it to you soon. She would have been very pleased with you. Not just with how well you have grown physically but in your heart too."

Sarah smiled briefly at the praise. "What do you think she would have thought of these last few days? We have all been through so much."

"Most Sojourners have. If the way was easy, more would have followed and stuck to the path."

Her face shifted to the ground. "I know." And she did. It was instilled in every one of the congregation as soon as they could walk. It was part of their core—a foundational issue—and yet at times she wished it wasn't. Wished for an easier life in an easier time when the sky was blue, the land was lush, and people and animals were happy and plentiful.

"We have to remain faithful, Sarah."

"I know." She raised her head. "But sometimes it is not easy to do."

Her father shared a knowing nod. "If everything was easy, then there would be nothing to strengthen our faith. And we need to be strong to make it through the days to come." Now it was Sarah who withdrew into herself. The thunder crackled overhead—louder and closer than before. "No matter what happens, we still have our tents and will be dry tonight. The rest will come in time."

"This would be the third time in less than three days we are looking to dwell beside some walls."

"Not dwell!" Desmond was alarmed at the term. "We are merely using a safe place to camp. And the patriarch only had us briefly stay behind the walls of the village. We camped outside the citadel, do not forget."

"The two are very close, Father, you would have to agree."

"We have to trust in the patriarch and the Sovereign. Whatever is decided is the best choice possible."

"It is not so much resting behind the walls, but seeing so many empty dwellings," she continued. "I do not remember ever seeing as many as we have now."

"You are young," he assured her. "We will come upon a town or village filled with people soon enough. The whole of Annulis cannot be empty."

While he'd meant it as a ray of hope, Sarah wasn't so sure she could take hold of it. There had been pockets of land she'd traveled before that had been empty of man or beast for days at a time, but this . . . This was something different. At least that was what she felt in her heart; it wasn't really anything that made sense logically. She also couldn't shake the sense of the days to come being darker still. And while she didn't like it and did her best at ignoring it, the sensation remained just the same. She prayed she was wrong.

"How old do you think it is?" She was eager to get her thoughts back on the present. "These walls do not look as old as the last ones we saw."

"I have seen older, but yes, this has seen many a century. I doubt even the patriarch could place its age."

"But why build something so far off in the wilderness? There is no river, no lake, just this old empty road."

"It was probably built for a brighter day, like many things in years past. And who knows what the land looked like before the Burning Cascade and Year of Night."

"At least there are no more Marauders or locusts," she added. "I wonder where they went."

"Why? I would think you had your fill of them."

"I have. It would just be good to know so we could avoid them in the future."

Sarah felt the first of a fine mist in the breeze. It had been increasing for some time—a small precursor of what was to come. If any were in doubt, a loud crack of thunder tore through the sky.

"Let us hope they return soon," said her father. "That storm is going to make whatever the patriarch decides to do all the harder."

"There has not been anyone here for years." Caleb brushed some cobwebs away from the partially open door staring back at him.

Like the rest of the place, the door was weathered with age and covered with a fine dust gathered through the years. He, James, and five other brothers had made fast and thorough work of investigating what was in the very least a large town. A large, empty town.

"The walls look sturdy enough," said James.

He, like the others, was busy scanning through the empty paths and streets now partially overtaken by straggly patches of grass. Caleb joined him, taking in the thick stone walls. They appeared able to withstand just about anything. The Dwellers who lived here must have felt fairly safe.

"But no water yet." Caleb opened another door with a cautious hand. Behind it was another empty room. They had come across several in their searching. This one had the look of a larder. There were heavy wooden shelves lining the walls. From the ceiling rafter dangled fat lines of knotted rope. He supposed these could hold bags of grain or perhaps dried meat to keep them from rodents or other vermin. Little good it did them now.

"We will not be able to go much further without it." James continued his inspection of one of the ropes.

"No." Caleb joined him. "But at least we have not seen any more of those locusts."

"Thank the Sovereign for that," said Allen. He was the same age as Caleb but of a much lighter disposition.

"The rope looks good," said James. "And we might be able to use those shelves for firewood."

"It is a start," said Markus, a more dour-faced man in their company. All stopped at the sound of the rolling thunder echoing across the room and outside in the street.

"We need to hurry," said Caleb. "We still have more to search. Perhaps the Sovereign will show us some grace."

"Let us hope so." James made his way from the room. "From what we have seen so far, this place has been picked down to the bones."

Back out in the street the men continued walking. They would come back for the rope and wood, marking the path to return with more men to help take what they could in the morning. More hands made lighter—and speedier—work. Right now they needed to finish marking any further places of interest.

"What do you make of this?" Markus stood beside another open door. This one was a good distance from where the others had been looking.

"We are not going to be able to look into every room," said Caleb, moving for the area. "We can only take a quick look and keep walking; otherwise we will be here all day."

"You might want a longer look with this," Markus persisted.

"You find some water?" James was hopeful.

"Not quite." Caleb peered more thoughtfully into the doorway, unwilling to move. A moment later the other men crowded around him.

"Do you think it is a shrine?" Markus inquired without taking his gaze from what Caleb thought could be something like an indoor garden. Caleb wasn't one to know the rhyme or reason for why Dwellers did what they did, so he couldn't even pretend to make sense of what was before him, but it was his best guess.

In the most basic terms, there was a statue in a center of a square room. The statue stood on top of a block of stone, around which a square outline of earth was made. There were scraggly remains of old plant growth around and in the dirt. The soil was still damp from the small opening above, where the recent blood rain must have poured through, but what was once rooted in the soil had died long ago. The fat shaft of light pouring from above helped one focus on the statue in the otherwise dark room.

Caleb had never seen such a statue before. It wasn't of a woman but a man wearing a breastplate over a flowing robe. The image was carved into stone with such great skill that it seemed able to breathe—and quite possibly would if anyone turned their attention from it for even a moment.

"It has to be a shrine of some kind," he said, pointing out some smaller stone votive tables on either side of the statue. "That would be where they burned the incense."

"And how do you know about that?" asked James, rather curious.

"I have seen more than enough shrines for my liking," he replied. "And far too few honoring the Sovereign too."

"But the Sovereign was never depicted," said Markus. "No statue, drawing, or anything other than that crest."

"Which came later," added Caleb.

"So whom did they worship, I wonder?" James gave the rest of the room another survey. "I thought all the Dwellers were enthralled by their goddesses. If this is a shrine, then this would be—or could be, at least—the sign of some god. It is the first I have seen anywhere."

"I do not think that really matters now, does it?" Caleb was to the point, like always. "His name is dead and gone, along with the rest of the stewards."

"I think we found all we are going to find," offered Markus. "Unless we stumble upon some lost cow." He grinned at his humor.

Caleb didn't share such levity. "Okay, back to looking. The rain will be on us soon enough. We only have the light for a little while longer. Let us make full use of it."

"No one has been in there for years," Caleb told Bram after he and the others had returned from their search. "It has been picked clean of everything. Only the walls remain." It was misting but not raining, but that was going to change fairly soon. As if to emphasize the fact another clap of thunder rolled across the dark gray skies.

"No water?" Bram repeated what Caleb had just shared.

"Nothing that we could see."

"We could not even find a well," added James.

Bram had been hoping they'd find at least some sort of supply. It seemed foolish to make a secure dwelling with no access to a spring or river of some kind. "It is completely empty?"

"Yes," James began before stopping to share a look with Caleb. "Well, apart from the shrine."

"Shrine?" Bram raised an eyebrow. "Another goddess?"

"Yes and no," said James.

"Which is it?"

"There is a statue, but it is not of a goddess. It is of a man. It is not like anything we have seen so far," James elaborated. "It also seems out of place."

"How?"

A louder thunderclap shook everyone's bones. This was followed by an increase in the mist. It soaked into their skin and clothing, offering slight relief from the grim residue deposited in the previous blood rain.

"Perhaps it would be better if we showed you."

"We should all go," said Bram. "If it is empty, as you say, we have a safe area outside the walls where we can pitch our tents and make camp." He paused, considering again the charcoal-gray sky. "Hopefully, before the rain begins."

Turning, he raised his voice, saying, "Let us move forward and set up camp. While this place is also empty, it would be wiser to keep to the open area outside it."

It thundered again, increasing the need to get moving. Bram took the lead, James and Caleb at his side. He wasn't going to run or even jog but did his best at keeping a brisk pace, allowing what he hoped was enough time to look over the key sites behind the walls before it got too dark to do much else. Eventually, they reached the walls, and after he directed the congregation as to where to set up the hearth and their tents, he asked for James and Caleb to show him their find.

No sooner had he set foot beyond the old gates than it started raining. Regardless, they pushed on. Bram wouldn't let them turn back for anything, not while they had some light and the rest of the congregation was focused on setting up camp. He needed to find out as much as he could, so when morning came he'd be able to make the wisest decision possible. And the more time he had to think and pray, the better.

Caleb and James had been right. The place was deserted. Deserted and picked clean of any sign of even basic habitation. It seemed centuries old, which could easily put it at the same age as the citadel they had just left. Here and there in the corners were fat wads of spider webbing and the occasional pile of dust that had accumulated over the years, but nothing else.

Bram welcomed the sight. No locusts and no Marauders made just about anywhere seem hospitable. He was beginning to wonder about all these fortifications. And empty ones at that. It could mean they were either close to a large city, like he thought, or near part of an outpost of the older Mundian Empire. The former offered some hope of finding supplies. The latter could mean there was nothing but empty shells of the past in all directions.

"Where is this shrine?"

"This way." Caleb took the lead.

All three were long since soaked, but none cared. It actually felt rather nice. Bram's eyebrows weren't itching anymore, and his scalp and beard felt much better. It wasn't a full bath, but it was better than nothing. Bram followed through the maze of streets. Finally, they came to an out-of-the-way area with an unexpected small room off of the road.

"I am surprised you were able to find your way back out after all these twists and turns."

"It was lighter then," Caleb explained, "and we had others with us to help."

"So this is it?" He studied the figure in the center of what was clearly a space carefully designed to provide light and water for whatever had been growing in it. The rough rain fell through the opening, creating a puddle in the dirt.

"Do you recognize it?" asked James.

"No." Bram had never seen anything like it in all his years. But Annulis was a large place, and there were one hundred great cities at one time—many of them departing the world throughout the various ravages over the centuries. "But it is most certainly a shrine," he said, pointing out the smaller votive tables on either side of the statue.

"Just what I thought." A faint hint of pride traced Caleb's face.

"Though not to the Sovereign," said Bram, wringing some water from his beard. "This must be someone else."

"But not another god?" James took a closer look.

"I do not think so. There has long been only one god. Even when the cities rebelled, they turned to goddesses instead. This must be for something else entirely."

"Whoever it is," said James, continuing to stare at the statue, "they certainly wanted to make it look as lifelike as possible."

"Yes," said Bram, "but it does not concern us. This place is old and empty. We will have to see what can be salvaged tomorrow. Right now—"

A great blast of thunder brought a fresh torrent of rain. It was falling so fast and hard, the puddle around the statue was splashing mud in every direction.

"Right now it looks like we have to brave this rain and head back to the camp." He began making his way from the room. "I will need your help winding back through this warren."

James and Caleb hurried to oblige.

CHAPTER THIRTEEN

A Looming Threat. A Cunning Answer.

"If not for those locusts, we would have had them." The soldier standing before Corbin finished giving his account of the recent battle with the still-approaching Pyri.

Corbin had brought the warrior into his private room shortly after what remained of their force returned to Larom. His quarters were a secure place to talk. He needed to be sure what they said was safe from any passing eyes or ears. It wouldn't do having rumors fluttering around the people. They were already talking about what they'd seen of the returning forces. He didn't want to give them anything further without getting out ahead of it. He was pushing a strong narrative about defending against and even *defeating* these crazed fanatics. He didn't want to lose it, even if things weren't working as they should have.

"How many Pyri fell?" Corbin watched the captain carefully for his reply. Well, the new captain. Corbin had just promoted him, since the other had died in the fighting. He wanted to be sure he knew what he was dealing with. He'd learned in the heat of battle things can get skewered, and this wasn't the time to start straying from the facts.

"I-I don't know. We pushed hard, but those locusts took their toll."

"Do you have even a rough idea?"

"Under one hundred."

"And we lost about half our numbers, you say?"

"Like I said, sir, if we'd been able to continue without these locusts, we would have won the day."

Corbin didn't like the math one bit. And he liked the fact that so many fled from their posts even less. The retreat surrendered the town to the Pyri, taking away a prime location where the crows could stop on their journeys. So even if these Pyri moved on, a prospect he doubted more and more with each passing day, they still were out a secure staging post. Perhaps it was time to tighten the rations even more—until things were more in his favor.

"So we're left with a much larger army marching on our walls than anticipated," he reasoned aloud, which sometimes helped him in working through issues from various angles. So far it sounded just as bleak when spoken as it did in his thoughts, but perhaps he wasn't seeing that missing angle just yet . . .

"If not for their cavalry, they would have fallen faster, even with the locusts."

"So they're *that* formidable, are they?" Corbin couldn't fathom anything being able to withstand their bolts and shields so effectively. Especially when the previous encounter had gone so well. This should have been a strong polishing off of their forces, weakening them to the point where Larom would finally have a numerical advantage. Where he could secure that victory—that very *visible* victory—in the eyes of the people.

"But even with their cavalry, they wouldn't be able to do much against these walls should they besiege us."

"I'm not interested in surviving a siege." Corbin peered out the window beside him, eager for something to capture his attention. Nothing did. The empty streets outside the clear glass panes only reinforced the truth of his limited options and resources. "We don't have enough supplies to endure as long as they'd probably want to stay— which is until we're dead. These fanatics won't rest until everyone's dead or submits to their flaming bird god. And didn't you say they had those flaming rods too?"

"Quite a few, sir." The captain grimly nodded.

"A good blast from those, and they could burn their way inside."

"With respect, I wouldn't advise going against them again before they arrive. If we get cut off outside the walls, you'd be sorely outnumbered."

"Not to mention we'd suffer more casualties," Corbin said, pointing out the obvious rather bitterly. He was starting to see the cracks in his narrative wall. If they developed any further, it would come crashing down on everyone. Things were so fragile, he worried about every breeze of contrary thought blowing through the city.

With such a diminished population, it didn't take long for rumors to spread. These were trying, troubling times, but they could still endure. Only if he could keep things going for a little while longer. If he could hold the façade together, he was confident he'd weather the storm, as would most of Larom with him. That was the hope, but he didn't have any idea how to bring it to pass.

"You know the walls are secure and well manned," the captain continued, "and all the army is now behind them. We can attack from the gates, should we find opportunity to do so. We needn't be stuck behind our walls."

"Not the best strategy, but I'll keep it under advisement."

"It's probably the wisest . . . and we could take the dead behind the walls," added the captain. "It would be safer than sending out men to gather what they could."

"There is that, I suppose." Corbin could see the benefit in keeping any bodies close. The fewer men he had to risk in securing any supplies, the better. "And you're sure those locusts flew off to the east?"

"Yes, sir. They should be well into the Ashen Fields by now."

"Let's hope they stay there. I'd prefer dealing with only one enemy at a time." Corbin rubbed his chin in thought. "You mentioned they offered terms of surrender before you rode out?"

"Yes, sir. I think it's something they have to do, even if they know the gesture will be rejected. It's part of their religion."

A sudden epiphany flooded Corbin's previously dark future. "We may be able to use that in our favor." He focused again on the captain, smiling. "Thank you, Captain. I think we're done here. Let Martin know I'd like to speak with him."

"As you say." The captain turned for the door.

"Oh, Captain?" Corbin's words turned him back around. "There's no need to share any information about your encounter with the Pyri other than that you were able to reduce their number. There's no need to have anyone worried about locusts or a larger force of fanatics marching for our walls."

"Understood, sir." The captain left.

Corbin stared out his window. He still saw the same empty streets as before but also a way he could make them into a clever net for snaring these wild-eyed zealots. A smile traced his lips as the pieces of his plan came together.

"It's a fine idea." Mother Astra sat across from Corbin in his private study. The grand priestess, like all the priestesses of Laroma, wore a black short-sleeved gown with black sandals, a thick crow-feather cape draped over her shoulders. On her head was a black shawl with crow feathers worked into the hem. Her medium-length sable hair blended into her somber attire.

A small wooden table rested between them, draped with a dark blue cloth. The study was more lavish than Corbin's common room and more private. It, too, had clean windows letting in light but also nicer furniture and decorations. There was nothing too lavish, but it spoke to Larom's previous grandeur. The study was part of the official office of the princeps and was used by whoever was elected.

Corbin had been in office for so long, however, he'd made it into a kind of permanent residence, adding more personal touches, like the tapestry on the wall behind him. Its subdued colors displayed a confident and strong Corbin standing like a god in his own right. He seemed to survey the landscape like some mighty emperor, looking for his next city to conquer. It came close to crossing the line of making too much of oneself, but only came just up to the line. Even still, Corbin kept it in the study, hidden from just about anyone's eyes.

"I take no credit," said Corbin. "It was all the blessing of Laroma seeking to help her people and great city." He'd just finished sharing his plan about how they'd defeat the Pyri. After the fine-tuning he and Martin had made a few hours ago, he felt it was more than possible they'd meet with success. He wasn't about to take the glory for himself—not right away and not with the priestesses. Part of his narrative wall was keeping everyone united on as many fronts as possible—for appearance's sake, if nothing else. The status quo could be a powerful thing—even an ally—if one knew how to use it properly.

"She has been merciful," Astra agreed. The black eye shadow above her gray eyes enriched her overall mystique, an impression which Corbin had long assumed all of her order wished to convey. Image was crucial, he knew, and never more so than these days. Even the string of black beads across her forehead and the silver charms dangling from it were part of the larger whole—conveying the image she was the true voice for the great goddess who watched over her people and city.

There was a sort of beauty in all of it, he supposed. And her youthful features didn't hurt in highlighting the overall impression. She was much easier on the eyes than the former grand priestess, who'd died the year before at an advanced age. But even in death, she'd provided for her order. The priestesses consumed her out of both necessity and a sense of honor for her many years of service.

"So you approve of the plan?" Astra was the first and most crucial part of the scheme. He knew Martin and the army would be behind him, but Astra's role carried more risks.

"It's a good plan," said Astra, "playing right into their false assumptions."

"But it can only work with the right person laying the bait in the trap. Martin assures me he's able to do his part. I need to know about you and your sisters."

"If we go unarmed and in our full regalia, I don't think they'll give us any trouble," said Astra.

"They might," Corbin gently countered. "They're not fools, just fanatics."

"You did say they were all men?"

"From what I understood."

"Then it's probably been months since they've seen any halfway decent-looking women." She smiled. "I'll take the most attractive sisters and make sure we're in our best form. I think I know how to handle some men."

"I'm sure you do." Corbin smirked. "I just wanted to be sure you understood your role and the dangers that come along with it. If anything went wrong—"

"I'd provide for the city in death as I had in life." There was a truth to the statement he could admire. That didn't mean he shared the sentiment. He personally wanted to live more than die, if given the choice. "What?" She seemed amused at what she must have seen playing out across his face. "You thought we'd all be living forever?"

"It's not that," he replied. "I'm just surprised you're so serene at the prospect of your own death."

"In the end we all share the same fate. No matter how many smiles and tears we share, or how much mirth we make, the flesh will still be picked from our bones." It wasn't the most cheering picture, but he let it go. He wasn't in the mood to debate the matter, not that he would really anyway. To each their own. As long as it didn't affect his plan or position, he could care less.

"I'm told they're keeping up a good pace," he continued. "They probably should be here in a few days, if not sooner."

"The sisters and I will be ready," said Astra. "We will stand with you and the army in a united front, making it clear the people have to follow through."

"They will, once they understand the reasoning."

"Not to mention the extra bodies this would-be siege would bring us." Astra was pleased with the thought. "Laroma is truly outdoing herself. She might as well be marching animals right into our pens and larders. It might even last through winter and spring."

He thought that might be stretching things but let it go. They would take things as they came, like they always did. "That's assuming we can keep most of them alive. These Pyri are fanatics who'd rather die than surrender."

"Your men will just have to be careful in how they wound them. Wounded is preferable to dead."

"Of course," said Corbin, rising from the table. "With any luck we'll have things cleaned up in a day and this whole group of wild men behind us."

Astra took to her feet. "With a feast to honor Laroma for her kind graces."

"I'm sure there will be much to celebrate," he added. "I'll leave you to your priestesses."

"We'll be sure to keep you and this plan in our prayers," said Astra, turning for the door.

Corbin watched her depart, already plotting the next steps and preparations. They wouldn't get a second chance.

CHAPTER FOURTEEN

A Heart Broken. A Troubling Discussion.

Waking so close to towering stone walls was still unsettling but not as much as it first had been just a few days prior. Sarah wouldn't say she was getting used to it, only that it was an odd sensation that she hoped to avoid in the future. The silence of the morning was also odd. The sound of the animals had been so interwoven with her daily routine; its absence was jarring. So too was the sight of their five carts being pulled by people.

But she couldn't do much about it; none of them could presently. For now she was rested and dry. A little hungry, but far from suffering the wrenching pangs of starvation. She also felt cleaner thanks to last night's rain, for which she was thankful. They'd been able to collect some of the water too, adding some relief for the children and others long in need of slaking their thirst. It wasn't the best option, but it was better than nothing, and for now she, like all the rest of the congregation, would take what small boons she could.

"You sleep well?" Her father offered to help her rise.

"Yes. And you?"

Most of the congregation was awake, already going about their regular tasks. For the most part it looked like just another day. And, in truth, she supposed it was. Trials aside, there were still things in need of doing and matters in need of attention. "I hope you took enough sleep. The last few days have been long."

He pushed her concern aside. "No longer than any others." He appeared strong and healthy. That was a good sign. He'd need all his strength in the days ahead. They all would.

"I have decided a group of us should take another look behind the walls." Bram's loud voice drew everyone's attention. "We might be able to find some items of use. The rest of us will prepare to depart. I would think no more than two hours would be needed. I leave Brother Caleb in charge of choosing the team accompanying him."

"Brother Nathan must not be pleased," said Sarah, recalling his objection to looking around the village earlier.

"We did find a few good things the last time we made a search," her father reminded her.

"And a few not-so-good things," she reminded him.

"Brother Desmond?" Caleb's voice carried their way. "Would you care to join us in our search?"

"Seems I have been chosen," said Desmond before raising his voice to the approaching Caleb. "I would be happy to, Brother." He started Caleb's way, then stopped, turning back to Sarah. "Can I trust you to pack up and be ready when I return?"

She knew he was teasing her, as they both knew how capable she was. But she also wondered if he was reminding her of her responsibilities, given her previous distraction at the village, when she'd been taken more with observing James than the task at hand.

"Of course, Father."

Satisfied, he joined Caleb's group. A short while later they were behind the walls, leaving her alone in her world of tents and bedrolls. Sarah was so engaged in her tasks, she didn't even hear Tabitha approach.

"There you are."

"Where else *would* I be?" She continued rolling her bedroll.

"Maybe behind the walls with me."

Sarah stopped, looking up with a curious eye. "But Caleb did not pick you with the others."

A mischievous smile crossed Tabitha's lips. "I found my own way inside."

"You went against the patriarch's orders?" She'd known Tabitha to be more independent than others but never so disobedient.

"It was for a good cause," she continued.

"Your own?" Sarah stood.

"For *your* benefit."

"How would disobeying the patriarch be for my benefit?"

"I saw James enter when he thought no one was looking."

Sarah didn't think she heard that right. "James? But Caleb did not select him for the group either."

"I know." Again there was that mischievous grin.

"But why would he go off by himself?"

"All I know is he is alone now for you to talk to him."

Sarah's heart leapt at the thought. "But he could be anywhere. That place is huge, and if my father catches me—"

"I followed him," Tabitha interrupted. "I know just where he went, and if you hurry we can get right back to him. Unless you want to stay here and tend to tents and bedrolls." Sarah couldn't contain the giddiness plastered over her cheeks. "I will take that as a no."

"Please do."

She took a look around the camp. Everyone was busy with various tasks, and the elders were talking with Bram. No one would notice if they snuck away for a few moments.

"It will have to be quick," she advised.

"I am not going to rush you," said Tabitha. "You might find once you get talking neither of you wants to leave the other's side."

"Tabitha!" The rebuke was mild.

"It could happen." She shrugged. "But first we have to get you together."

She took hold of Sarah's hand. The two carefully and nonchalantly moved for the gate. A few well-placed strides, and they cleared the opening entirely. Once inside, Tabitha burst into a run. Sarah took off after her. She wasn't really paying much attention to the scenery, just focusing on following on Tabitha's heels as she led her down a series of narrow streets. She was amazed anyone living here didn't get lost every time they tried leaving their house. It was such a confusing mix of twists and turns. If not for Tabitha, she'd surely have been wandering in circles.

"Shhh . . ." Tabitha slowed, motioning for Sarah to do likewise. "I think we are getting close."

They had neared a kind of intersection, an open area where several roads met. In the center were a few stone benches. All were empty except for the one on which James sat. Only he wasn't alone. Beside him was Malena. That by itself might not have been so troubling a sight, but they were doing more than just sitting.

James and Malena had wrapped their arms around each other and were kissing quite passionately. The familiar nausea returned. Sarah could say nothing; she couldn't even move. It was like she was a statue, unable to do anything but stare in growing sorrow with the knowledge that whatever she would have wanted between her and James would never be.

"Oh, Sarah." She felt Tabitha's hand on her back. "I am so sorry. If I had known . . ." Tabitha never finished. She probably realized there was no reason to. Nothing more needed to be said.

Tears were falling down her cheeks before she knew they were there. With that awareness was a growing desire to flee. She didn't want to look anymore, even if at the moment she couldn't pull away. The image would forever be scarred in her mind. She'd grow old and gray, and it would still haunt her. The only thing she craved now was running as far away from this place as possible. Surprisingly, her rigid body exploded into life, racing back the way she and Tabitha had come.

Bram sat among the elders, listening to their thoughts. All of them had gathered in a circle, sitting on the ground. It was an old custom elders and patriarchs and matriarchs had enjoyed since any could remember. Bram wasn't going to change it for anything. He'd already made some alterations in the last few days, with unpleasant results. Best to stick with what was known and right. It had served them well for all these years and would continue doing so until they breathed their last.

"We cannot keep up like this, Brother Bram." Milton stated the obvious. His thick eyebrows came together in a troubled expression. "We need food and water."

"I know," he replied. "And if we keep finding these empty places, I fear the worst may be upon us."

"What has the Sovereign shown you?" Anna was curious, leaning forward.

"I have searched his will," said Bram, "but have found nothing."

"No signs?" she asked, clearly intrigued by the lack of guidance.

"I have sought, but all I see are these empty places and open spaces," he confessed with no small degree of displeasure. "I am beginning to think we may have taken a wrong turn along the way."

The elders' faces became grim. Questioning the direction was the same as questioning the one leading the congregation. And if Bram was questioning himself openly, then it was a serious matter.

"What are you implying, Brother Bram?" Mathias's voice was especially raspy this morning. "Are you saying you wish to step aside?"

"I am saying I would like some answers. Not just for our direction but with what we have seen. I cannot get past the skulls in the village or those words carved into those walls. It has to mean something, and the longer it goes unanswered, the more I fear we miss something important."

"Do you think it a sign from the Sovereign?" Milton carefully inquired.

"It is a sign of something," said Bram. "These empty citadels and towns mean something—I fear they are connected somehow, and we are not seeing it."

"We have seen many empty towns and villages over the years," said Anna. "The Dwellers leave them as their numbers dwindle, they are raided by Marauders, or other things."

"But how many have we found that were all empty in the same area?" Bram countered. "I have seen my share of empty places, as have you, but never have I seen whole regions deserted. And no animals either? Have you noticed that we have found nothing in the wild? Not even a rabbit."

"There are still crows," offered Thomas, obviously trying to brighten the dark picture Bram was painting. It didn't help.

"Yes. Crows." His eyes traced the circle, regarding each face in turn. "And no water to speak of, and no Dwellers to trade with or ask if there are any better places where we could sojourn."

Mathias snorted. "We are not looking for comfort, Bram. We look for the Veiled City. The heralds all said it would not be easy, but if we prevailed—"

"And how can we prevail if we starve along the way or die of thirst?" He didn't mean for his rebuke to be so harsh, but what was said was said. "I do my best each day to follow the path. I search and seek as best I know how, but if we have lost our way—"

"We have not lost our way!" Mathias replied loud enough to turn a few heads from the congregation. Bram preferred keeping their discussion private, even from Caleb and James at times. Some things didn't need to be known by everyone.

"*If* we have lost our way," Bram continued calmly, carefully emphasizing the first part of the sentence, "we need to find it."

"*Have* we lost our way?" Milton stared Bram full in the face, eye to eye.

Bram paused. He didn't know what to say or if he should say anything at all. "I am not sure," he finally answered. "But I think if we do not find something better soon, we should look at turning our path in a different direction."

"Without the Sovereign's guidance?" Mathias wasn't pleased with the idea.

"I have faith in the Sovereign and his heralds," Bram assured them as well as himself. "If we have strayed in any way, he will be faithful and return us to the path. If we but follow, he will guide us."

"We have been speaking but have not really said anything that we did not already know." Anna's comment cut through Bram and many of the other elders like a knife.

"I cannot share anything but the truth," said Bram. "I trust you only do the same."

A pause settled over their discourse. When it was clear no one was going to disrupt it, Bram spoke. "Have you any thoughts on those locusts? We have avoided them thus far, but I fear we might cross their path again."

"I have never seen or heard of their like," said Milton, "as I have said before. But all this talk of fear, Bram—it is not like you, nor us. We live by our faith, not fear. The world has enough fear, which we have already seen and lived through. We need to keep our faith in the midst of it, not worry about what horrors may yet await us."

"With age comes wisdom," added Mathias. "We have weathered times of trouble before. I am confident we will make our way through this if you do not lose your faith in our cause and place."

"I am more concerned about the congregation." Bram found his voice was surprisingly low. "All these empty places and spaces can rob them of their faith—in each other, in us . . . even the Sovereign. I would like to spare them that if I could."

Mathias sighed. "Then what do you propose?"

"I see us moving down the road for at least one more day. If we find nothing else—no other signs or omens—we will consider something new."

There was another long pause.

"Agreed," Mathias said at last.

"I think it a fair idea," Milton added.

Anna nodded. "One more day. Let us keep our eyes and ears open."

"And it looks like they are ready to leave." Thomas nodded to the congregation, who were getting the rest of the materials, meager though they now were, packed into their carts. "Perhaps we should get ready as well."

"One more day," Bram muttered, joining everyone in taking to their feet.

Sarah said nothing. She didn't even try to think about anything other than making sure the bedrolls were taken care of and all was made ready for their upcoming departure. She'd taken enough time away from her duties as it was. Tabitha watched, careful not to get in her way.

The process was agonizingly slow. It was as if the world had become trapped in honey, and she had to use all her strength and focus to get her simplest chores finished. Most of the others had finished packing. This only made her stand out all the more.

"Do you want to talk about it?" Tabitha asked.

She paused, about to say something, but happened to catch sight of James trying his best to sneak back into the camp. Tabitha followed Sarah's gaze.

"There is nothing to talk about," came Sarah's reply. "We both saw what we needed to see. I wish James and Malena well." She was surprised by how smoothly the words came to her tongue, even though when spoken they soured her stomach.

Tabitha gave her a strange look. Sarah didn't like it, feeling as if she had to give it an answer. "He never knew how I felt, so I cannot blame him for anything. The blame lies with me. I should have told him how I felt sooner. And now I have to live with that." Her shoulders sank with the words. It was the truth, and it was best if she accepted it.

"You should not blame yourself, Sarah."

"Then who *do* I blame? If I had at least told him, he would have known and perhaps would not have been so taken with Malena."

"And what if he refused you—and to your face, no less?"

Sarah paused, contemplating the concept carefully. She hadn't given the scenario much thought. She was so focused on the sight of James and Malena's embrace, little else mattered. So what would have happened had she been able to speak with James directly? Suddenly, a wash of thoughts and emotions flooded her thinking. Tabitha waited patiently as they swirled about her mind.

"Well?" she asked at last.

"I-I do not know." And that was the truth. There were so many things that could have happened. So many ways things could have played out— for good or for ill—none of them certain.

"He might have already decided on Malena some time ago."

"I thought you wanted to comfort me." Sarah frowned.

"I cannot comfort with lies, only the truth. It might not be welcome all the time, but in the end it will be the most appreciated."

Sarah sighed. "Thank you, but right now I wish to keep my thoughts to myself."

Tabitha picked up Sarah's bedroll. "I hope you understand I never wanted to cause any pain."

"Of course I do." Sarah grabbed her father's bedroll. "You were trying to help."

She started for the nearest cart, Tabitha beside her. Neither spoke as they deposited the bedrolls with the rest of the supplies already inside. Both noticed Malena had returned and was making a show of packing up another cart some yards away. Neither Sarah nor Tabitha said or did anything, not even returning the smile and nod Malena innocently offered upon discovering both of them watching.

"The men have returned." The news brought everyone's attention to the gates. Caleb and her father were at the head of the band. They had a few things in tow but it wasn't an impressive sight.

"I do not see any water," said Tabitha ruefully.

"Maybe they found some in smaller containers." She tried sounding more optimistic, even though such sentiment was far from her at the moment.

"How did it go?" she asked once her father had gotten closer. The rest of the men went to the carts, seeking spots for the goods they had taken. Caleb made a beeline for Bram and the elders, obviously eager to make a report.

"We found a few things," her father replied. "There was some wood we were able to salvage and some pieces of old rope but not much more than that. This place has been picked over quite well."

"No water?" asked Tabitha.

"No water or food," he declared. "But I am sure we will find something along the way."

"I suppose I should return to my parents before we depart. Brother Desmond." Tabitha politely nodded and departed.

"Did you get bored waiting for us?" her father teased.

"No. I was able to keep busy, and Tabitha kept me company."

"You feeling all right? You look a little pale."

"I am fine."

A commotion broke out across the congregation. The men moved forward, the women and children just behind them. Confused at the sudden activity, Sarah searched for the cause. Marching up the road was a group of men.

"Get behind me, Sarah," said her father, pushing her behind him.

They all wore armor and carried strange-looking shields at their sides. It seemed like some sort of tool—a series of daggers bent around the shields' round metal lips. Not skilled in the use of weapons and armor, she didn't know if this made the shield harder to use but was sure it made it more intimidating. So far they didn't have any weapons drawn, but she could see the swords sheathed at their waists, ready at a moment's notice.

"Are they more Marauders?" she asked with a lowered voice.

"I do not think so." Her father's eyes never departed the men. "They look more like Dwellers."

"Is that the same crest we saw in the village?" Sarah focused on the image clearly visible on their shields.

"It looks to be." She couldn't miss the concern in her father's voice.

"What are they doing out here?"

"I think we are about to find out."

CHAPTER FIFTEEN

Help for the Path. The City of Last Resort.

"Hello and well met," said what Bram assumed to be the leader of the group of men closing the remaining yards between them and the elders. He wanted to get between the congregation and these strangers, allowing for a more private discussion.

Each was clearly sizing up the other. It was to be expected whenever two new people crossed paths. Even Sojourners, when Bram was younger, were careful in meeting other congregations. But these weren't Sojourners nor Marauders. They were all obviously Dwellers.

The fronts of their cruel-looking shields were painted white, making the black crow profile quite visible. The gray circular nimbus behind the crow's head helped emphasize the bird's narrowed white eye. It seemed to be staring right at them with great interest, clearly mimicking the ones bearing the emblem.

"Are you Laromi?" Bram inquired cautiously. It wasn't safe to assume anything—especially with strangers.

"We are," said the other. "From Larom itself, in fact. We weren't expecting to find anyone so close to the city, especially Sojourners."

"You have seen other Sojourners?" Bram was momentarily filled with hope.

"Not for a long time," said the Laromi's leader. "Maybe in my father's day, but you're hard to miss."

Bram hid his disappointment. "How far away is your city?"

"Not more than a day," the other replied with the same measured tone. "You looking to make a visit? I thought you Sojourners weren't ones for cities."

"It is not our custom," explained Bram. "But after encountering some Marauders we find ourselves lacking in supplies. We would be thankful for anything you could spare. We would also be willing to pay or trade what we have for anything you could part with."

"We might be able to help you out." A strange expression graced the leader's face. He turned to the others in the group. "Laroma definitely seems to be smiling on us." The others grinned. Bram wasn't quite sure how to read those smiles, but they didn't raise any immediate concern, and so he let it pass.

"Where were you headed before you ran into those Marauders?"

"As the sparrow flies," said Bram.

"A little vague, isn't it?" the other jested. "You go following after birds, you're bound to get lost." The rest of the soldiers shared in a small chuckle. "How many are in your party?" Their leader surveyed the rest of the congregation.

"We are some one hundred souls," answered Bram.

"One hundred . . ." the Laromi pondered aloud, seeming to create a rough tally of those he could see. "And not just men and women but children too. We don't get too many of those around these parts these days."

"We are open to anything you may be willing to share." Bram gently pushed the main thrust of this conversation along. In his previous dealings with Dwellers, he'd found it wasn't wise to stray too far from the objective. "We do not want to hurt you in order to help ourselves."

"Oh, I don't think that would happen. In fact, I think you'd be most welcome at Larom."

"Really?" Bram looked the others over carefully.

"Oh, yes." The Laromic leader smiled.

"And you speak for the leader of your city on this?"

"He'll probably be so thrilled to see you, he'll throw a large banquet." Some of the other Laromi snorted, while others' grins only widened.

"They would not have to do that," Bram assured him.

Experience had shown the more honor Dwellers showed someone, the more they expected in return. Often that meant paying higher prices for various items because of the extra effort they'd made. It wasn't outright dishonesty but in keeping with the morality of the many Dwellers he'd encountered throughout his life.

"We do not intend to stay long," Bram continued. "Only see what we can trade or purchase from you and then be on our way. We would not even go behind your walls, but simply remain in our camp."

"Let's deal with that later. For now, if you're open to it, we could lead you back to the city. It might be safer anyway, given your previous encounter with those Marauders."

Again Bram paused. Could this be the Sovereign bringing them back on the path? They had just been discussing it, and now these men had come the very same day. "A most generous offer," he said, glancing at the rest of the elders out of the corner of his eye. "If you could give us a moment."

"Of course."

Bram took a few paces back and huddled with the elders. "I am inclined to accept their offer. If we can get some water and supplies, it would go a long way."

"As we have already discussed," said Mathias.

"I do not agree with their swords," said Thomas, "but if they are not Marauders, I can overlook them . . . temporarily."

"So you agree, then?"

"It is not for us to make the final decision," said Milton. "You are patriarch."

"After our discussion I cannot help but think this a sign, but I would feel much better if you were with me on it."

"We are with you," said Anna. "It could be no coincidence these have arrived just after you shared your thoughts. Clearly, the Sovereign is watching over us and guiding us."

The other elders gave similar assent.

Encouraged, Bram and the elders returned to the Laromi. "We will take you up on your offer."

"Wonderful." The Laromi's leader held out his hand. "I'm Danrin, by the way. Figure we might as well know each other's names. We're going to be walking for a while."

"I am Bram," he said, cautiously taking Danrin's hand. "Let me inform the others and then we can depart."

Bram made his way back to the congregation, who were eagerly waiting for word of what just transpired. "We have just been told there may be a chance of us getting some supplies at a city called Larom. These men will lead us safely there." There was some murmuring, but that was about it. Bram took it as another good sign.

"How far away is this city?" asked one of the sisters from the back.

"Not too far," he replied. "About a day, I am told. So make ready to depart. We will leave at once."

"Do you mind me asking why you are so far from your city?" Bram asked Danrin. The two of them walked side by side, the rest of the men blending around the patriarch, Caleb, and James. The rest of the congregation followed a handful of paces behind them.

"We're out on patrol."

"Patrol for what?" asked Caleb.

"For anything," said Danrin. "This isn't the safest place on Annulis, as you've probably already discovered."

"We have not seen much of anything," said Bram. "Aside from the Marauders, all that has crossed our path has been empty towns."

"Laromic towns," James added.

"Times are hard for everyone," said Danrin. "The princeps has decreed we should bring all the people we can into the city."

"Would that not cause greater problems in your city?" James softly inquired.

"Just the opposite," replied Danrin. "It actually helps Larom survive."

"But who would farm your food and see to your livestock?" Caleb wasn't following the reasoning.

"You said you've been to some of the towns"—Danrin gave Caleb a solemn glance—"so you know how that's been working out."

"But how would bringing more people to the city help?" James wrestled with his thoughts. "Would that not be bringing more mouths to feed with nothing to feed them?"

Danrin smiled knowingly. "It's not as bad as you think. You'll find out soon enough."

"So you still have supplies you can spare despite the increase of your population." Bram was impressed. "You must have quite a surplus."

"Laroma has blessed us with more than enough bounty." This brought a few chuckles from the other Laromi, but a hard stare from Danrin choked them off. "You'll see when we get there."

"With such a bounty, are you not worried about Marauders?" asked Caleb.

"They're not what they once were. But if they *did* try anything, they'd wish they hadn't."

The finality of the reply made Bram seek another topic of discussion. "That place where you found us. It did not look like the other village we saw. It did not even have a statue of your goddess inside."

"That's because it's not Laromic. It's been empty for a long time. I think it was something of an outpost during the empire."

"There was this statue we found inside," said James. "It was of a man and smaller than the statues of your goddess."

"That would be the emperor. Well, an impression of what he was supposed to look like."

"It looked like a shrine," James continued.

"Yeah." Danrin sighed. "Some people liked to honor him like a god at times. Those that didn't know the truth." He changed his tone, taking in Bram with a curious eye. "So where were you really headed before we crossed paths? You're not really following after sparrows, are you?"

"We follow the path to the Veiled City." Bram welcomed the chance to speak of more familiar territory.

"And what path's that?" asked another of the soldiers from beside Caleb.

"As the sparrow flies," Bram replied.

"Was that a joke? I didn't know you Sojourners had a sense of humor."

"It is the truth."

The following lull in conversation allowed Bram the chance to work out the best phrasing of his next question. "You mentioned many of your people are being called to the city. We came upon a village less than a week ago that appeared freshly deserted."

"Like I said," explained Danrin, "that's not unusual."

"They had left a child hanging from a tree," he continued. "Would there be any reason why? She had to have been dead no more than a couple days prior to our arrival."

"Was there a placard around her neck?"

"Yes. It read 'thief.' "

"Then they probably left her as a warning."

"A warning for who, though?" James was clearly eager for answers. Bram guessed they all were. "If there was no one there to see it, what good would it do?"

"Don't know and don't care," came Danrin's terse reply. "We have to do what we can to stay alive. Maybe they didn't have the time to dig a grave or figured the crows would take care of it."

"Speaking of that," Bram said, cautiously moving to his next concern. "We happened upon something else that perhaps you could explain. We found some skulls with markings showing where their flesh had been stripped away." Danrin exchanged some glances with the other Laromi. All seemed uncomfortable with the idea, which Bram thought was normal. But while he took the unease at the news as a good sign, it didn't provide any answers. He decided to press a little more on the topic, hoping for some greater insight. "Do you know any reason why they might have done this?"

"No."

"There was also a rhyme we found carved in someone's private room. I have been trying to make sense of it myself, but perhaps you might know more than I do. It said: 'The crows have come to rip and tear, to take us all into their snare.' "

"No idea." Danrin was quick again with his reply. "People sometimes can't take the strain and go mad. It's happened more than a handful of times. It could be nothing but crazy ramblings from some shattered mind. It wouldn't be unusual for someone to kill someone else in self-defense for acting out that madness. Like I said, dark days for some."

"I see." Bram let the matter drop. Clearly the topic was a dead end. And he had no desire to risk anything further by upsetting armed men.

"Let me ask you something." Danrin kept his eyes on the road as he spoke. "You've been traveling the area for a while. Have you seen any signs of an army out there?"

"An army?" Bram was surprised. "Nothing but the Marauders."

"These would be people with a flaming bird crest on their shields and banners. Anything like that?"

Bram shook his head. "Are you saying there is another army out there?" The Marauders were bad enough, but a whole other army roaming about?

"Rumors." Danrin waved away his concern. "More stories, probably. But it's wise to look into any threat, as I'm sure you know."

The conversation after that was rather limited and sparse, giving each time for thinking and hoping about what came next. The hours moved past, until finally the tall walls of Larom rose into view.

"There it is." Danrin proudly pointed out the sight for all to see.

"Never have I seen anything so large before." Caleb's voice revealed the same mixed emotions the others of the congregation shared. He, like many of his age, had not seen a city up close in all his life. Indeed, it had been decades since Bram had last seen one himself, even from a distance.

"Yes," said Bram, "it is rather impressive."

For a moment he doubted himself for coming this way. Perhaps he had missed the Sovereign. Perhaps this wasn't the right path. Perhaps—no. He was confident he was right, and so were the other elders. "In an abundance of counsel you should carry out your plans," the old saying went. And he had that and his own faith to guide him. This was the right choice. They just needed to see it through to the end.

"You should see the inside." Danrin's face beamed. "We should be there within the hour."

Bram renewed his efforts, putting more vigor into his already tired legs. Time enough to rest once they reached the gates. Obeying their patriarch's command, the rest of the congregation fell into line, some shuffling, some marching for those hard stone walls. The sun was fading as the congregation made it within plain sight of the tall stone walls surrounding the city.

"Look," said Caleb, motioning to the stone crows perched on the walls on either side of the strong gate.

"Crows," muttered James. "You really are quite focused on them."

"They're sacred to our goddess," Danrin explained, lifting his shield to emphasize his point.

"We will wait here," Bram told Danrin. "You will need time to speak with your leader and—"

A loud grating sound captured their attention.

All watched the slowly opening gate with great interest. Behind the thick doors was a small company of men dressed in the same strange armor as their guides, each carrying a type of crossbow Bram had never seen before.

"It looks like they beat you to it." Danrin smirked.

As one this new company of men moved forward, eating up the space between the two groups until at last, with a few yards between them, they halted. One in their number, whom they surrounded, wasn't dressed in armor but a pair of black pants and white shirt over which were worn a black vest and burgundy cape.

"What is the meaning of this, Danrin?" asked the man in the vest.

"We came upon them in the road," Danrin returned.

"*All* of them?" The other was quite impressed.

"Yes."

"My, my, Laroma has surely blessed us—and before our other guests arrive too. *Quite* the blessing." The same man raised his right hand in greeting. "Peace to you. I am Corbin Camden, princeps of Larom."

Bram stepped forward, falling back on the old customs that had served them well for decades. "I am Bram, patriarch of this congregation."

"And quite a good many people they are." Corbin scanned the faces of those farther back on the road. "Strong and healthy to a one, it seems."

"Thank the Sovereign for his mercies," said Bram, "but we will not remain so, I fear, unless we replenish our supplies. We lost what we had in a rather unfortunate encounter."

"The Pyri?" Corbin shared a glance with Danrin.

"Pyri?" Bram was confused. "Are they another group of Marauders—these Pyri?"

"The Pyri are something much different. They'd be hard to miss—them and their flaming bird standard."

"Ah, Danrin spoke about them earlier."

"They haven't encountered them yet," Danrin informed Corbin.

"More good news." Corbin was genuinely relieved. "Is this all your number?"

"Yes."

"It's getting late," Corbin continued, gesturing at the darkening sky for emphasis. "Contrary to what you might think, not all who call Annulis home are callous. I can see the journey has worn hard upon you. You are welcome to share our hospitality. In fact, we've just begun restocking our supplies."

"I was telling them just that on our way here," offered Danrin.

"Of course." Corbin's smile seemed strange to Bram, but again he pushed any fears aside. There were many strange ways among the Dwellers. "Please accept our hospitality, such as it may be."

"A kind offer," said Bram, "but we do not look to impose, only to see what you might be able to spare before resuming our journey."

Corbin's smile deepened. "I'm sure we can work out an agreement to satisfy each other. In fact, your arrival might very well call for a feast."

A sudden burst of excited murmuring erupted from the congregation. "You need not go to such trouble." Bram tried tamping down that excitement before it got out of hand. They had some means to get basic supplies, but nothing that would allow for a feast. Best not to even get any hope up for such a thing and be spared any disappointment. "We shall be happy enough to enjoy what you can spare. And we still have some coin to pay for what we require."

"I insist. And we'll give you a fitting place of honor at the table. What do you say?"

Bram looked back to the congregation's faces—faces that were now lit up and shining more than he'd seen in days past. He searched out the elders. Their faces were stoic, but their eyes spoke of commitment to anything he decided. He gave a nod and turned back to the Laromi.

"We would rather not enter the city, but if that is the only way for a deal to be struck, I suppose we can agree to it this once."

"Excellent."

Behind the gates, Larom was a strange sight to the congregation walking down the clean but worn streets. Sarah clung close to her father as they were led through a large gathering of Laromi. She couldn't shake the thought they were watching her with an unnatural amount of interest.

"I do not feel safe here," she whispered.

Desmond tugged Sarah closer. "Just keep walking."

Ahead of them was Bram, with Caleb and James at his side. They too were on edge. Though the Laromi didn't show any outward signs of aggression, something heavy lingered in the air. Something weighty that grew even more oppressive the further they advanced into the courtyard.

Trying to distract herself, Sarah shifted her focus to the tall statue of the city's patron goddess. This one was much larger than the one in the village. But though it was grander in some ways, it was also worn and tired, like much of the city, she noticed, and even the people living in it. What held her eyes the most, though, were the crows. A handful of the stone-carved birds perched at the statue's feet, gazing over all they could survey. For a moment they seemed almost ready to take wing.

"Still more crows." Her father followed Sarah's gaze.

"The crows have come to rip and tear . . ." Sarah repeated the words she wouldn't soon forget.

"Put it out of your mind. It is not any of our concern. We just need to get through this meal, take some rest, and then we can return to the path."

"They seem so . . . similar." Sarah studied the crowd of Laromi who had gathered to meet them.

"The same could be said of us by them, I am sure," said her father. "The Dwellers have their own ways and manners. As do we. It is best we do not linger long among them. It is not our place to try and make sense of things that do not concern us."

"I know. We stay to the path—as the sparrow flies."

Her father shared a small side hug. "And we shall be back on that path soon enough—fed and with enough provisions to see us through. Have faith in the Sovereign and the patriarch."

But any warmth Sarah had been feeling was instantly chilled by the sound of the gate closing behind them. And then came the echoing thud of the large plank dropping into place and locking the doors tight.

Corbin, who still was leading them, came to a stop and turned round to address all gathered in a loud voice. "People of Larom, the doors have now been locked, the walls secured. We are safe from any harm Annulis would set before us. We will endure whatever these foolish fire worshipers send our way." Sarah shot her father a curious glance, but he motioned for her to stay silent. "And now we see how Laroma continues shining upon us. The crows have returned with this fine group of people. A *healthy, strong* group of bodies."

"The crows?" Sarah heard Bram ask.

Danrin smirked over his shoulder, eyes gleaming with a dark mirth. "Just a nickname. Those sent to round up people for the city are called crows."

The blood fled from Sarah's face. "The crows have come to rip and tear, to take us all into their snare," she muttered. Only now it wasn't a strange saying but something very real. Something very terribly real.

"And they have served Larom and Laroma well." Corbin's expression changed. The kindness and goodwill fled from his face like water draining from a burst skin. In their place was something cold and hard. It almost reminded Sarah of one of the Marauders' masks.

"And with such a large return, it's fitting we should have a feast worthy of such news. For here is a celebration truly worth celebrating."

"Guards! Help prepare our guests for the feast." No sooner had Corbin given the order than some soldiers rushed forward, taking hold of the adults in the congregation while others lifted the younger ones over their shoulders.

"Father!" Sarah screamed as a set of rough hands took hold of her wrists. These pulled her toward the chest of a leering soldier. She couldn't escape his grasp no matter how much she tried.

"Sarah!" Her father struggled with two strong Laromi of his own. "It will be all right. Do not be afraid. We shall—"

He was cut short by a hard blow to the back of his head.

"Father!" Sarah again tried breaking free but was restrained.

Her captor started dragging her deeper into the city. She couldn't see where exactly, as she was being pulled from behind, but continued her feeble struggles.

"What is the meaning of this!" Bram shouted as she was dragged past the patriarch. He stood defiantly before Corbin. James and Caleb were at his side, faces clenched in rising rage. "You offered us a place of rest."

"Yes, I did," said Corbin. "And you'll get all you need in the dungeons."

James sprang into action, brandishing his dagger. Before he could take more than two steps, another soldier ran him through with his sword.

"No!" Sarah felt the tears flow at the sight of James dropping to the cobblestones, blood dripping from the corner of his lips. Caleb tried taking out the soldier with his own dagger but was just as quickly dispatched.

"Looks like we have our first course." Corbin almost snarled in his glee.

Sarah shut her eyes, willing the horrid images from her mind, but it was no use. They were burned deep inside and wouldn't depart no matter how hard she tried.

And then the tears really flowed.

She barely registered the world around her. Swallowed by her sorrow and drenched in fear, she was vaguely aware of being led through part of the city and then eventually down a dark hallway with Sophie, Tabitha, and a sobbing Malena. Their captors would eventually shove them all into a lightless room behind a wooden door that was slammed back into place as quickly as it had been flung open.

She'd always remember the set of cold eyes staring back at her through the rectangular slot near the top of the door. There were some muffled words followed by laughter, and those same eyes departed, leaving only darkness and dread of what was yet to come.

CHAPTER SIXTEEN

Preparations and Fear. A Questionable Omen.

"There it is." Elliott didn't realize how excited he was until he heard his own voice. They'd finally arrived within sight of Larom. The city was nestled in a plain at the base of the Kondis Mountains. With the Ashen Hills to the south, it was framed perfectly on three sides, letting the Laromi focus only on the east, where the road directed the Pyri toward the city gates.

"It's still a good distance away," cautioned Sir Pillum. "But it's nice to see the walls."

The road leading up to Larom's closed gates was well maintained, getting better, in fact, the closer they drew to the city. And while there hadn't been any further ambushes or assaults, that didn't mean they weren't on the lookout. The slower gait they'd adopted was for the infantry's benefit. If they were suddenly called upon, they'd do better not having endured a forced march. It was also for the good of the horses, so they'd have the strength for a fast gallop—and charge—if needed.

Elliott was riding a new horse beside his master. He still kept the sword at his side but didn't have any armor or anything else to defend himself when the fighting came. Not that he was actually expecting to see combat. That last encounter with the Laromi in the old town had been an abnormality; this time he imagined he'd be back in the camp like normal. He was actually getting used to the gnawing sensation in the pit of his gut growing stronger as he approached the stone walls.

Ever since his first taste of real battle, a sort of nervous churning had been taking place in his stomach. He thought at first it was only the rush of battle and his nerves dealing with the aftermath of it all, but the sensation stayed as they secured the perimeter. It was there when he woke in the morning, staying with him all throughout the honoring of the dead and the burning of the town. And as they mounted up and left, it still remained. It just didn't go away—only kept up its gnawing. Its slow, numbing chewing on his insides. He didn't know what to make of it and wondered if it would ever leave. But that had been this morning.

Amazingly, the longer he rode, the less he noticed the sensation. It was as if with each passing mile it was deepening—making itself more and more a part of him. He wondered if that was what knights felt all the time. If so, someone as experienced as Sir Pillum probably didn't even know it was there anymore.

Thinking of his master, Elliott turned his way. There was something else he was contemplating this early afternoon. "Do you think they're already watching us?"

"I'd hope so. Otherwise, they wouldn't be very wise. I wouldn't put it past them to spring a surprise attack—even an ambush or trap of some sort."

"Do you think we'll get there before nightfall?"

"We might, if we keep this pace. Though it would be foolish to try a night battle. Calix is right. We'll be fighting at first light tomorrow."

"Do you know how many there may be?"

"No. Not until we see them arrayed. And even then, they might keep more behind to man the walls."

"And how are we going to defeat their walls?"

"The same way as we did with the towns."

"But these look much larger and stronger." Elliott inspected what he saw of the defenses from his current position. He wasn't a grand strategist but could see that these walls were in much better repair than the previous ones they'd encountered around the more ramshackle cities they'd vanquished in the early days of their campaign. The Laromi were certainly proving to be a challenging foe.

"If we let what is outside guide our faith, we will always be weak. For what is outside is corrupt and subject to lies and deception. But if we look inside and keep our sights on the truth, we won't know fear, only confident expectation of what's yet to come." Turning to Elliott, he added softly, "It's not wrong to acknowledge you have fear, Elliott. All of us are tempted from time to time. But it would be a sin against Pyre to think we are unable to do what he's charged us to accomplish."

"I'm sorry, sir," Elliott repented, which made Sir Pillum's brow wrinkle. "Sorry for what?"

"For doubting we'd succeed."

"You weren't doubting me, but Pyre, who sent me and you—along with this whole army—to spread his truth."

"I'm sorry, sir. It won't happen again."

"I'm not mad at you, Elliott." Sir Pillum's voice remained soft. "I'd be lying if I said I or anyone else here never thought such things. We're all human and subject to doubt. But I'd spare you some of the struggle I had to suffer before gaining a greater hold of the truth.

"A warrior who wavers in his belief is really of little use. He's already slouching toward defeat. To win the day we need to be fully committed to our beliefs, which will give us the strength to persevere and see victory when all others have fallen."

Elliott let the wisdom soak into his mind and heart. There was truth there. Truth he wasn't about to squander. Truth that made the faint gnawing in his gut fade even further into the background of his consciousness.

"You sound more like a priest today, sir," he teased.

"I did hang around quite a few growing up." Sir Pillum joined in the same spirit of levity. "And don't worry," he added. "That gnawing in your gut will go away soon enough."

Elliott went wide eyed. "How did you know about that?"

"You just had your first battle. It's a common thing. Once you get through this next one, things will settle down again."

"So it isn't there forever?"

"No. It might return sometimes before a particular battle, but once the swords start clashing and arrows flying, it'll fade away." The relief at those words poured over Elliott like cool water washing away every concern—both old and new.

"So this is what it's like to be a knight?"

"Just a small part. But, like I said, if you keep your faith in what you should, things will work out for your good. Pyre will see to that."

"Wise words, Sir Pillum," said Calix as he rode up alongside them. "I trust your squire will heed them."

"Elliott has proven nothing but faithful and more than willing to strive for his best. I'm confident he'll make an excellent knight when the time comes." Elliott silently soaked in his master's praise.

"Let's hope so. There's still much work to do. You've spied their walls, I'm sure."

"We have, sir," said Sir Pillum.

"What do you make of them?"

"Not much. I'm sure they'll have men on the ramparts, though. For show, if nothing else."

"I'm expecting archers and infantry and at least one ambush before we get too close. Keep alert and be ready to move if called for. I don't trust this open wilderness. It provides too much cover and the perfect ground for an attack. If anything happens, I'll need you to lead one of the two wings I'm dividing the Salamandrine into."

"I'll be ready, sir," said Pillum.

Calix nodded and rode on to another group of knights, no doubt to share more plans with them.

"The leader of your own wing?" Elliott was amazed. "Have you just been promoted, sir?"

"It sounds that way, doesn't it? Still, I wouldn't put too much store in it. We've lost a good number of men these last few days, and some of us will have to do more than before."

"Still," urged Elliott, "Commander Calix could have chosen someone else to lead the second wing. The honor is certainly yours, sir."

"Yes, I suppose he could choose another, which is why I don't plan on letting him down. I'll need your help in this too. So keep alert for anything."

"Yes, sir."

Sarah sat in her cell. She had been separated from her father and left alone with Malena, Tabitha, and Sophie. She didn't know where the rest of the congregation had been taken, but it was clear from what she could recollect they had been grouped by age and sex. They had taken the adults' daggers along with the men's remaining staves, making sure all were totally defenseless. Once done, each group was introduced to their cell.

No one spoke above a whisper, and even then they kept what was said to a minimum. There wasn't really anything *to* say—not anything any of them wanted to keep dwelling on—and so each found other things to keep from getting snared in their fearful thoughts.

The smell was the worst. It had the tang of something she might know, but then another aspect wrapped around it that was at the same time foreign and uncomfortable. She wouldn't put a name to the actual odor. If she didn't acknowledge it, it was easier to put out of mind. Though that was rather hard to do, given it was everywhere. At least with the cell door closed, it wasn't as bad as when they first arrived. She dreaded to think she might be getting used to it.

They'd been herded deep into a dark series of tunnels winding in various directions. It reminded her of a beehive with individual cells for holding them and the rest of the congregation. Shoved inside and locked away, they would clearly have no escape. Yet another thought she didn't want to dwell on any longer than she already had.

"Do you think they will feed us?" Malena had finally stopped crying long enough to speak.

They all had wept at first once the door slammed shut, but Malena had outlasted them all—and for good reason, Sarah supposed. She'd just been parted from James after making her feelings known. While she didn't enjoy seeing her suffer, Sarah could be thankful she hadn't done the same and didn't have to suffer the pangs of losing what might have been with James while also wading through the fear she already was enduring for her father.

"Let us hope they refrain," said Tabitha. "If they kept us starving, so much the better—for all our sakes."

Sarah agreed wholeheartedly. The less they had to do with any of these Dwellers, the better. But she didn't think they were going to give them much time. Already she was pushing down the icy dread slowly ascending from her stomach at what lay on the other side of that door . . . What sort of death—she stopped herself. It wasn't doing anyone any good to focus on such things. She needed to keep her mind on something else, something brighter . . .

Sophie retched again into the small bucket she kept between her legs. A fresh wave of pity washed over Sarah at the sight of the pale-faced girl who had kept so much to herself all her life. And now, when she needed it most, she had no one really to latch on to for some strength and comfort. How terrible a thing to be so alone when surrounded by others. And yet Sarah herself didn't know what she could do or say that might cheer her. Instead, each had to endure in their own way.

Another hacking cough emptied more bile into the bucket. They'd first encountered it upon their arrival. She assumed it was for collecting their waste, but it collected Sophie's vomit just as well. Thankfully, Sophie's sable strands were held back by the leather straps on her ponytail, keeping the hair from getting anywhere near the bucket or her mouth.

Sophie raised her head and wiped her mouth. Not much was coming up anymore. When they had first been locked inside, she was already pale but started shaking violently, followed quickly by the vomiting. Sarah could tell she wasn't sick, just terribly overcome with fear. Her green eyes no longer held their usual glimmer. Now they were haunted things framed by a lined and troubled countenance, aging her more than her years.

"Better?" Sarah asked.

Sophie could only nod, closing her eyes as if by doing so, she could will the whole cell and everything else away.

"But they have to have food," Malena insisted. "They told us they had food."

"Were you even *listening* when they led us away?" Tabitha's voice had a clear edge to it Sarah had rarely heard. "*We* are the food."

"Surely, one cannot truly survive in such a manner. They have to have something else hidden away. We cannot be the only thing they . . ." Malena's voice faded as the revelation soaked in.

"How long do you think we will stay here?" Sophie dared to ask in her weak voice. "Do you think they will keep us locked up until—until they have need of us?"

None dared reply to the horrid question. Instead, they all took another look around the cell. Apart from the door, there was nothing but stone walls. The floor was hard rock and the ceiling was the same. There was no getting out. There was nothing they could do but sit and wait.

"Do you think they will start with the patriarch?" asked Malena.

"After the others have been . . ." Tabitha stopped upon seeing the fresh tears welling in the corners of Malena's red-rimmed eyes. "Best not to think about it," she instead advised.

"But who would be next?" Malena insisted. "First James and Caleb and—"

"Malena." Tabitha's voice was like steel. "You need to think about something else—*all* of us do."

"But what else *can* we think about?" There was a growing whine in her voice. For all the sympathy Sarah could muster, the question still grated on her nerves. "All of us will never see the light of day again. We will never see our loved ones—" She choked on the words.

Sarah found her annoyance melting into compassion. Before she could think, she found herself reaching out and consoling Malena, who readily accepted it.

"It will be okay. We will make it through. We just have to keep our faith in the Sovereign watching over us." She was amazed at how close the words sounded to something her father would have said. Perhaps she was becoming more of an adult than she realized.

"I do not know if I can. I already have seen my love fall by the sword." The words further melted Sarah's heart. She wouldn't have wished such sorrow upon anyone. "Do you have any idea what that is like?" She pursed her lips, keeping the sobs lurking just under her breath.

"I have an idea," Sarah softly returned as the two stared into each other's eyes. "And I know it is terrible."

Malena believed her. She wiped away a fresh tear. "How could the Sovereign let such a thing befall us?"

Sarah didn't have the answer, but tried anyway. "We got out of the danger with the Marauders. And that looked very grim."

"Not as grim as this."

Sarah didn't have any reply. For as troubling as the encounter with the Marauders had been, they'd still had a chance of escape if they could have fled the barracks. But being underground in this cell was different, and on top of that there was the horrible fate awaiting them, haunting their thoughts just as thickly as the sickening odor permeating the air.

"It will be okay," she found herself repeating.

Malena started crying again. Sarah looked to Tabitha, who mirrored her own feelings of fear and confusion. It only made the room seem darker.

Once more Sophie retched into her bucket.

"We camp here." Calix's command was repeated throughout the ranks. "Off the road and facing the walls."

Elliott took to the order, as did the rest of the army, his master doing likewise. They hadn't seen anything all day. Sir Pillum was hard to read, but others showed signs of not liking it one bit. As the day waned, that disfavor only increased.

"You think they'll try for a night attack?" Elliott asked Sir Pillum. His master had already dismounted and removed his helmet.

"If we keep a good watch it won't matter. See to the pavilion while I talk more with Calix."

"Yes, sir," he said, taking Bakan's reins and trotting off with the rest of the squires and infantry making their way to a suitable position far enough off the road to serve as their camp. Thankfully, they'd have enough grass for the horses. It was one of the good things about being in these fields.

Once the perimeter of the camp was defined, it was second nature to find his place, and Sir Pillum's pavilion within that. He had gotten so good at it, he almost didn't need to think. In fact, he was halfway through the process before he realized he was actually doing it.

Soon enough the pavilion was pitched and the horses were brushed and brought to the corral, where they joined the rest munching on grass. As the sun was setting, he broke out his simple folding seat and began working on Sir Pillum's shield, polishing it as carefully as he ever had. He wanted it to look its best for the coming fight. He'd tackle the helmet next before delving into the armor upon his master's return.

"As diligent as ever." Sir Pillum's praise roused Elliott from his work.

"I just finished," he said. "I can start on your armor once you—"

"No need," said Sir Pillum. "I'll sleep in it tonight. Can't be too careful so close to the city. And dawn will be here sooner than we know it. Besides, we need some time to get you outfitted."

Elliott's eyes widened. "You're going to give me armor, sir?"

"Well, it'll be infantry armor for the most part, but we can add a few knightly touches."

"What for, sir?" He couldn't hide his confusion.

"Calix wants everyone outfitted. He thinks it best, since we've lost so many in the last few battles, to get everyone on the best footing to at least defend the camp. So all squires and camp workers are getting their taste of battle."

"Thank you, sir."

"It's nothing, Elliott, just something practical. You'll get a shield, sword, and helmet from the Salamandrine and then the rest of the armor from the infantry. You won't look pretty, but it should help level the field if anything does come your way."

"I'll take whatever you can spare, sir." Elliott was more than overjoyed at the prospect. This was much better than just staying behind in the camp. In the very least, he'd be able to feel more a part of the coming battle—maybe even offer support in some way if needed—getting yet another taste of what his future might hold.

"I figured you would." He shot Elliott a smile.

"Will I still be allowed to fight on horseback?"

"Of course. How else can you continue to improve if you stay on foot? Now, let's see about getting you used to everything while we still have some light."

"Really?" He was almost beside himself.

"I'm not about to leave you all dressed up with nothing to do. Besides, it will be good practice and a way to show me what you've learned so far. It's about time to test you on it anyway."

The rest of the evening was a blur as Elliott was outfitted with his own armor. He wasn't a knight yet but was much closer than he'd ever been. Sir Pillum had gotten his hands on a Salamandrine helmet and a leather brigandine shirt, like he said. He was able to find a pair of matching pants that would fit him well enough and a Salamandrine shield in good condition.

"How does that feel?" Sir Pillum inspected his newly attired squire.

Elliott rolled his shoulders and flexed his arms. "I think it feels fine?"

His heart was close to bursting with the excitement of actually wearing armor. Normally that wasn't something a squire was allowed until he was knighted. His lack of experience meant he wasn't entirely sure how it was supposed to feel. He knew the ins and outs of the various components, of course—had to so he could keep Sir Pillum's armor in good order—but knowing the function of something wasn't the same as using it yourself.

"Not too tight?"

"No."

"Here." He handed Elliott his sword. "Try swinging it."

Elliott did as instructed. There might have been a slight tightness across his chest, but it loosened with more practice swings.

Sir Pillum drew his sword and started sparring with him, much to Elliott's delight. They'd practiced before, of course, but those were just drills. He rarely got the chance to actually spar, and never in armor.

"Try that shield too."

Elliott raised it and blocked another of his master's swings. He wasn't going too hard on him, but to his delight, Elliott kept up with the repeated swings and counterattacks.

"Not bad. You should be able to hold your own. Though I wouldn't get too carried away until you're in some proper armor." Sir Pillum sheathed his sword.

"Yes, sir."

"Now, how about I show you how to get in and out of things quickly? You took some time before. A knight needs to be able to don his armor as quickly as possible, whenever the need arises."

"I'll do better, sir."

Sir Pillum smiled. "Relax, Elliott. No one is expecting you to be perfect your first time. And this armor is a little mismatched as well. The first thing you need to do is relax your shoulders . . ."

Sir Pillum walked him through the process of donning and doffing his armor at least a dozen times. Finally, when it was too dark to see well enough to continue, both retired for the night. Elliott was too excited to sleep. For the first hour he lay on his bedroll, eyes searching the heavens. Already he envisioned the battle to come. And while there was that same gnawing in his gut, he now knew how to confront it.

As he studied the stars, a streak of light caught his eye. It fell in a diagonal line over part of the sky. One moment it was a white-hot line, and the next it had faded as quickly as it had appeared. Unsure of what it was, he wondered if he should wake Sir Pillum. That thought was quickly dismissed. He needed his sleep just as much, if not more, than Elliott. If it was something, the priests would know about it. They were good about keeping abreast of such matters.

For a moment he toyed with the idea it was his own personal omen. If it was, then what it was supposed to signify remained a mystery. And while it was fun to speculate on such matters, it didn't get him any closer to falling sleep. Finally focusing on clearing his mind and slowing his breathing, Elliott drifted off into a dreamless slumber.

CHAPTER SEVENTEEN

A Surprising Welcome. A Selection of All.

awn came much too soon for Elliott's liking. It wasn't that he wasn't excited—he was. He just didn't know how tired he'd been and could have done with a few more hours' rest. There would be none of that, however. A knight needed to be ready at all times, sleep or no sleep. And with the city so close, they weren't going to waste a single moment. He tended to his chores and duties as normal. Unlike his master, he hadn't slept in his armor. Now he donned it and his helmet and fixed the shield so all was ready.

He knew he probably looked a strange sight upon his horse when compared to the rest of the Salamandrine, but didn't care. He was armed and armored and going into his second battle in less than two weeks. It was time to get a taste of being a knight and see from the frontlines what it was like to put a city under submission.

"Sleep well?" Sir Pillum was making some final adjustments to his armor at Elliott's side.

"Well enough."

"A little excited, I'm sure."

"Yes, sir."

"Well, stick close to me, and I'll help watch your back." A tingle raced down Elliott's spine. That was something only one knight would say to another. One who trusted his fellow brother in arms.

"Yes, sir."

"Remember, we have protocol first. We need to offer them the chance to accept Pyre's mercy. Should they fail, we bring about their judgment."

"And then offer the remnant one last chance," said Elliott, nodding. He wasn't about to forget something he'd seen carried out again and again over the last three years but knew Sir Pillum had to do his part in reminding him.

"All right," said Sir Pillum, mounting Bakan. "Once we ride to—"

He was interrupted by a small rock striking his left shoulder. Both he and Elliott watched it land near his horse. It didn't appear particularly interesting, and it hadn't caused any damage.

Elliott craned his head. "Where did *that* come from?"

Sir Pillum also looked around. "Maybe it got picked up by some fluke wind. Stranger things have happened."

"Laromi in the camp!" A lone cry cut short their discussion.

"Laromi?" Elliott looked to his master.

"It can't be an army," said Sir Pillum. "We'd have heard it sooner."

"Then what could it be?"

"Only one way to find out. Come on." He moved Bakan in the shout's direction. Elliott followed. The two made their way to the edge of a strange gathering. Thirteen dark-clad women of various ages with crow-feather shawls over their heads stood opposite a line of stone-faced Pyric soldiers.

"Who are they?" Elliott kept his voice low.

"Priestesses of their false goddess," answered Sir Pillum.

Elliott was surprised. He'd only known the priests at Pyrus and those who traveled with the army. He'd never seen any other servants of these false goddesses. None of the towns or villages or even the cities had kept any; all they had in the way of worship were those statues in their center courtyards, what remained of their false religion a long-hollowed-out husk.

"How come we haven't seen any of them until now?"

"They must have left for the safety of the city."

He supposed that made sense. The smaller towns and villages weren't well defended, and from what he could tell, the people weren't too devoted to their goddess.

"Who here speaks for you?" said one of the priestesses, stepping forward. She was slightly older than the rest but not by much. She, like the others, had dark-painted eyelids, adding a strangeness to her already dark garb and overall appearance. She also wore a whole cape of crow feathers in addition to her shawl.

"I do," said Calix, taking a few steps forward. Milec was close at his side, only a few paces behind. The rest of the Pyri parted, allowing them a straight path to the woman. "And who are you?"

"Astra, grand priestess of Laroma."

"And why have you come so brazenly into our camp?" Calix looked the woman over from head to toe, obviously not impressed with what he saw. "You realize we have little love for those who promote the worship of a false goddess."

"We've heard," said Astra. "And it's because we've heard that we've come out to meet you before you set yourself against the city. We ask for your mercy."

"Mercy?" Calix and Milec exchanged a curious glance. "The only mercy Pyre offers is in submission to him and his will."

"So we've also heard."

Calix and Milec exchanged another glance. Elliott shared their uncertainty. This wasn't anything like he'd expected.

"So you're offering your surrender?"

"We have been sent by the princeps of Larom himself. He wishes to avoid any further loss of Laromic lives. He sees no other way but to surrender and pray for the best."

"You'll forgive me if I find that somewhat odd," Calix replied. "After our previous encounters with your soldiers, I wasn't expecting something so . . ."

"Rational?" Astra raised an eyebrow.

"Unlikely," Calix continued. "If you're playing for time—"

"No." Astra was adamant. "We have come unarmed and openly to you. This is what the princeps wants, and we are in agreement with him."

"And what about your people?" Calix took in the rest of the priestesses behind Astra. "Do *they* share the same conviction?"

"They go where Laroma wills and the princeps says," replied Astra, smiling. "And we speak for Laroma."

"Hah!" Milec stepped forward. "So you admit you make up your so-called goddess's will. You wouldn't dare speak for her if she was real. No god would endure misrepresentation with any degree of leniency."

Astra's smile only deepened. "Spoken like a true priest."

Milec's chest swelled with pride. "And I know whom I serve, and it's not myself."

"Laroma has always been an easy goddess to serve. Her will is never far from our own, and she never requires much from us outside what we already believe."

"And so you'd just abandon her now?" Milec continued. "I find that hard to believe."

"As I said"—Astra's demeanor remained as calm and pleasant as if she were speaking with an old friend—"her will never deviates from our own."

"Convenient." Milec snorted.

"Yes. Very."

"And how many are in the city?" Calix narrowed his eyes, as if he could pierce through any deception like an arrow through a chink in armor.

"Less than there once was, but enough," replied the priestess. "Close to a thousand altogether." Elliott was amazed at the low figure. From what he could see, it could easily hold ten times as many occupants.

"That includes your army?" Calix was clearly doing his own math.

"Yes. So you can see part of our reasoning for surrender."

"You also must renounce your false god," Milec reiterated. His face was stern, brown eyes alert and shifting between Astra and the rest of the priestesses.

"We know." Astra surrendered a soft sigh. "And I do so with a heavy heart. But if it will save the city and citizens"—she removed her shawl—"then the greater good be done."

The action was copied by the other priestesses, providing an image Elliott found unsettling. He noticed he wasn't alone in his unease. It wasn't so much the way the women looked but more the uniform nature of the action itself. That combined with the exact same appearance each conveyed made it seem as if they were looking at a dozen identical sisters or a series of reflections.

"Then as head priest of this army, I accept your surrender," said Milec.

"As do I, as commander of this army," added Calix.

"We're pleased to hear it." Astra gave a small nod. "We shall lead you to the city and there open the gates to you. The princeps will officially surrender, and that will be the end of it."

"And if you're trying to play us false—"

"We have no desire to tempt your wrath," Astra assured Calix. "We've seen enough of that already."

"Make ready to follow these women," ordered Calix. "Once we've secured the city, we can conduct a proper Selection."

"So much for my armor." Elliott sighed.

"We're not inside yet," Pillum advised. "Nothing is certain until the city has been secured. So keep alert until then."

"Yes, sir."

"For the glory of Pyre!" Calix shouted.

"The glory of Pyre!" came the thundering refrain.

The army moved into action, following the former priestesses of Laroma. They moved slowly and silently, which only made Elliott more impatient to get inside the walls.

"Patience," said Sir Pillum, obviously noting his restlessness. "Don't lose your focus. Many victories have been lost at the last moment when someone let their guard slip." Elliott kept this truth in mind as they trotted up to the gates and waited for them to open.

They weren't accompanied by the whole army. Most of the Salamandrine and a good number of the infantry had come, but the rest remained behind to keep the camp and guard against any betrayal or anything else unexpected.

"They still have men on the ramparts," Sir Pillum observed. "Keep your shield ready should they decide to fire any bolts our way."

But no bolts came. The soldiers only eyed them from above, ever watchful as the gates finally opened. Elliott didn't really know what to make of the city. He'd only seen Pyrus and a few other anemic examples they'd encountered, but there were some obvious similarities. All of them were large and walled and had thick gates, but the citizens inside these walls and the soldiers staring down at them were very different.

The crows decorating the gate and visible across the rest of the city were the next obvious difference. He really couldn't see what the attraction to the creature was. It wasn't a fearsome beast someone could rally behind for courage and inspiration. They weren't even really that heroic. They were nothing more than scavengers. Again, not the most inspiring mascot for a great city to embrace.

Calix waited until the priestesses were inside, then raised his hand for all to see. "Forward." The soldiers complied, stepping in formation until they too had been swallowed by the gates. Behind them came Elliott and the Salamandrine.

Inside, Elliott was taken aback by a large gathering of Laromi facing the Pyric forces. He'd never seen so many of them in one place before. He was used to smaller populations, and seeing them all waiting and apparently ready to submit to Pyre was quite the sight.

None of them were soldiers. All were civilians or perhaps a mix of civilians and soldiers who'd cast off their arms and armor. He wondered why only those on the rampart remained on the walls. For a moment he worried they were being surrounded but quickly put it out of mind, confident in Calix's decision and Pyre's protection.

He still couldn't get over how all of them resembled each other. He'd seen this before, of course, but on this larger scale it was almost unsettling. It was like he was looking at fragments of a mirror holding the same reflection. The longer he looked, though, the more he noticed slight variations in body shapes and facial features. It wasn't much, but it was enough to add some personality to this uniform population.

"I'm Corbin Camden, the princeps of Larom," said a black-haired man with hazel eyes who advanced a few paces the army's way. In most respects he resembled the other Laromi around and behind him. His chief distinction came by way of a vest and cape worn over his otherwise identical outfit.

"And you speak for your people?" said Milec, stepping to the front of the Pyric line.

"I do," said Corbin.

"And is what this false priestess says true? Are you willing to submit to Pyre's mercy?"

"We are willing," said Corbin. "And we welcome it."

"With men still watching your ramparts?" Calix made sure his voice was loud enough to reach those ramparts. "You'll forgive me if I don't feel entirely comfortable with your surrender."

"And you'll forgive me if I'm not totally sure you'll accept it. But since one of us has to take the next step, let me remove any doubts." Corbin motioned to the soldiers on the wall. They departed their posts, making their way to the courtyard. Elliott couldn't see any other soldiers in sight. None on the walls. None around them. None anywhere. They truly had surrendered without a fight.

"Are we sure we can trust them?" Elliott whispered to Sir Pillum.

"Trust in Pyre, and in his priests," he whispered back. "The Selection will reveal the truth."

"Is this all of your population?" Milec was already thinking along the same lines.

"Yes," said Corbin.

Milec stared at the princeps. Elliott could feel the thickness of the air. He wanted to rush forward and do something—anything—to break through the tightening sensation, but he held to his training and didn't budge nor make a sound.

"Then prepare yourselves for Selection," Milec said at last. "I will give you the honor, Calix," he informed the commander. "It should be yours with such a victory."

"The true victory comes from Pyre, who aided his servants," countered Calix.

"Quite true," Milec returned, "and he has favored us all this day. Since you're already lined up, we shall begin."

"If that's what you wish," Corbin calmly returned, though Elliott thought he might have caught a flash of something else just behind his eyes. "Though there isn't any rush."

"The sooner Selection starts, the sooner we'll know your fate. We shall await the others to join us from the ramparts."

"We don't have to do this right away," Corbin continued in his same pleasant manner. "We'd be happy to entertain you—"

"First the Selection." Milec was adamant. "The rest can come later, as Pyre wills."

"See that they're lined up properly," Calix told some men. "And take a head count. We were told almost a thousand people. Let's make sure they're all here."

A handful of the nearest infantry started lining up the Laromi while some Salamandrine started counting heads. All waited for everyone to get into place. The priests joined Milec, awaiting their part. The rest stood at attention, not sure what else to do. Elliott didn't blame them. Nothing about this day had been ordinary so far. Finally, a Salamandrine counting heads raised their voice.

"One thousand exactly."

Calix gave Milec a nod, who returned it in kind.

"I trust our intentions are now proven." The princeps gave a small nod to Calix, who was already focused on what was to come, letting Milec step forward and begin Selection.

"Submit or be slain." Milec began with the familiar opening words. "These are the words of Pyre and Salbrin, his herald, for all of Annulis."

"Praise be to Pyre and his herald, Salbrin," recited Elliott and the rest of the army.

"The time has come to select your fate," Milec continued. "Commander Calix, please approach."

The commander stepped in front of Milec, eyeing those assembled with a purposeful gaze, moving from right to left. "There is coming a judgment to this world," he said at last. "A great fire that will burn across all Annulis. But Pyre in his mercy has allowed an escape. There is only Pyre!" Calix shouted. "Great is he and single in power!"

"Great is Pyre!" Elliott joined in the army's shout. He noticed some in the crowd were alarmed by the decree and wondered if they might be having second thoughts. Maybe not all of them agreed with their leader. They'd all find out soon enough.

"You have before you a choice," Calix continued. "Side with a false goddess who cannot help you or take the hand of mercy Pyre extends." Raising his fist overhead, he shouted, "There is only Pyre and his people!"

"There is only Pyre and his people!" Elliott and the other Pyri repeated the refrain.

"Those who wish to be purged from this world's corruption and look forward to the Great Conflagration with joy instead of fear, step forward. Pyre is not one to deny you a choice, for he wishes to have loyal followers ready to carry out his commands. You are free to choose whom you will. Today you can step forward and submit to Pyre, the true god, or you can remain as you are and in the end face the cleansing that is to follow."

"Those who submit to Pyre, step forward," said Milec, continuing the Selection.

There was an uncomfortable pause across the assembly. Corbin looked over the gathered people, first to his left, then right, nodding to each group in turn. He also found the priestesses behind him, and nodded. As one the whole mass of people moved forward. Elliott had never seen such a thing. There had always been those who wouldn't take Pyre's offer, but to see not a single one refuse him . . . that was something he almost couldn't fathom. Even Astra and her priestesses stepped forward without any hesitation. He was dumbfounded.

"Looks like you have your answer," said Sir Pillum.

There was another pause as Milec allowed for any wavering. When it was clear all would remain true to their choice, he said, "So be it. Selection has ended. Your fate has been sealed."

"All of you will find your place in Pyre's plan," said Calix. "Some in the army, others in its support."

"Wonderful," said Corbin with an authentic joy Elliott found hard to question. He approached Calix and Milec like a man greeting long-lost friends. "This calls for a feast. I trust you won't object."

"You have enough food to feed my men?" Calix doubted the prospect.

"Oh, we have plenty to go around," Corbin assured him, grinning. "In fact, we just recently received a fresh supply. Come, take your rest until then. I'll show you and your top men the city so you'll know what you've won."

Calix turned to another knight. "Set up a watch for the walls, and I want a patrol on the streets—*all* the streets."

"There really isn't any need for that," said Corbin. "We're all friends now."

"As long as there are those who won't side with Pyre," explained Calix, "we must always be vigilant. You'll learn this soon enough."

"I'm sure I will." Corbin motioned for Calix to enter the rest of the city. "Please, let me show you around."

"We'll need to topple that statue too." Milec pointed his blaze rod at Laroma's statue. Elliott noticed a few of the priestesses twitch. "And then we must burn any temples to your former false goddess." This made more than half the priestesses clearly uncomfortable. Only Astra remained entirely stoic.

"After the feast," Corbin assured him. "You'll have all the help you need. Let us honor you and our new alliance first, and then seal it by doing as you say."

"Very well," Milec relented. "It could make for a fitting end to such an occasion."

"Exactly. Now, let me show you the wonders of Larom."

Bram did his best at moving along, but it wasn't easy given the constant tugging of one of the Laromic soldiers on his arm. Behind him, another prodded with his sword. Unable to use his staff, he was slower than his capturers would have wanted. He didn't know how much he'd come to depend on it until he was deprived of it. He also no longer wore his cloak or cowl. Both had been taken from him when the two soldiers leading him down the dimly lit hallway had pulled him from his cell.

He had no idea of the time of day. The torch-lit halls and dungeons made it impossible to discern. Not that it really mattered. The stench he'd endured since his imprisonment was getting stronger and didn't sit well with him. It wasn't just a carnal smell, but something more stomach turning. It was something that lingered long in these halls and dungeons, until it seeped into the very stones. He already knew what it was, of course, but didn't want to bring himself to the point of fully acknowledging it if he didn't have to.

"Where are you taking me?" He didn't expect an answer but asked anyway. He hadn't been spoken to since he'd been shoved into his empty cell.

The worst was the guilt weighing heavily upon him. He'd failed. Failed the rest of the congregation. Failed himself. Failed the Sovereign. He should have never entered the city. No matter how much they needed supplies . . . But it was pointless to blame himself. What was done was done. And now . . .

"Keep moving," said the soldier behind him with another prodding of his sword. "You'll see soon enough."

Bram was led right into the source of the growing stench: a horrid kitchen splattered with blood and globs of entrails on various stone slabs and gore-crusted tables. Hooks and chains hung from the walls and ceilings, some with human body parts still attached.

"The crows have come to rip and tear, to take us all into their snare," he muttered.

It all was terrible. And to think they were doing this to their own people. He knew Dwellers weren't the most honorable at times, but the Laromi were the worst of their kind. They consumed their own people in hopes of seeing another day. Except it wasn't much of a hope at all. They were all on a dark spiral taking them deeper into that darkness. There wasn't anything to it but death and despair. And the worst part was Bram suspected most had known it at some point. The self-deception would have come after, when they coaxed themselves into a false reality from which none would willingly awake.

"Here's the guest of honor," said the soldier tugging Bram to the Laromi in charge of the slaughterhouse. There were two of them, dressed in equally vile clothing stained and splattered with all sorts of visceral material. Their aprons were also smeared and stained with things Bram didn't want to try to decipher. "How many more you going to need?"

"Corbin said he wanted a feast," said the one who appeared to be the younger of the two. Given their hard expressions and dirty faces, it was hard to tell just how old either was. "Nothing too big, mind you, but decent enough." He scratched his stubbly cheek in thought. "About two adults should do it."

"All right. We'll start with the old ones first." Bram's heart plummeted into his stomach at the idea of the other elders sharing his fate.

"He doesn't look too tough," said the second man, giving Bram the sense of being a cow before the butcher. "But we don't want to take any chances."

He gave a nod.

Bram felt the sword pierce deep into his back. It was like a blazing stick had been shoved into his body. The subsequent removal of the blade sliced even more of his muscle and organs.

"Get him to the table before he collapses." The cook who'd spoken first motioned to a grim stone slab tilted at an angle.

Bram couldn't resist their efforts even if he wanted to. His strength was fading. Already he could barely shuffle his feet. By the time they laid him against the sour-smelling stone, he was having trouble breathing and felt as if his whole lower body was encased in ice. This cold traveled up his hands and arms and chest. His eyes couldn't focus. He could barely hear anything. All he sensed was the stone against his back; everything else had faded. There was nothing he could do. It was done . . . and so was he.

Bram expelled his last breath and departed Annulis.

"How are the horses?" Sir Pillum asked upon Elliott's return.

He'd taken both his and his master's mounts back to the camp so they could graze and rest. There wasn't any reason to have them in the city. In his absence Calix's orders had been carried out, and much of the city appeared well under control. The Laromi appeared to be going about their normal business, while some of the infantry manned the walls and gathered with Salamandrine in the center court. These were occasionally swapped out for others assigned patrol duty. Those who weren't assigned a patrol, like Sir Pillum, tried to appear busy with the rest of the army free from any duty.

"They're all fine," said Elliott. "Have you just been standing around all this time, sir?"

"More or less. The Laromi are returning to their business, while Calix, Milec, Drenn, and the other officers are being shown the sights."

"This isn't like any Selection I've ever seen."

"True." Sir Pillum nodded. "But since such a large selection has never happened before, it's hard to know what to expect next."

"Maybe it's a sign of Pyre's favor. Perhaps the Grand Conflagration is going to happen sooner than we thought."

"Maybe." Sir Pillum focused on Larom's painted idol. "Though it would be nice to tear that statue down."

Elliott took in the idol anew. It was the most well maintained of any statue he'd seen. Not that it made any difference. An idol was still an idol—fit for little more than rubble. "When morning comes, it will fall."

"If it doesn't, we'll have more than enough eager volunteers to take on the job. It isn't sitting well with most of the men—the priests especially—but we have to stand by Calix's and Milec's orders."

"I'm sure they know what they're doing, sir."

Sir Pillum smiled. "You sound more like a knight all the time." Elliott returned the grin. "Still, it wasn't much of a fight for you."

"There will be more."

"Yes, there will. All the way to the eastern coast and then beyond that."

"Would we really go farther?" Elliott was taken with the idea, but somehow it seemed too elusive—too much like some fanciful dream. "I know we've taken many other places with other armies, but is there really anything outside the Sea of Mundus?"

"We go as far as Pyre and Salbrin say. Like you said, we already have the fleet out taking what it can, but once the continent's secured, any other pockets remaining must be taken for Pyre. Only then will our service be complete and Pyre honored."

"Yes, sir." Studying the statue again, Elliott asked, "What do you think they see in such things?"

"Besides the pretty face and figure, you mean?"

Elliott clearly didn't hide his shock well enough, which only seemed to increase his master's amusement. "What? You think your master was a pious priest? I do have a woman waiting for me back in Pyrus, you know."

"No, I didn't, sir. I never heard you speak of it until now."

"Well, it was a private matter, I suppose. And the less you speak of it, the less you have to think of it, I guess, too." Elliott couldn't miss the small twinge just on the outskirts of Sir Pillum's voice.

"So she is waiting for your return, sir?" Elliott said as much as he dared, not wanting to pry too much into his master's private affairs but also not able to fully resist the desire to explore this new facet he'd never known of Sir Pillum.

"For me or Pyre—whoever arrives first. We've been betrothed for four years now. And that woman is well worth the wait, let me tell you." Pillum stopped as if coming to himself. Elliott allowed his master the time needed to recover. The knight sighed, expelling whatever he might have been thinking from his mind.

"But back to their goddess." Sir Pillum returned to the statue. "They've deluded themselves so long they can't tell it's a lie anymore, and if you keep teaching a lie long enough it becomes hard to break free."

"Except today."

"So it seems." The words weren't entirely flat, but not entirely filled with a great deal of faith either.

"Do you really think they have enough food to feed all of us?"

"I doubt it. Maybe the priests and some officers, but not much more than that."

"Then why say they do?"

"To impress. Either that or to get on our good side. The people are still tainted, don't forget. They've yet to fully embrace Pyre and adhere to his teachings. Don't look so glum." He patted Elliott on the shoulder. "A few more days of camp rations won't hurt you."

"I'm surprised *you* weren't invited to the banquet, sir."

"Me?" Sir Pillum laughed at the notion.

"If they are looking for men of rank, they'd do well to choose you. Commander Calix appointed you to lead a wing, after all."

"True, but we never fought that fight."

"But the honor should—"

"Don't worry about my honor, Elliott. We don't serve Pyre for honor or distinction but out of reverence and a desire to spread his mercy. In the time to come, all will be rewarded with what is right. For now we only do what we are ordered to and so glorify Pyre in the process." He stopped and smiled. "I suppose I'm sounding like a priest again."

"Maybe just a bit, sir."

"It's still true, and as the days wear on, we'll be entrusted with more responsibility. Salbrin and all of Pyrus are counting on us and the other armies across Annulis. We must not forget that."

"Yes, sir." A greater sense of sobriety enveloped Elliott. Sir Pillum always had a way of inspiring people with his strong dedication to the truths of Pyre and the duties to which he'd been entrusted. Again Elliott was reminded of just how much he had to live up to when he finally stepped into the Salamandrine's ranks.

"What do you think they'll serve at the feast?"

"Still hungry, I see."

"Just curious is all. There wasn't much to take in the towns, no livestock and hardly any grain, and I haven't seen anything here either."

"Yet," Sir Pillum cautioned. "You haven't seen much because we've been kept in this courtyard. There could be storage bins and other larders kept for sieges and winter. This place might even make a decent headquarters. But don't worry. I'm sure whatever they offer will be fitting for such an event."

A clattering sound caught their attention. It came from a few yards away near an open spot in the courtyard. Curious, both knight and squire went to investigate and found a small pile of rocks. They resembled the one that had struck Sir Pillum's shoulder earlier.

"More wind, sir?" Elliott adopted the previous explanation as they squatted over their find.

"Maybe," he said, searching the late afternoon sky. "I don't see any clouds, so it's not a storm."

"Maybe they fell from the walls."

"Maybe." Sir Pillum wasn't convinced. He picked up a stone, turning it in his hand. "Let's keep alert, though, just in case. And while we wait for the commander and the others, you don't have to remain here." He rose, causing Elliott to do the same. "You might as well get some rest in the camp. We'll see to keeping order until Calix returns. There isn't much else that needs doing right now. And something tells me you might be hungry."

Elliott couldn't keep the grin from showing. "Yes, sir."

CHAPTER EIGHTEEN

A Grisly Dinner. Confrontation and Conflagration.

"Please, enjoy our hospitality." Corbin motioned Calix to a seat on his left in the large dining hall they had entered.

Like much of the city he, Milec, Drenn, and a few other officers and priests had seen, this room was rather utilitarian. In fact, much of their way of life, he was starting to suspect, was of a very workmanlike nature. Even the dishes and silverware placed upon the table were rather common.

"I'd rather have seen more of the city," Calix said bluntly. They'd only seen perhaps half of it in their tour. What he did see wasn't impressive—just empty buildings and larders. Nothing that gave him any hope there was anywhere near what they needed for supplies.

"You'll see the rest at first light, after we see to the statue of Laroma," came Corbin's confident assurance. "For now let's celebrate our new union." He motioned again to the table. "If you would do us the honor."

Calix sighed and took a seat at the oval table. The rest in the delegation followed his example, dominating one side of the table. Corbin, Astra, and a few other priestesses and Laromic soldiers of rank, whose names Calix still hadn't learned, took the other.

"So what is a princeps, exactly?" asked Drenn, genuinely curious. "We haven't come across that title in any of the other cities."

Corbin was happy to explain. "The Laromi have disposed with rank and class. We're a truly egalitarian people where all are equal in rights and place."

"Which must explain your unique sense of dress." Milec smirked. "Astra and her priestesses are the exception, of course."

"Our forefathers realized that clothing was tied to class and rank. Those who had more showed it through their dress, and those who had less couldn't help but show it as well. It was just one of many inequalities among the people. One of the changes they made was instituting a uniform code of dress. If all wore the same attire, there would be no distinction, and each would act and treat the other as their equal."

"I don't see that working too well," said Calix. This was milder than what he was truly thinking, but he kept his thoughts to himself, since it really didn't matter what these people did before Selection. Their old ways were now behind them and soon would be turned to ash.

"There were challenges at first," Corbin openly confessed, "but once all property and possessions were made communal, things got easier to enforce. And in the later generations, none could recall what it was like before we'd reached the place of total harmony with each other. I'd like to think it's one of the reasons why we've survived as long as we have. Whereas the other cities and people go to war among themselves over rank and privilege, titles and possessions, we're all united in a common purpose and existence."

"Yet you rule them," Drenn continued, softly pointing out that one glaring blemish on their otherwise perfect ideal. "Doesn't that mean you're above them?"

"I hold the office of princeps." Corbin didn't miss a beat. "It is an elected position anyone can assume. It simply means a first among equals. There is always a need to keep and marshal consensus on matters. All I do is facilitate the will of the people." It sounded innocent and humble enough, but Calix didn't believe a word of it.

"Well, that will change now that you're under Pyre." Milec's comment stirred a faint flutter of emotions on the priestesses' faces. Calix was sure the others hadn't missed it.

"I suppose it will." Corbin's enthusiasm diminished a degree. "But first we must feast."

"You really didn't have to make a meal," said Calix. "We're used to living on rations. And any food you did have would be put toward that end." It was the truth, and he felt obligated to offer it. They hadn't had too many meals offered them by those they encountered—none, in fact—since setting out on their campaign. Like everything else with this whole encounter it was more than a little disconcerting. Even so, Calix forced himself through the unease. He kept reminding himself this was far from a normal Selection. Perhaps Pyre was showing them what to expect in the lands ahead.

"I thought it only fitting to celebrate our new alliance, and since the food is already prepared, it would be a shame to waste it," Corbin continued, in a manner Calix could see was genuine.

"You honor Pyre by honoring his servants." Milec accepted the sentiment and its speaker.

"How can one do anything *but* honor them?" answered Corbin. "You opened our eyes to the truth, and we will be forever thankful."

"So what are you serving?" Calix was actually curious. "I didn't get the sense you had anything on hand during our tour."

"I think you'll be pleasantly surprised." Corbin motioned to one of the soldiers standing by the door. "It's a miracle in its own right that we have anything to share at all."

The doors opened, and ten nearly identical Laromi entered. Each carried a covered silver platter and wore a white apron around their waist. The men took up positions around the table, setting the silver platters in intervals. When they had finished, each took a place behind the Pyric side of the table.

"The smell is rather familiar." Milec sniffed at the platter nearest him. "Don't you think?" he asked Calix.

"Perhaps." Yes, there was something quite familiar about that smell . . .

"Please." Corbin motioned to the silver platter closest to Calix. "I insist you start first. All of you." He gestured for every Pyri to lift a lid.

Calix went first, the others slightly after him. When the lids were lifted, all were shocked to see what rested on their silver platters. Before them were pieces of not cattle or lamb or some other animal but human beings.

"What's the meaning of this?" Calix was on his feet, staring down at the face of a bearded old man with closed eyes. The singed hair on his head and beard added a sinister aura to the cooked flesh of his features.

"It's a glimpse of your future." Corbin motioned to the apron-wearing men behind Calix and the other Pyri.

These drew their weapons from hidden sheaths under those white aprons and set upon the Pyric delegation. Before any could react, they were run through. Calix felt the blade slide through his armor and upper back into his midsection. It was a fatal wound. He'd bleed to death in the next few moments.

"You'd think your god would find smarter followers," Corbin mocked. "You really thought a whole city would just turn over to your fantasies without even *trying* to defend itself?"

"Infidel!" Milec hunched over the table, gasping for breath. A sword had pierced through his left lung. "You will all *burn* for this. Pyre will—"

The Laromi behind Milec ended his words with a swift chop to the neck. His head hit the table, landing in a nearby platter.

"Thank you," Astra snarled. "It was about time he shut up."

The rest of the delegation were similarly slaughtered.

Calix could do little but watch in shame and rage the undoing of all his hard work and service to Pyre. He had been so faithful—had fought so true. And now, to see it all end like this—through deception and his own folly. He should have put every one of them to the flames—razed this city at first sight. Protocols be damned.

"Wait," said Corbin when they were about to put Calix to his final end. "Leave him alone for a moment. He *is* our guest, after all."

"You haven't won anything," Calix growled, collapsing into his chair. "There's still an army in your city and we—"

"Will be easily defeated." Corbin leered over Calix, smug in his own imagined brilliance. "You've walked right into our trap. Even now things are playing out as they should."

"Pride blinds you to the truth."

"You speaking of yourself?" Corbin chortled.

The words stung Calix harder than they should have. "Maybe . . ." His heart was throbbing. He could feel the blood draining from him with every beat. "But you've made a terrible mistake. When . . . Salbrin hears of this . . . he will . . ."

"Do nothing," Corbin finished for him. "Because he can't do anything. Not to Larom. You may have taken some towns and villages, but you'll never get the city."

Calix smiled through the pain. "You really think you've won."

"Of course."

"Then you . . . don't know . . . the power of Pyre . . . nor his people . . ." He could already imagine the revenge they'd extract upon this debauched and depraved people.

"Oh, but I think I do, Commander," said Corbin. "Keep to the plan," he told the others in the room. "Give the signal and take the rest. We'll have as many as we can alive, but if they're willing to die, we'll just celebrate with a larger feast." The soldiers and aproned men hurried from the room.

Turning back to Calix, Corbin continued his mocking discourse. "You see, Commander, I exploited your weakness and won."

"We have no weakness." Calix's hands were cold and he felt weaker by the moment, but he wasn't about to show Corbin or the others if he could help it.

"Your fanatic faith is your weakness. You're so careful to offer conversion—to save others from your fearful wrath—never imagining someone would take it and turn it against you. In a way, I suppose you could say you're a victim of your own beliefs and success."

"Well done." Astra was clearly delighted. "Things couldn't have gone any better."

"There's still some fighting to do." Corbin took his knife and fork and began slicing into the cut of meat on a platter across from him. Thankfully it was too butchered for Calix to get a clear sense of where on the unfortunate soul's body it may have come from. "But with their leadership gone, their confusion will be to our advantage."

The princeps retrieved a steaming chunk and offered it to Calix. He managed to spit a bloody wad onto it with what strength yet remained.

Corbin frowned. "Such manners. Yet another of your people's failings."

Calix felt his head fall to his chest. His thoughts were fuzzy and vision spent. Only his ears still worked, though his hearing was fading too with every ragged breath.

"Praise Laroma for her ever-increasing bounty and wisdom," he heard Corbin tell Astra.

"And her limitless favor and love," replied the priestess. "She truly is a goddess worthy of her people."

All Larom was quiet. Pillum didn't like it. He was used to the sound of camp life, where something was always going on. Here in this open and thinly populated city, the silence was more annoying than restful. Finally deciding he'd had enough of the courtyard, he started exploring the rest of the city. So far he'd seen a lot of empty buildings and not much else. He didn't know what Corbin had been so excited about showing Calix and the rest of their leadership. There wasn't anything useful anywhere.

The walls would help keep most threats at bay, but inside there was nothing worth taking. He could almost see Calix's face as he tried keeping up the diplomatic airs while his anger simmered at having his time wasted. Pillum was sure the others weren't that pleased with the tour either.

And yet in a way walking through the streets made Pillum homesick for Pyrus—for Marian, his betrothed. He'd been gone for so long he was starting to consider the open wilds of Annulis his home. He wouldn't be the first knight or soldier to think that way. Many who'd left on campaign were sure they'd never see Pyrus's walls again. It was their sacrifice for the higher good. And they'd be rewarded when the time came.

And yet it was the thought of Marian's dark eyes and flaxen hair that comforted Pillum in times of unrest and distress. His faith was his anchor, yes, but his love for Marian had been his hope of enjoying any remaining good in this world. And yet he knew he would cast it all aside if called upon by Pyre. He would give his last drop of blood to secure his god's will. No cost was too great to be paid. And Marian's belief and support of this only deepened his love for her.

He was just as surprised as Elliott when he'd mentioned Marian earlier. He hadn't planned to share such things with him until he was a little older and Pillum could talk with him as an equal. He was sure Elliott would find himself tempted at times by an attractive smile and alluring gaze from some fresh-faced woman. But he'd just blurted it out, upsetting any previous plans. He supposed it wasn't all that bad. If anything, it helped deepen their bond, made Pillum seem more human, more approachable. And that was what was needed when Elliott would take his oath and join the ranks of the Salamandrine officially as a knight.

And while it did cheer his heart at times, such as now, to think upon his beloved, Pillum knew it did little good to dwell on such things all the time. For he'd learned from others in the camp that the longer you let your focus and love turn from Pyre and the mission, the more you open yourself up to compromise and self-doubt, even a slackness of duty. And so as much as part of him would have liked to linger on thoughts of Marian's willowy frame, he cast such thoughts aside and settled himself in the here and now. The present which he would have to occupy in order to secure that brighter future Pyre had promised for all.

He supposed he'd have to start looking for a new squire before long. With Elliott's induction, Pillum would have to begin the process all over again. It was bittersweet, as he really had grown to like Elliott, but it wasn't like Elliott would be leaving his side, just that he'd have to take on the responsibility of training a new squire from the beginning. And who knows, there might even be some Laromic boy who could take that place. Today was teaching all of them nothing was too far outside the realm of possibility.

Pillum was making his way around the corner of another empty building when something caught his eye. He thought he saw some movement in the doorway of a building lining the street. Curious, he moved closer. When he did, two Laromic soldiers rushed out of the opening. Surprised but not immobilized, he pulled his sword and faced them. The first slashed wide, allowing Pillum a chance to sidestep the attack.

"What are you doing?" he asked his attacker. "You've sworn yourself to Pyre."

"Not me," the other replied, repositioning himself for another attack.

"And you?" Pillum asked the other Laromi, who was pacing like some cautious dog.

"I'm for Laroma." He found his courage, striking with a strong lunge Pillum was barely able to parry. "We all are," he continued.

Before Pillum could inquire further, about twenty Laromi streamed out of the same building where the first two had been hiding. Each of them held one of their blade-spinning shields.

He didn't have much time to act. Either run or fight. He couldn't do both. The odds were against him, but that wasn't the crux of his thinking. If there were this many hiding about the city willing to attack any Pyri who crossed their path, there could be more. The rest of the army should be warned.

"Sir Pillum!" The shout came from another knight galloping toward him on horseback. With him were a handful of infantry. Pillum recognized him as Sir Lane, a well-seasoned warrior with a steady and strong sword arm.

Suddenly, the odds looked more in his favor.

Pillum turned and took out the Laromi nearest him with a strong jab clean through the neck. A quick jerk freed the blade and cleared a path for another Laromi.

A swift turn of his weapon, and Pillum lopped off the other's sword hand.

The man screamed and dropped to his knees, clutching the bleeding wrist. Pillum's fellow knight was upon the rest, slashing and bringing his horse's hooves down upon them.

The rest of the Laromi did the best they could with their shields, but the infantry slowed any momentum they might have had. After a couple more Laromi fell, their boldness fled along with them.

"Let them go," said Lane just as Pillum was about to dash off after them.

"And have them free to harass others?"

"They aren't the only ones. They're springing up all over the city."

"What? How many?" Pillum wasn't sure he'd heard that right. The whole city in revolt? What was going on?

Lane was grave. "If they stick just to the city and our own men, then we're outnumbered."

"Then we need to get to the camp and—" The sound of shouts and battle stopped Pillum in midthought.

"It looks like they've sprung their trap." Lane pointed out the fresh column of black smoke rising from the direction of the courtyard.

"Smart." Pillum thought aloud. "They take our senior leadership and unleash a surprise attack. Our discipline will hold, though."

"But not forever," said Lane.

"We need to find Calix and—"

"There's no time, and where would we look? This city is empty and huge."

"You said there were other places the Laromi had attacked you from?" The beginning of a plan was forming.

"We were on patrol near the dungeons when they first attacked."

"They have dungeons here?" Pillum supposed it wasn't out of the question. He just hadn't been used to seeing the people they'd encountered actually using them. So much of the cities and towns had been nearly deserted ruins that not even the most basic buildings remained in use.

"They have a pretty extensive run of them not too far from here," Lane continued. "I don't think they wanted us to find them when we did. There must have been close to fifty hiding in them. Our patrol must have prompted their attack."

"That *is* pretty extensive." Pillum imagined how many more soldiers could be lurking just about anywhere in the city. Perhaps those thousand who bent the knee to Pyre were just a ruse. What if there were twice that number about and armed? Three times as many?

"They could have gotten more in there, too, if they weren't being used," one of the infantry informed them.

"They're being used?" This further piqued Pillum's interest.

"The cells had prisoners inside," explained Lane.

"Who?"

"They looked like Sojourners," said another soldier.

"Sojourners, really?" Pillum hadn't been expecting to see too many of those in this campaign. From what he'd heard, they'd just about vanished from Annulis.

"Must have fallen for one of the Laromi's traps," the same soldier continued.

"But that wasn't all." Lane's face was grim. "After the Laromi fled rather than fight, we searched through the dungeons and came across something even more treacherous. They're eating people."

"*What?*" Pillum nearly shouted.

"There was this room like a kitchen with a hearth and butchering tools and . . ." Lane paused, obviously working hard to maintain his composure. "They were cutting up human bodies and cooking them."

"Corbin's feast . . ." Pillum didn't dare speak anything more. Everyone already knew what he was thinking. "We have to assume Commander Calix and the others are not going to be coming back."

"So what do we do?" asked another of the infantry.

"We need to strengthen our numbers and turn the tide," said Pillum, thinking. "Have you found any more patrols on your way here?"

"Some," said Lane. "We sent them on to warn others and take out whatever Laromi might arise."

"And how many Sojourners did you say were in those dungeons again?" An idea was starting to come together. If they hurried, it might even stand a chance of succeeding.

"We didn't look in every cell, but there could be close to fifty or sixty."

"Not enough to do much of anything but cause some chaos." Pillum's musings raised Lane's eyebrow.

"You going to tell me what you're thinking?"

Tiny falling rocks began bouncing off Pillum's and Lane's armor. Above them, Pillum could see the sky was filled with blazing pebbles.

"How far away are those dungeons?"

CHAPTER NINETEEN

A Treacherous Trap. A Curious Liberator.

E lliott was outside in the camp when he first smelled the smoke and heard the yelling. "What's going on?" He, like the rest, stared at Larom's walls with growing wonder.

"Do you think they toppled the statue?" asked Ryan, another of the squires, in obvious enthusiasm.

"They would have called for us if—"

"Look. There." One of the infantry pointed out the fresh collection of Laromi on the walls. Armored and armed Laromi. Elliott barely had enough time to register the sight as the gates opened and out spilled still more Laromic warriors thirsty for blood.

"Get the horses and sound the alarm," said Sir Mitchell, a nearby knight. "Mount up and defend the camp. You too, Elliott," he added. "With Sir Pillum and the others still inside, we need you and everyone who can fight among our ranks." Elliott nodded grimly and went for his horse, praying he could don his armor before the men had neared the camp.

He was so focused on getting ready for battle Elliott almost missed the small pebbles falling to the ground like hail. After a few had rapped his head, he finally lifted his gaze. The early evening sky was clear but streaked with lines of light and fire. It reminded him of what he'd seen the previous night. Only these streaks weren't flashing and fading. They were increasing in both frequency and duration. But pebbles weren't much of a nuisance, and while the sky wasn't the most inviting, he still had a duty. He resumed his run for the pavilion and his armor.

"Archers, take out as many as you can," arose a new order.

With Calix and the officers in the city, it fell to the next-ranking members to coordinate the camp's defense. Elliott barely registered the twang of arrows flying overhead. Finally at Sir Pillum's pavilion, he laid hold of his makeshift armor. Carefully but quickly he managed to slide the shirt over his head, making any needed adjustments. A few moments later he was as ready as he'd ever be. Sword and shield in hand, he dashed back into the chaos, eager for his horse.

It was harder to ignore the pebbles with his helmet on. As he raced, he had to focus to keep from getting distracted by the constant tapping on the metal. The shape of the helmet only helped amplify the thumping, making it harder to hear the shouts and commands of his acting superiors. Finally, he was in sight of the horses and the other knights hurriedly mounting them. Leaping onto his new steed, he pulled on the reins and joined in with the rest of the Salamandrine.

"Ride. For Pyre and glory."

"Pyre and glory." He joined the rest in the refrain. And for a moment he actually thought he was a real knight. A real knight charging headlong into a very real battle.

The hooves thundered as the distance to their foes shrank. Instantly, he was among them. And just as instantly the knot in his gut returned at the sight of their grim shields in action. Their spinning blades passed his waist and chest more than once. If not for his fast dodging, they would have come much too close for his liking. A few more attempts were shoved back by his shield. He thanked Pyre for his favor and sought entry for his sword among the press.

He punched through a few times and even scored a cut but nothing substantial. If only Sir Pillum were here. He would have cut through this mess in short order. He wondered how he and the others were faring behind the walls. It was clear they were betrayed, but how soon had they known, and how devious was that deception? Did they have enough advance warning to hold their ground and defeat their enemies or . . .

Another sword strike rattled Elliott's shield, returning him to the present. As the streams of sweat traced down his back, he finally made his first instant kill. The Laromi was chopped at the neck and shoulder and knocked down to the ground.

Being mounted had its advantages.

From the glimpses his helmet afforded, the infantry were doing well too. They had taken some ground and were making progress in knocking the Laromi from the walls with more arrow fire. But the Laromi weren't letting up with their crossbows any time soon.

"Regroup for a charge." Elliott heard the command bellowed from amid the battle.

He had never charged before, but there was nothing for it. Disengaging, he joined the other knights at the camp, where they were assembling their formation. "We press hard and keep going all the way to the gates. The infantry will keep our backs."

Elliott found a place among them toward the middle. It made the most sense given his weaker armor and lack of experience. This way the momentum of the others would carry him forward and compensate for any defects in his approach.

"Now!" The one leading them raced forward.

Once more the earth thundered, and once more Elliott found himself racing for the enemy. The formation held, hindering him from doing anything but keeping his horse in pace with the others. Those on the outside and front swung and cleaved with their swords. There was no rhyme or reason, just the intention of doing as much damage as possible to as many Laromi as possible. It was also needed to clear the way. The horses helped some, but a sword swing into your enemy's face was rather hard to successfully protest.

Together they steadily advanced, trampling, slashing, and even kicking down those who tried standing in their way. The gates hadn't been closed after the Laromi's charge, tempting Elliott with hope of easy access.

A few crossbow bolts scored hits on an exposed horse or fellow knight, but for the most part, between their shields and their own infantry's arrows, much of the assault was hindered. But there was another threat.

The pebbles were now joined by larger chunks of flaming rocks, these falling intermittently and mixing with the pebbles. Some were even large enough to cause some pain. He witnessed a couple knocking some Laromi to the ground and bloodying another. His thoughts immediately went to the horses. They were much more exposed to the threat. And right now they were all that gave the Salamandrine an edge in the fight.

"Shields high!" Elliott reacted without thinking, bringing his shield up above himself just as another volley of crossbow bolts fell.

They had to funnel their numbers into a straight line of two abreast so they could get through the gates. This slowed things and removed Elliott from the safety of his previous position. The change gave those on the ramparts time to send more bolts Elliott's way while some eager Laromi brought their swords into action. Thankfully, there were only a few of them, and the Salamandrine were continuously moving forward.

Carried in their wake, with the help of a few strong strikes of his own, Elliott was in line and racing through the gates without a second thought. He wasn't sure what he might have found behind the walls, but nothing could have prepared him for what greeted him.

The clash of arms he expected, but not such a swarming force as was on display in the courtyard. This wasn't the meager group he'd first seen when they'd entered the city. Obviously, they'd lied and kept their forces in hiding until their plan was ready. He didn't see Calix or Drenn or the other officers anywhere, but there was a great deal of chaos about, and it was hard to catch direct sight of just about anyone. Not to mention most of the knights inside were on foot, forced to wade through the melee like everyone else.

Orders were bellowed, but there wasn't much that could be done. Elliott was part of the press and had to find a way to make his way through it. There was no room to maneuver in such a mess of bodies—both living and dead—and the horses were already hard enough to control in close quarters.

Thankfully, the pebbles had stopped, but in their place fell more of the larger rocks. Some of them flew harder and faster than others, shattering into the walls with enough force to knock out chunks of stone. Others struck down anything crossing their path. Some victims were Laromi, but others were Pyric infantry. A handful of Salamandrine suffered dents in their armor, but Elliott couldn't see too many taking greater damage amid the wild melee.

"Cut them down!" came another command. "Press them back and keep the line."

Some well-placed sword strikes vanquished more Laromi, creating a path deeper into the courtyard. The enemy, while superior in numbers, was still distracted enough for Elliott to pass through mostly unmolested.

He pushed in deeper, mindful of his horse and the crowd of bodies around him making it harder to move the longer he fought. But if he was going to hold the line, this was about as good a place as any. The others with him seemed in agreement. Each planted themselves in their new position and worked on clearing out the enemy so they could secure some locations for the infantry.

As he kept his sword swinging and blocking repeated attacks, Elliott kept one eye on the rest of the battle, mindful of any new threat. The Laromi didn't appear to be fielding more men, but they weren't falling down so easily either. In fact, too many knights littered the courtyard; more than a dozen horses were riderless. Still, it appeared they had the upper hand . . . for now. But there was no sign of Sir Pillum. Elliott prayed wherever he was, he was all right and able to defend himself from whatever he might be facing.

"Here it is," said Lane, bringing his horse to a stop before a squat stone building. It didn't look like much from the outside, but it did look secure.

The rocks kept falling, actually picking up in intensity and size since Pillum started running after Lane. And surprisingly he'd made good time, keeping up with the horse better than he might have thought given the current ordeal.

"And they came from inside?" Pillum moved closer, cautiously observing the area. The size of their group had grown. They'd been able to find handfuls of other Pyri eager to unite amid the growing chaos. They now had another knight and about ten more soldiers in their party.

"All of them," Lane repeated.

Pillum drew his sword. "Let's take a look." Lane and Sir Janis, the other knight, dismounted, joining the rest of the infantry behind Pillum. "Take the horses too. They need some shelter as much as we do." He moved for the thick door in the center of the windowless stone wall.

It was slightly ajar.

"There shouldn't be anyone left inside—apart from those in the cells," said Lane.

"Just being sure." Pillum prodded the door open with the tip of his sword.

He cautiously made his way forward. There was nothing inside but a set of low-burning torches affixed to the walls. By the dim light he spied another door. This one was reinforced with iron patches on the bottom, top, and side where the hinges joined the walls. It too was open, more than the previous door had been.

"What's the smell?" Janis scowled as he entered the room, leading his horse behind him.

"You don't want to know." Sir Lane kept his horse in tow. Surprisingly the ceilings were tall enough to allow for the beasts, which was to their fortune, as none really felt confident leaving their horses unmanned during such a time of upheaval.

"Why don't you lead the way," Pillum offered Sir Lane. "It'll be faster."

Lane left his horse with Janis and led them to the next door and the hallway behind. It descended into the depths of what must be the dungeons. Pillum counted more than six dead Laromi along the way.

"We ran into a little resistance the last time," explained Lane, noticing the other's interest in the bodies.

"Tough fight?" asked Janis.

"Not really." After the hallway came a circular room.

"Where are the cells?" Pillum remained alert. His legs felt like they were coiled springs set to release at any moment.

"Behind that door," Lane answered, pointing, before leading them into the winding corridor beyond. The smell was much stronger down here. It was a terrible thing Pillum couldn't remove from his nostrils or throat. And the further they went, the worse it got.

"Over here." Lane motioned to a nearby cell door.

Pillum looked through the tiny window cut into the old wood. There were three middle-aged men inside. Their strange beards, cowled heads, and common dress told him all he needed to know.

"They're definitely Sojourners," he said, moving back to his fellow knights. While he hadn't seen any himself in his life, he'd been instructed enough in his training to know them upon first sight.

"So what's your plan?" Lane crossed his arms, awaiting Pillum's answer.

"We use the Sojourners as a distraction. We set them free and herd them into the fighting. With the added confusion, we might be able to turn the tide."

"It might work." Janis was open to the idea. "But they're such a small number. Do you really think it would be worth it?"

"It's the best we have," Pillum countered. "And I'd rather have them die than more Pyri."

"There is a truth to that." Janis nodded.

"So can you break down these doors?"

Two infantrymen went into action, chopping away at the wood. "We're going to need more Pyri too," he told Lane and Janis. "Take your horses and see how many you can round up." Both departed at once, no doubt happy to be free from the dark tunnels and overpowering stench.

Pillum joined some others on a new door, hacking away with as much strength as he had. They didn't have the luxury of time. The longer they took, the more of an advantage the Laromi could exploit.

After a couple of cells were breached, they found their rhythm and the right method for breaking the doors. The process sped up, and things were moving along nicely when Janis and Lane returned with more men: six soldiers.

"This is all we could find." Janis sounded slightly disheartened with their results, but Pillum wasn't about to hold anything against him.

"It will do for now," said Pillum before pointing out the work still before them. "Two to a door. Follow the pattern, and you'll take them down quickly." The newly arrived rushed to some cell doors and started their work.

They'd taken the Sojourners they'd freed and grouped them at the front of the hallway, keeping them under guard. None of them said a word, only watched with careful, fearful eyes. So far they'd found some men and women and were getting ready to free some children.

"You going to wait until all of them are freed before you move?" Janis studied the clump of Sojourners with a curious eye.

"We don't have time," said Pillum. "We'll start with this group and then send them in a stream after that. It's going to be the most effective when we first release them."

A door shattered, followed by another. All watched the small children stream out of their cells and join the other Sojourners, who were more than happy to receive them.

"A few more doors should do it." Soon three more were broken, and a handful of older men and women emerged. "This will be good. Send the others after me," Pillum said, motioning to a few soldiers. "With me. You too, Janis." Turning to the Sojourners, he said, "If you want to live, you're going to have to run."

Pillum watched their eyes widen.

"Well?" No one did anything, merely stood in place. "Get going." The soldiers started waving their swords and prodding them toward the exit. "Run for the courtyard. If you can make it through, you're free to go."

"And if we do not?" asked one of the older Sojourners.

He ignored him, lifting his sword and rallying the fellow Pyri with him. "Run!" They all charged at top speed, driving the Sojourners before them.

Outside the rocks were still falling. Only now they were even larger. This could work in their favor too. It reminded him of those locusts, in that there was no way they could bend the situation to their will. The sounds of battle increased as they all neared the courtyard.

"Go and hurry the others along," Pillum told Janis. "We can take it from here." The other knight nodded and turned his horse around, galloping back the way he'd come.

"Keep going!" he shouted back at the remaining men before stopping entirely after catching sight of something he didn't want to believe.

The battle beyond was forgotten; his gaze couldn't leave what was just a few yards from him. At the back of the courtyard stood Corbin and a line of Laromic pikemen. On top of each pike was a freshly severed head. A freshly severed *Pyric* head.

His eyes only fell on two of those heads before a rage rose in his gut. Corbin was saying something, but it was lost on him. The blood was pounding in his ears. Pillum rushed full speed at the princeps before he even knew what was happening.

"Again!" A priest shouted above the fray.

Elliott still had no idea where Milec was in this mess. He imagined the priest had joined his brothers in setting fires with their blaze rods. Some of the flames had been put out, but others remained, consuming more of the city. Elliott heard the sound of another rush of flames but didn't have time to look back. His eyes were set on the threats assailing him from all sides.

The Laromi had renewed their efforts, and Elliott was suffering for it. His arms were sore, and he was drenched in sweat. A few more hits on his shield, and he didn't know if he'd be able to keep it aloft any longer.

Worse still, the flaming rocks hadn't ceased, only increased. And not just in frequency but also in size. Some were as big as fists. Those struck by these died an instant, messy death. And there was one the size of a head that hit the walls, shattering a hole wide enough to ride a horse through.

"It's the Great Conflagration!" a half-crazed priest shouted while scanning the carnage with eyes that didn't really see what was transpiring about him. "It's come at last, and we are not ready." He dropped to his knees, casting aside his blaze rod in his frantic panic. "Forgive us, Pyre. We have—"

A fist-sized rock struck him on the head, stopping his petition in a spray of blood and brains.

Elliott didn't have time to register much of it. He was lost in his own world, battling for his life. Once more a Laromi slashed at his legs. Once more he blocked the attack. Thankfully, his horse was still holding. There were a few wounds here and there, but they weren't deep, only glancing at most. He didn't know how much longer his luck would hold and didn't have any desire to push things to their limit, but there was little else to be done.

He brought his sword down with all his might, cutting into the shoulder and neck area of his attacker. The warrior retreated with a yelp of pain.

The other Laromi continued their efforts, holding back nothing. In the time since the Salamandrine rushed the city, a new boldness had washed over the enemy. Elliott didn't like it one bit. He couldn't imagine how Sir Pillum kept up as he did in these battles. Training could only get you so far; it was clear something else was needed.

A sound of trumpets stilled the fighting. Each side scanned the courtyard, eager for a sense of what was happening.

"Is that ours?" asked a nearby Pyric soldier.

"No." Elliott shook his head. It was clear from how the Laromi were reacting they didn't know what was going on either.

"Warriors of Pyre." Corbin's voice rang out across the courtyard. "Behold your leaders."

Elliott couldn't believe his eyes. A group of Laromic pikemen had fanned out behind the Laromic line. They had arrived from somewhere deeper in the city, no doubt from where Calix and the others had been invited to join in the feast.

Each pikeman proudly displayed a head at the top of his pole arm. He could see Calix's head clearly from his position. The other officers of the army were also there. Drenn's head was the easiest to spot thanks to his bright red hair. He even found Milec's head among them. Thankfully, Sir Pillum's was missing from their number. He breathed a little easier, but that didn't help with the fact their leaders had been killed.

Though the armies might have stopped, the rocks did not. More Laromi and infantry were taken from the fight and more holes in the walls and ground materialized with booming crashes. But it wasn't enough to wipe the gloating sneer from Corbin's face nor quell the rage boiling in the Pyric ranks.

"Infidels!" A shout erupted from beside Elliott.

"Kill them all!" came another. "They've proved themselves unworthy of Pyre's mercy." And with that, the battle was renewed.

"You ready to join them, boy?" asked a snarling Laromi on Elliott's left.

He dealt the man a swift kick in the mouth. To Elliott's surprise, there was still enough strength in him to send the Laromi to the ground.

A new commotion drew his attention back to Corbin and his pikemen. Behind them were what appeared to be a rush of people breaking up their line. But these people weren't Laromi or Pyri. Men, women, and children dressed like simple villagers ran like mad through whatever opening they could find. The result was confusion and disarray in the Laromic line.

"Stop them!" Corbin ordered. "And secure the dungeons. We—"

He was interrupted by Sir Pillum's sword running him through. With him were a few other knights, who hacked into the pikemen.

Elliott's heart leapt in his chest.

His master was alive!

Sir Pillum was giving orders, but Elliott couldn't hear them. Whatever Pillum might have been saying and planning, Elliott knew he needed a horse. Kicking his own in the sides, he made for the knight, slashing left and right with renewed strength.

Some of the men fled before the wild charge, but others dared defy him. These were met with a flurry of steel and the pointed corners of his shield. He was beginning to see why his master enjoyed using the tactic so much.

He didn't look back to see how each of his victims fared. His eyes were set on Sir Pillum. A few breaths later, he was close enough to hear his voice.

"We keep the pressure here," he was telling all within earshot. "The prisoners will give us an edge, but we can't take it for granted. Get a horse and take down whomever you can."

"Sir Pillum!"

The knight looked Elliott's way. "Elliott?"

"Here! Take my horse, sir."

"You stay on—I'll ride behind until we find a free one." Sir Pillum climbed up behind Elliott and his saddle. "You holding up?"

"Better than I expected, sir."

"Then you have to learn to expect more of yourself."

Elliott couldn't suppress his grin. "Yes, sir."

"Now, get me to a horse so we can finish putting this city to the torch."

CHAPTER TWENTY

Chaos on Every Front.

S arah stared at what remained of the cell door, unable to move. She, Malena, Tabitha, and Sophie had huddled together when the first sword struck the wood. Why they were hacking through the door was beyond any of them. If their captors wanted to get in, they had the key. It wasn't until the door finally splintered and was torn away that she realized the reason: those on the other side didn't have a key.

The first face that had poked through the new opening wasn't Laromic. He was dressed in armor but not the kind she had seen before on the Marauders.

"Who are they?" Malena could barely whisper loud enough for Sarah to hear.

She couldn't bring herself to respond. There wasn't anything she could say anyway. She didn't have any answers. And that was perhaps the most terrifying part of all of this. There was some clamor outside in the hallway, but most of what was going on was out of sight. Though from what she could hear, it was quite destructive.

"What do they want?" asked Tabitha.

"I do not know." Sarah finally found her voice, small as it was.

There was nothing any of them could do but back further away from the opening, hoping perhaps this stranger would somehow miss them in the cell's shadows.

"Get out!" the armored man in the doorway shouted.

None of them moved, which only provoked him. "You want to get out of this with your life?" he asked.

"Y-yes," Sarah stammered.

"Then run!" Each of the girls looked at the others, seeking further answers.

"Now!" The shout sent them on a mad race for the hall. "Keep to the left." The advice followed them down the hallway.

As they ran, Sarah saw other cells had been opened—just about all of them. She was hopeful they'd spot some familiar faces in passing, but each of the cells was empty.

"Don't stop." Some of the same men were following at their heels. "Keep it going!"

"Where are the others?" she finally managed to ask as they moved around a corner. The hall was relatively empty apart from some slumped bodies. None of them were Sojourners—all Laromi.

"Probably in the courtyard by now."

Sarah slowed as they neared one of the bodies. She couldn't help it. It was almost instinctual. She needed to take a closer look. The man was clearly killed in some sort of conflict. There was blood across the armor on his chest. His mouth was agape and eyes wide open, glaring back at her, empty.

"Don't stop," said one of the men from behind, shoving her forward. She noticed an older man watching them as they passed. His armor was made of metal plates covering most of his body.

"This the last of them?" he asked the men behind Sarah and her friends.

"Almost," came the reply from one of the men. "Just five more cells left."

"We can manage," said the older man. "Go with these and see where you can help shore things up."

The words made little sense to Sarah, who was focused on just keeping her feet moving in tandem with each other and not falling face first onto the cold stone. The others with her were doing the same. Even Sophie was managing well, the former unease and nausea quickly forgotten.

They eventually made their way outside. It was night, but the sky was ablaze with what she thought were falling stars—until one struck a nearby building and knocked a hole in it.

"What is happening?" Sophie's fear had returned.

"I do not know," said Sarah, sharing some of the same unease.

"Come on," said one of the men behind them, shoving them into a group of others from the congregation. Sarah counted ten in all, these mostly younger men and women. All appeared well, from what she could see. A small blessing amid everything else.

"You get to the courtyard and just keep running," another armored man instructed them. "Don't let anything stop you. You get free, you get to live."

"Why are you doing this?" Malena dared to ask.

"For the glory of Pyre," he replied. "Now run!"

"Cut them down," Sir Pillum ordered.

With his master once again on a horse, all seemed right with the world. Elliott was beside him, his own horse still strong. He was doing his best at keeping up the fight, even though he was beyond sore and near exhaustion.

The tide was turning.

Assailed by swords and the never-ending flaming rocks, the Laromi were being pushed back into the advancing infantry. The remaining priests were making their own progress with their blaze rods. Soon enough they'd be able to put the whole city to the ash heap and finally be done with it.

Elliott took a swing, and another Laromi retreated a few paces. "We almost have them," he told Sir Pillum.

"Not yet, but Pyre is with us." He moved ahead, seeking more room to maneuver. When he did, Elliott noticed those around him staring up with fearful faces. Curious, he joined their gaze.

"Sir Pillum . . ." He wasn't sure if his master could even hear him; his voice was trembling.

"What is—"

He stopped when he viewed the scene that was slowing the battle across the courtyard. The rocks had grown in size. The small pebbles and fist-sized stones were gone. Now the sky was filled with head-sized ones.

And there were many of them . . .

"It's the Great Conflagration!" shouted one of the knights.

Elliott was thinking the same thing. How could it not be? That frantic priest had been right. The end of all things was close; he just never knew how close. And had they really failed like that same priest had said? Or were they in the final battle before the end, as some said would happen before Pyre's return?

"What do we do?" Elliott could barely get the words out of his mouth.

"Make for the gates!" Sir Pillum shouted.

Laromi and Pyri alike took the advice, instantly shifting their focus from killing each other to running for their lives. But not all followed the action. More than a handful of priests dropped to their knees in humble submission.

"We welcome your judgment, mighty Pyre!" Elliott heard one of them praying as he galloped past. He wished he could summon the same faith but wasn't able to do anything but keep himself galloping—trampling any Laromi unable to outrun his frightened steed.

The rocks pounded into the walls, streets, and people. This was instantly followed by the wails and screams of the dying mingled with explosions of toppled wall and shattered stone. He nearly avoided one that crashed to his front left. The impact shook the earth as he raced past. The flaming debris brushed his cheek and the horse's side. His mount snorted in protest but kept pushing through. It seemed self-preservation was working well for both horse and rider.

"Keep riding!" Sir Pillum shouted from somewhere on Elliott's right. He didn't dare to check where, keeping his eyes locked front and center.

The closer Sarah and the others of the congregation got to the courtyard, the more chaos they encountered. There were dead bodies everywhere.

Some were Laromi. Some were these new people who had set them free and were hurrying them toward the courtyard.

The fallen horses were the strangest sight. She hadn't seen a horse in quite a while. Seeing them crumpled on the ground with blood pooling under them only heightened her sadness.

The flaming rocks kept coming, striking indiscriminately and powerfully all unlucky enough to cross their path. It was as if she were reliving the Burning Cascade.

"There it is," said one of the men prodding them along. "You're on your own now." He joined the others in pushing their way into the wild fray.

"Sarah." Tabitha gave her hand a strong tug. "We need to get out of here."

Not wasting a breath, Sarah and the others raced for what they assumed were the gates. The night had grown thick, cloaking in darkness anything that wasn't lit by the small fires spreading throughout the courtyard. It didn't take long for everyone to separate. Only Tabitha, Sophie, Malena, and herself remained together. They weaved through the fallen, maneuvering around the swords and combat, making sure they didn't take a sword in the gut themselves.

"Sarah, look out!" Tabitha's warning came just in time. A Laromic soldier would have taken off her arm at the shoulder. Instead, she was able to turn and avoid it.

Tabitha didn't share the same fortune.

Another Laromic blade thrust into her chest and rammed clear through her body.

"Tabitha!" Sarah screamed.

Her friend stared down at the wound, seemingly unable to process its presence. Sarah ran to her as she fell, holding her aloft as the Laromic soldier was himself run through by one of the other armored men they'd been fighting.

"Let me go," Tabitha urged. "There is nothing that can be done."

"No. We can find someone. They can bind the wound."

"You cannot bind *this* wound, Sarah. I am done with Annulis. I just wish I could have found the Veiled City before . . ." She collapsed into Sarah's arms, lifeless.

"I am sorry, Sarah." Malena remained at her side, face wet with fresh tears. Sophie was ashen, frozen in horror. "But she is right. There is nothing we can do. We must get out of here."

"Tabitha?" Sarah's voice was as weak as she felt.

Her friend said nothing more.

Sarah wept.

"Help me," she pleaded.

Malena froze. "I-I cannot. I am sorry, Sarah." Still crying, she dashed into the churning press swelling at the gates.

"Sophie, come and take an arm," she said, motioning for Sophie to help carry Tabitha. Instead, Sophie's gaze grew distant as she slowly shook her head. The haunting expression on what had once been such a kind and lovely face chilled her to the bones.

"We are all going to die," Sarah could hear her mutter. "We are all going to die." The words were louder this time.

Sarah watched fear consume her. Her face twisted into a horrible mask of terror before she wildly darted off. Sarah could only watch her go, helpless to do anything else.

Another burst of falling rocks struck, killing some more people and damaging more of the walls and buildings. If she didn't keep moving, she could very well be their next victim.

Shaking with fresh sorrow and tears, she took hold of Tabitha's body with both hands and pulled. Grunting and sobbing, she dragged the body through the bloody bedlam. Thanks to the fresh chaos birthed from the raining rocks, she was able to make her way without incident. She was thankful for that. Truly, even now, the Sovereign must have been watching over her. But it was still far from easy, and there were plenty of obstacles she had to work Tabitha's body through as effectively and respectfully as possible.

It felt like forever, but eventually Sarah reached the gates. But that wasn't the end of her trials: the people would not let her pass. Each was maddeningly pushing their way through in hopes of getting out and free of what was becoming a tomb. She had dragged Tabitha's body as long as she could, but her arms and shoulders were already burning. She wasn't sure if she could go any further, much less get through the crowd.

Escape was looking impossible. She prayed for the Sovereign's mercy and hoped for the best. But from how things appeared, this wasn't going to end well for anyone—whether Sojourner or Dweller.

"Out of the way." A panicked Laromi shoved her aside.

She watched him get close to the gates before a flaming rock struck him in the neck, killing him. Even so, with such a death so close to them, the people didn't care. Some continued fighting each other for passage; others simply tried worming through the mob, focused only on the freedom they apparently thought was just a few feet away.

Sarah turned and saw a set of horses gallop nearly right on top of her and Tabitha. She was barely able to dodge the hooves and yank Tabitha's body out of range before they sped past. While jarring and frustrating, the event did have a silver lining. It opened a swath she could exploit. Taking hold of her friend, she found a reserve of strength and headed toward it.

"Make way!" she heard an armored man on one of the horses shout into the fray. It did little good. The people weren't going anywhere if they could help it—other than outside of the city.

"Make way!" Sir Pillum shouted at the mass around the gates.

Laromi and Pyri alike were pushing through them all at once, hindering anyone from getting through. More rocks fell around them, reducing a small portion of their number, but it did little good. Those that fell were overcome by others, who scrambled over their cooling bodies, and the problem was created anew. Enraged, Sir Pillum began cutting Laromi down. But this too did little to speed up the process, only clogging up more of the area with bodies.

A fresh wave of flaming rocks struck the city, this time making gaping holes in some buildings and causing enough damage for a whole section of the outer wall to fall. The debris landed outside the courtyard, allowing a fresh avenue of escape for the many who rushed for the new opening. Some of these were the escaped prisoners who joined the Laromi and Pyri, creating a new mass of bodies.

"Look!" A shout brought every face heavenward. Above them was a cluster of even larger rocks. These had to be twice the size of the previous head-sized ones.

Elliott's heart jumped into his throat. "What do we do?" His master was stone faced. "Sir Pillum?"

Everything slowed around him as Sir Pillum took in the scene.

"You need to get word to Pyrus and tell them what happened here." He spoke with the same graveness etched across his face. "There isn't enough time for anything else. I'll make a way for you."

The tears were flowing, stinging the corner of Elliott's eyes. "No, sir. We can both—"

"No. I'll make the way and you get word back to Pyrus. Salbrin and the Quorum need to know everything. No matter what, we have our orders and our mission. It needs to be completed. Now stay close. The opening won't remain clear for long." He gave his horse a kick and ran for the newly created hole in the walls.

"For Pyre and Salbrin!" Pillum rushed into the fray, clearing a path.

As ordered, Elliott followed at his heels.

Sir Pillum rode with a wild abandon Elliott had never seen before. Usually he was a wise warrior, knowing when to go on offense and when to back into defense. Now he was just attacking anything that moved. Some were felled and others retreated, allowing a break in the mass of people. Elliott slid through the opening and was through the walls and on the other side a moment later.

"Hurry, sir!" he shouted with all his strength. "You can still make it."

But no sooner had he spoken than it was overrun with Laromi and even some Pyric soldiers intent on living a while longer. He'd lost sight of Sir Pillum completely.

"Ride, Elliott!" He heard his master's shout. "Ride!"

Elliott forced his horse into top speed, never looking back. Not even when a tremor shook the earth, knocking him from his horse. This was followed by a great flash, lighting up the night.

And then everything went black.

Sarah stopped. Her arms weren't able to continue, and her back was sore beyond belief. She was in the mix of everything, dodging flaming rocks and angry people alike while protecting Tabitha's body as much as possible.

It was a losing battle.

"Tabitha," she said. "I am—"

"Look!" One of the armored men lifted his hand to the sky.

Scores followed his direction, Sarah among them.

At first she didn't believe what she saw. It was too impossible to comprehend, but yet it was there: a cluster of large flaming rocks was falling fast. And they were about to land right on top of them.

Cries and curses flooded the air. Fear thickened around her along with the new insane rush of people seeking an escape. She watched, horrified, as men literally tore into each other like wild dogs. Gone were any formalities of civilization. Now there was just a frenzied, hopeless madness.

Another large stone struck a section of the wall a few yards from the gate and shattered it, creating enough of an opening for people to pass. This new avenue wasn't wasted. Scores jostled for the fresh escape route—all heedless of the uneven section of wall remaining. The stone trembled, then an even larger section collapsed and buried the very ones rushing for it.

Sarah saw her chance.

"I am sorry," she told Tabitha, rising to her feet. "Please forgive me."

She ran for the now even larger opening, ignoring the thought that she was stepping over the bodies just beneath the rubble. She reached the opening and went through it but kept running. She knew that flaming cluster of rocks was coming ever closer.

Braving a look back, she watched a ball of flame descend into the city. She willed her legs faster.

She was huffing hard when the earth shook under her feet. An eyeblink later, a burst of force slammed into her, shoving her to the ground. There was some heat and a deafening clap that echoed between her ears, and then everything was silent, empty blackness.

CHAPTER TWENTY-ONE

A Grim Morning.

A brilliant light flooded Sarah's eyes as she forced her eyelids open. She couldn't see anything clearly because of the brightness. She rolled to her side and waited for her focus to return. It was clear from the light it wasn't evening anymore. It looked more like dawn. She'd lost a whole night, but the sky was clear. Not a flaming rock in sight. Feeling more herself, she slowly made it to her feet. She wasn't in any pain, only suffering a slight twinge of stiffness here and there. She took that as a good sign.

Apparently she was still in the same place she had fallen the night before. She didn't see anything or anyone moving about as she scanned the terrain. The road was empty, but there was a large group of brown and white tents a short walk away. She could make out some fluttering white banners among them. While some of the tents had been flattened by last night's rockfall and others had been burnt, the banners appeared unmolested. The red bird image on them was something new to her. It appeared as if made of fire. A strange sight, but it didn't help her at the moment.

Bodies were strewn across the open field and the camp. Most wore the same armor as the people who had freed her from the dungeons. But there were plenty of Laromi in the mix. All had either been killed by the enemy, pummeled by the rocks, or even both. The worst were the dead horses. Thankfully, there weren't too many.

No body moved.

No sound was made.

For once in her life Sarah had a taste of what it was like to be totally alone. She had never known anything like it, having had the congregation around her since birth. Without them, it was like she was living in another world.

But there was still hope. If she had survived, it stood to reason someone else had too. Turning from the camp, she studied the area leading up to the city. There were more bodies—both Laromi and the ones they were fighting—but she saw some brown cowls and cloaks among them too. Some of the congregation had escaped the walls but not their former captors' swords. But that was outside the city. There might be something better behind the walls.

And then she actually saw the city.

What remained of Larom was little more than ruins. The once-strong walls had been toppled in sections, exposing the broken buildings and still-smoldering mounds of dead and debris inside. The gates had been broken and burnt. Rubble of all sorts had been flung in all directions. Some stones even rested a few handbreadths from where she stood. If they had gone any farther, she might have been killed where she lay.

Once more she was thankful for the Sovereign's protection.

It was then the smell hit her. It was a heavy, smoky odor at first, but with it was the telltale stench that had permeated the dungeons. Thankfully the fresh holes and openings in the Laromic defenses allowed her a clearer view without having to draw so near the stench. Not that what she saw was much better.

The bodies had fallen at random; others had clumped together into gruesome mounds, these most common where people had been seeking escape. Some were burnt to the point of not even being recognizable as humans. Others had been felled by sword.

"Sovereign have mercy," she heard herself say.

It was all that could be said.

The destruction was greater than she could have imagined. The death toll even worse. While she didn't hold any fond feelings for her captors, she didn't delight in their deaths either. And certainly not in this sort of death—which she wouldn't have wished upon anyone. Yet even from her position it was clear there was more to search through, which meant she'd have to get into the bowels of the courtyard after all.

So much for staying clear of the stench.

She made her way through what remained of the city walls, carefully noting the bodies she passed. She saw far too many familiar faces, counting twenty or so members of the congregation who had died about a stone's throw from the gates. To be so close and yet still fail . . . Not that it would have been any better had they cleared the gates, given the fate of the others she'd seen earlier.

The hardest to bear were the children. Thankfully, there weren't many of them, but there were enough to stir up fresh grief. She did her best to avoid them, lest she find something too haunting for memory.

A moment later she caught sight of Tabitha's body. Surprisingly, she still lay where Sarah had left her the night before. For a moment she entertained the illusion Tabitha only rested. But the red stain on her blouse instantly dispelled such thoughts. Still, it had been a nice thought, and welcome. She stopped and brushed a few stray hairs off her dead friend's forehead, then moved on.

Nothing stirred.

No breathing.

No moans.

Nothing.

There were a few more faces she recognized, but more were Dwellers and the ones who had freed them from the dungeons. There was still no sign of her father, but she hadn't made it even halfway through the courtyard.

She spied a kerchief-clad head a few steps away. Curious, Sarah drew closer. The body was bent at a strange angle, hiding the person's face. Walking around the body, Sarah discovered it was Malena. Her eyes were still open, staring off into space. Her throat had been slit. The ruinous line across her neck marred her former beauty.

For everything she'd endured this last week, Sarah bore her no ill will. She might have envied her in some small degree, but she didn't hate her. She was part of the same congregation, a fellow sister on the journey. And now her journey was done. Bending down, she closed Malena's eyes, giving her at least some small kindness.

This done, she moved on, slowly making her way through the more tightly packed and partially buried and burned bodies. As she did, she took her time, searching the faces she could see and trying her best not to linger on the more destroyed ones when she could help it.

The smell of burnt flesh was even stronger but didn't turn her stomach as much as it might have. She'd become more tolerant of it during her time in the cell, though she could never imagine herself getting used to it.

She cautiously avoided the crater near the middle of the courtyard. About twice as wide as she was tall and slightly less than that in depth, it marked where the last large cluster of rocks must have fallen. Loose stone and earth still occasionally crumbled over the hole's lip, increasingly so as she skirted its jagged outline.

The impact was so great it had toppled the statue of Laroma. She'd fallen onto another group of unfortunate folks before getting pelted with still more flaming rocks. These had pummeled and crushed the statue quite heavily in places. Sarah supposed she could have taken that as an omen, but she didn't. There was far too much to process as it was, and she still hadn't reached the end of the courtyard.

The further she walked, the more challenging the maneuvering became. Not to mention the more grisly the bodies. There were more than a handful whom she couldn't identify as Dwellers or Sojourners. Pushing beyond, she happened upon the outline of another body from which she couldn't pull away.

The instant she spotted it, her heart stopped and lungs froze. She could only stand, unable to move. Suddenly, her legs gave out and she collapsed on her knees. Tears flowed like rivers as what strength she'd possessed drained from her body. And yet in that weakness she forced herself to crawl.

Finally, she came alongside the fallen figure. Gingerly, she lifted his crushed, bloody face. The chunk of rock resting beside his head made clear what had happened. Yet it didn't make it any easier.

"Father." She could barely get the words out of her mouth. There was hardly any breath. All of it was consumed with sobbing. Falling across his cold chest in her sorrow, she cried until the tears ceased flowing. She didn't know how long she lay there, only that at some point a sound returned her to her knees.

She caught sight of a young man to her left.

He appeared about her own age, with short brown hair and piercing green eyes. He was wearing the same sort of armor as the men who had freed her and the rest of the congregation from the dungeons. But that was last night. Things might be different now.

And then there was the sword in his hand and his hard stare. His face was unreadable, which didn't help either. Yet, unable to do anything else, she found herself staring right back.

APPENDICES

APPENDIX A

The Communal Hearth

This ritual is performed nightly by all Sojourners after making their camp. Once a central fire has been stoked, the leader of the congregation will begin the ritual, acting out key elements as needed and required for additional emphasis and reflection.

Leader: And what is our hope?

Congregation: The Veiled City.

Leader: So spoke the heralds, and so we have believed. For we know the truth. The Sovereign created Annulis to sit among the stars. And he placed upon it the city of Mundus and a steward to watch over it and teach the people the ways in which they should live.

And there was peace for a season.

Congregation: And there was peace for a season.

Leader: And from the mighty city arose stewards to tend to one hundred more, which sprang up across Annulis like great trees across the plains. Each had a steward descended from the first. And so the

Mundi spread across the world and stayed true to the Sovereign and his teachings.

Congregation: May it be so with us.

Leader: But in time the people looked to their own ways and thoughts, turning aside from that which they had known to be good and true for what they desired instead. And so there came strife, division, and unrest. City rose up against city. Each coveted the other, seeking enrichment and empowerment of themselves by diminishing others. But one cannot make his candle burn brighter by snuffing out another's. And while there were some who sought to hold back and still the divisions and discord, what had been released would not be contained. Rebellion had taken root and was now affixed firmly in the hearts of many.

Congregation: Sovereign watch over those who yet remain true.

Leader: Each of the cities tore into the other, raising up a new goddess to guide their way. In their pride and delusion they cast away the truth, holding to a lie with all their strength.

Congregation: Sovereign watch over those who yet remain true.

Leader: Even in Mundus they could not hide how far they had fallen. Though they still pretended their love for the Sovereign was as it was in the days of old, it was not. For the stewards were no more in the city, instead following after Maraud's example, becoming emperors instead.

But then came the heralds.

Blessed be the heralds and the one who sent them.

Congregation: Blessed indeed.

Leader: To all who would listen, they delivered their message faithfully. They condemned the cities and towns, the villages and people, for having fallen away from the Sovereign and the ways he imparted through his first steward. They spoke against the goddesses and strife, and condemned the emperors as nothing more than petty tyrants, having lost their place and right as steward long ago. But they also spoke of a war. A terrible war that was looming on the horizon.

Congregation: Let he who has ears hear.

Leader: For those who would be kept safe from the dark times and free from the corruption of the rebellious should seek out the Veiled City, whose builder is the Sovereign himself. The first city built before all others.

Congregation: Let he who has ears hear.

Leader: Those who heeded the heralds began their sojourn, as do we who follow in their footsteps. And those who stayed behind dwelled in their old lives, as they still do today. And though the others mocked the ones who first set out, their days grew darker and the terrible war came upon them. But those who sojourned were kept safe.

When peace returned to Annulis, the Dwellers thought the worst had passed, but those who held to the heralds' message knew better. For while all were welcoming peace and brighter days, there arose sudden and terrible destruction.

Fire rained upon the world.

It fell upon all Annulis in a burning cascade. The cities that remained were toppled, and great Mundus—that would-be empire of Annulis—was crushed into dust and ash and given the sea as a shroud.

Congregation: Let he who has eyes see.

Leader: For three whole days the fire fell. And on the fourth day there was darkness, which lasted a year.

Congregation: The Year of Night.

Leader: But that was not the end. For whenever it would rain, blood fell from the skies and added to the land's woe. Crops failed, people perished, and animals died. But we Sojourners were kept safe as the Dwellers continued to suffer. Even after the sun once more dared shine and the rains continued their days of blood.

Congregation: But the Veiled City still stands.

Leader: And it is the only hope for all who wish to escape from this wounded, dying world. For what the heralds have spoken shall come to pass. There is only it and nothing else. Everything has proven false and will soon fade away, but to those who find the Veiled City, peace and life are their reward.

Should I not find the city before my years grow full, recall all I have spoken this night. Pass it on to others who have taken the journey with you. Keep the truth before you and let it guide you onward.

Congregation: We shall.

APPENDIX B

Selection

The faithful of Pyre seek to share the truth of their god to all those on Annulis. Those hostile to the message are believed to have proven themselves enemies of both the god and the mercy he is said to be extending to those who embrace it.

Selection is the process by which the Pyri learn who is with them and Pyre and who is against. Conducted by priests and a selected member of the Salamandrine, it is put before every group a Pyric army comes across. The idea is that each has free will to select their fate and choose the course of action the army is to enact based upon that selection.

Those that embrace Pyre's mercy become part of the Pyri and learn more of the truth of Pyre and their glorious approaching future. Those who fail to show honor to their god are disposed of, which helps cleanse the world for their god.

The following is the main text of the ritual. The main priest presides, the selected speaker—a knight—provides the choice to the assembly, and the other Pyri present join in with affirming refrains of their faith.

Priest: Submit or be slain. These are the words of Pyre and Salbrin, his herald.

Praise be to Pyre.

Pyri: Praise be to Pyre and his herald, Salbrin.

Priest: The time has come to select your fate. You have no other choice. Sir *(name given)*, please approach.

(The selected knight approaches and begins the offering of their options.)

Knight: There is coming a judgment to this world—a great fire that will burn across all Annulis. But Pyre in his mercy has allowed an escape.
There is only Pyre!
Great is he and single in power!

Pyri: Great is Pyre!

Knight: You have before you a choice. You see the fate of your false god. She, like the rest, cannot save you. But it is not so with Pyre. There is only Pyre and his people!

Pyri: There is only Pyre and his people!

Knight: Those who wish to be purged from this world's corruption and look forward to the Great Conflagration with joy instead of fear, step forward.
Pyre is not one to deny you a choice. He desires loyal followers ready to carry out his commands. You are free to choose whom you will. Today you can step forward and submit to Pyre, the true god, or you can remain as you are and in the end face the cleansing to follow.

Priest: Those who submit to Pyre, step forward.

(Those who submit will now step forward.)

Will no more heed Pyre's call?

(Wait for one more moment to confirm their final choice.)

Then so be it. Selection has ended. Your fate has been sealed. Come forward and kneel. You will not be appointed unto Pyre's displeasure but in the Great Conflagration will enter into his favor. But these will share the fate of all who refuse submission to the great Pyre.

Let the purging begin!

(Knights and infantry slay the rejectors of Pyre's mercy, and a final prayer is offered before the fire is set on the bodies.)

Priest: Oh Pyre, we offer you this sacrifice. May it hasten your day. Praise be to Pyre the Purifier.

Pyri: Praise be to Pyre!

Priest: Now, my brothers, let this filth be cleansed.
Praised be Pyre!

Pyri: Praised be Pyre!

APPENDIX C

Pyric Funerary Rites

On the battlefield it becomes necessary to cremate the dead Pyric warriors who have fallen in the field along with the dead of the fallen enemy—those who aren't killed during Selection. The fallen Pyri are honored in this ceremony that involves the highest-ranking priest among them giving what amounts to a final blessing as they send the dead to their rest with Pyre. Those of the army who remain are also called to watch and see their fallen comrades off in a sober but still-uplifting ceremony.

The start of the rite calls for the priest to gather with some others and their blaze rods around the bonfires. The army stands farther back, watching and waiting to see the flames rise and share in their professions of faith and blessing for the deceased.

Priest: May Pyre's wings ever enfold us.

Pyri: And may his herald always lead us true.

Priest: As has been our custom since the first days of Pyre's herald, we look to honor those who have fallen in Pyre's service. Free from this corrupt, dying world, they're now awaiting the coming of the Purifier, eager for a world reborn.

Pyri: May he come quickly.

Priest: As Salbrin has said, all will be purified, even our flesh. And so we lay Pyre's kiss beneath his fallen warriors. May it burn as a beacon of hope for all who yet walk Annulis and serve as a pleasing sacrifice to our god, who has received these—his precious ones—to his breast.

(The bonfires are lit by the priests with their blaze rods.)

Priest: There is but one god.

Pyri: Pyre!

Priest: There is but one herald.

Pyri: Salbrin is his name!

APPENDIX D

Laromi

Laromi follow a path of living that sees the needs of the many outweighing the needs of the few. As such, they have formed a communal society with limited private property rights and a strong discipline in place to keep any one individual from standing out. This preference for the status quo has not stopped them from making some advances in technology, which they have used to keep from being vanquished by the Days of Blood.

This doesn't mean they are immune from hardship, though. And as they have suffered from the shortage of food and other things, they have started to turn on themselves, guided by the darker aspects of their philosophy and eventually embracing cannibalism to survive.

At first they chose the old and infirm of mind or body who were believed to be too much of a drain on the people, and then they turned to a lottery before deciding on a process of gathering up those from outside the city. And when that eventually fails, they will have nothing left but to turn on the inhabitants of the city and will face the very real threat, if nothing further is done, of killing off their own population in the name of saving the city-state.

Their leadership is unique in all of Annulis, adopting the "first among equals" concept of the princeps. Nowadays, with his complete control over the army, it's become little more than a dictatorship, which the people quietly endure with a nihilistic understanding of their final and fatal days ahead.

Crest or Symbol

The Laromic crest is a black crow with raised wings whose head is kept in a left-facing profile. A single white eye glares at the viewer, while a stylized gray cog rests behind the crow's head as a sort of nimbus. All this is over a white background. Most commonly this crest is seen on banners and shields and around the temple and palace.

Belief System

The Laromi hold to the patron goddess of their city, Laroma. She is supposed to be both the embodiment of the city and also its defender and patron. As with most of the cities of old, the Laromi have rejected the Sovereign as both an act of defiance and a sign of self-reliance over the old order. As with the goddesses of the other cities, there is a strong degree of civic pride mixed in with the religious devotion to Laroma.

Appearance and Dress

Like all humans on Annulis, Laromi possess olive skin and a variety of hair colors—from blond to red, brown to black, and all shades in between.

Men dress in brown or black pants with off-white or white shirts. A leather belt and boots complete the look, with the pants worn tucked into the boots. Most men are clean shaven and short haired.

Women wear black or brown skirts with white or off-white blouses. Their skirts fall to just below their knees, where the tall boots take over. Unlike the men, they keep their hair in a variety of lengths and styles. Both sexes, however, are modest and sparing in the use of other adornments and jewelry.

The sole exception to this custom is the princeps, who wears a burgundy cape draped over his shoulders, along with a black leather vest, to mark his rank as first among equals.

Weapons and Armor

When it comes to weapons and armor, only the army makes use of them. Soldiers wear chain mail shirts over brigandine leather pants. Each also wears fluted steel bracers and greaves along with an open-faced helmet with nose guard. Their shields are an offensive and defensive weapon: a round metal disk surrounded by an apparatus with terrible-looking teeth, which can be activated into a sort of functional chainsaw by means of winding a device on the back of the shield that moves the gears that are inside the shield itself. When fully wound, it can run for about three minutes. It takes about thirty seconds to completely wind.

As for other weapons, all make use of a short sword and a special crossbow equipped with a clip that holds five bolts. A spring-and-gear system allows for rapid reloading and release. It has to be wound up as well, but it makes up for this with quick firing without a lag for loading between every bolt.

Relations with Others

Laromi are open to meeting anyone outside their city, as it means they can substitute them for another Laromi on their plate. Sometimes they can also get goods and foodstuffs to trade, which allows them to delay the dark doom hanging over them.

As to the beliefs of others, they don't really care. Even their own worship of Laroma is lip service these days at best. Their greatest interest, however, is in the Pyri and the Marauders, whom they see as perhaps a greater threat than their own looming fate if these two peoples' growth continues.

APPENDIX E

Pyri

The Pyri are a people who hail from the city of Pyrus or have been added to its ranks through their crusades. The ancient city was taken over and now is ruled by Salbrin and his Quorum of Septet. All traces of what they were before have been scoured to make room for the new truth of Pyre. For the Pyri are devoted to Pyre and his herald, Salbrin, who endeavors to give all a choice before the Great Conflagration comes: death or a sworn allegiance to Pyre.

With their militant message, they are fast becoming the dominant force on Annulis, and all others must take up arms against them or join them for fear of being slain, as is the fate of all who find themselves crosswise of Pyric purpose and beliefs.

Crest or Symbol

All Pyri hold to the sacred emblem of Pyre, which is a phoenix crafted out of yellow flame over a white background. A red version of the phoenix is placed over a white background for the army to wear, and some of the higher-ranking priests have a golden emblem instead.

Belief System

All Pyri hold that Pyre is the only hope of getting out of Annulis alive. A great firestorm is coming to destroy the planet, but when it arrives those who have sided with Pyre and await their time of purifying will be kept safe to inhabit the world to come. All others will be consumed in the cleansing fire.

Appearance and Dress

Like all humans on Annulis, Pyri possess olive skin, with hair ranging from blond to red, brown to black, and all shades in between. Civilians tend to adopt robes and shirts and billowing pants for men and dresses and saris for women. Both sexes wear leather shoes or sandals with thick belts being a favored adornment, along with anything phoenix or flame related. Men tend to keep clean shaven, with all men keeping their hair short. Women tend to keep their hair longer, but some opt for a medium length as well.

Weapons and Armor

The general population is not allowed to carry weapons. Only the army is allowed to make use of armor and weapons. In this way the population is controlled and the army supplied with the equipment they need to carry out Salbrin's decrees.

Relations with Others

All who don't honor Pyre are held to be infidels fit only for death. This is the belief that is impressed and instilled upon all Pyri. Those who seek to deviate from this truth are in turn commanded to repent or are killed for such blasphemies. There is no middle ground, for all hold to Salbrin's message of Pyre returning to save a pure people who have been put through the crucible and are now fit for the new world to come.

APPENDIX F

Sojourners

Sojourners are a migratory people who are loosely connected in simple groups that often are related to some degree by marriage or other matters. Such groups wander the world in search of the Veiled City, which they believe is their future. Many on Annulis naturally don't hold to this viewpoint and as such see them as nothing more than wandering beggars who are foolishly wasting their lives traipsing throughout Annulis for no reason. But since they are not a warlike people and sometimes do good by bringing much-needed goods and even news from outside their towns and villages, they are often tolerated and even traded with for limited mutual gain.

Each group is called a congregation and is headed by a patriarch or matriarch, the oldest member of the group. Under them are the elders, these being the next oldest. Other than this there is no real hierarchy, and each congregation strives for a system of communal unity, calling each other sister, brother, elder, patriarch, or matriarch.

Crest or Symbol

The Sojourners don't really hold to a crest, as such things are tied to the cities and those who dwell within them, and they don't wish to be connected to them in any way. However, they have adopted the sparrow as a symbol for their people, for it lives in the wild while also searching for cities and dwellings to make a home in. A fitting analogy for what some might see as their aimless wandering of Annulis.

Belief System

Sojourners have a very simple belief system. They hold to the traditions of the old empire and honor and venerate the Sovereign and chief stewards of Mundus, but they also believe the heralds and their call to flee their old lives and save themselves from destruction by going in search of the Veiled City.

When a Sojourner dies, they are buried in an unmarked grave in the wilderness, leaving no sign of their passing so that there is no reason to seek it out again in place of the Veiled City; nor does such a burial place draw anyone else who might try to loot or defame it in any way. Only their memory will go on with the congregation; the body is left to be buried in the past as they move ever onward.

Appearance and Dress

Like all humans on Annulis, Sojourners possess olive skin and variety in hair color—from blond to red, brown to black, and all shades in between.

All the men wear a beige or off-white long-sleeved tunic with black cuffs and collar. They also don brown pants with black cuffs, along with a simple leather belt and shoes with reinforced soles that lace up to the ankle. The men also stand apart from the females by donning a brown cowl upon their sixteenth year—a sign of entering into adulthood.

Men wear their hair combed back, not letting it grow longer than the base of their neck. Further, upon reaching adulthood and gaining his cowl, a male Sojourner is expected to grow a beard in keeping with their chosen style, which grows from under the chin rather than across or upon it.

Women wear a beige or dark brown long-sleeved dress with black collar, cuffs, and hem. They share the same shoes and belts as the men, as well as the brown cloak both wear, which is secured by means of a brooch. Women also wear a kerchief, which they gain upon reaching their sixteenth year to mark their passage into adulthood. This headdress consists of a cream-colored cloth that is trimmed in black.

Under the kerchief women are allowed to grow their hair down to the base of their shoulder blades but have to keep it in a ponytail, which is often neatly affixed with leather straps at the base.

Other than this, neither males nor females wear any sort of adornment other than a woven bracelet that husband and wife don to show they are married. These are matching sets, of course, and are made of leather or cloth or whatever other material might be available at the time. Any jewelry they come across is used for bartering instead of for personal adornment.

Weapons and Armor

Being people who seek a peaceful way of life separate from what they see as the debauched and warlike ways of the cities, Sojourners do not carry any real weapons or armor. They keep only a dagger at their side for everyday use (and as a last-resort form of protection), and a walking stick is the only other item that could be used as a weapon.

The dagger is bestowed upon both men and women with their kerchief or cowl as another sign of their higher position in the community and greater independence. The walking stick is mostly used by men and elderly women.

Relations with Others

Sojourners are unambiguous when it comes to relations with others. There is only them, Marauders, and Dwellers (those who dwell in cities, towns, and villages). The Marauders are seen as a group that should be avoided, while the Dwellers are useful on occasion. But they too are avoided for the most part and seen as corrupted, as are all those who have rejected the heralds and the Sovereign altogether.

Chad Corrie has enjoyed creating things for as far back as he can remember, but it wasn't until he was twelve that he started writing. Since then he's written comics, graphic novels, prose fiction of varying lengths, and an assortment of other odds and ends. His work has been published in other languages and produced in print, digital, and audio formats. He also makes podcasts.

ChadCorrie.com | @creatorchad

Scan the code for instant access to Chad's social media, newsletter, podcasts, website, and more!